Daddio Joe
ON THE RADIO

Daddio Joe
ON THE RADIO

A Nonsense Novel

JOE REMESZ

iUniverse LLC
Bloomington

Daddio Joe on the Radio
A Nonsense Novel

iUniverse books may be ordered through booksellers or by contacting:

iUniverse LLC
1663 Liberty Drive
Bloomington, IN 47403
www.iuniverse.com
1-800-Authors (1-800-288-4677)

ISBN: 978-1-4759-9235-9 (sc)
ISBN: 978-1-4759-9701-9 (ebk)

Library of Congress Control Number: 2013911741

Printed in the United States of America

iUniverse rev. date: 07/10/2013

CHAPTER 1

As a farm boy living near Winnipeg I was fascinated by the wonder of radio. Since my parents, Piotr and Stella Rubeck, were to poor to have one, I went to see our librarian, Catherine Livingstone, and she said to me with a punctilious look, "Joe, in the 19th century two young men—one an American, the other an Italian, were tinkering away in their workshop filled with complicated gadgets, most of them home made, and that's when radio first began."

Mrs. Livingstone, lovely and in her thirties, said that the American, Thomas Alva Edison, invented a recording sound in 1877 when he succeeded in putting his own voice onto a cylinder of wax thus inventing the gramophone. "Later, between 1879 and 1883," Mrs. Livingstone continued, "Edison invented a light bulb which put inexpensive and automatic lighting into most cities and homes of almost the entire world."
The farm we lived on still didn't have electricity.
Mrs. Livingstone went on, "About the same time an Italian engineer named Guglielmo Marconi was experimenting

with, no, not pizza, but radio waves in his attic in Bologna. Without connecting wires Marconi was able to ring a bell in a distant room by pressing a button in his lab. Then on the 12th of December 1901 he floated a four hundred foot antenna aloft Signal Hill in St. John's, Newfoundland. In 1/86th of a second Marconi heard a pre-arranged reply signal broadcast from Cornwall, England, 2,170 miles distant."

Mrs. Livingstone then said that when Marconi's radio was hooked up to Edison's electricity, the result changed the world in the field of communications and entertainment.

I soon discovered that the first radio receivers were crystal sets, simple gadgets in which a piece of quartz, about the size of a peach stone, was the receiver. Mounted on a base alongside the crystal was a piece of stiff braided wire known as the *cat's whisker*. Connected to the cat's whisker was a set of earphones, usually clamped about the ears of a radio nut, which I was becoming to be.

With a steady hand, the listener would probe the surface of the crystal with the cat's whisker. Certain parts of the crystal surface would be vibrating in tune with radio waves broadcast by near and distant radio stations. Within years of radio's invention the governments of Canada, United States and most nations, were scrambling hastily to make legislation controlling use of the new piece of technology.

By the time I was born during the Great Depression in 1930s, crystal sets had been replaced by more sophisticated receivers using radio tubes and powered by wet and dry cell batteries.

I can remember distinctly when I was five-years-old, that was two years after the end of prohibition and the average citizen could find entertainment in both bottles and radios, that my father trapped enough muskrats enabling him to sell the furs, go to an auction sale and come home not only with a radio but also an Edison gramophone. "The radio and the gramophone are a luxury which we must handle carefully," my father said.

The radio rested on a large box adorned with three dials, each calibrated into minute graduations. Behind the box and connected to it, was a large curved horn about two feet high looking like a giant version of the ear trumpet my hard of hearing mother used.

From the horn came the voice of a man declaring that Mackenzie King was elected Prime Minister of Canada. I was perplexed, confused, baffled. Who was Mackenzie King? And where did the voice come from?

"It's a trick," I said to my mother sitting next to me in a rocking chair and adjusting her hearing aid. Then as I pondered this thought, I recalled what Mrs. Livingstone had said about Edison, Marconi and radio waves. As I was trying to figure things out, the voice stopped and there was music, a piano playing. I wanted an explanation so I ran back to the library and Mrs. Livingstone told me that a gadget called *microphone* picked up sound waves and could travel long distances through air. At the end, a receiver, like the one we were listening to, converted radio waves into sound waves we could hear.

Throughout my childhood, as long as I could, I would sit in front of our radio, my ear glued to the speaker grill, my right hand twisting the station selector. There was skill involved as I twisted from 540 to 1600. A heavy hand could obliterate six minuscule signals in half an inch on the dial.

It was while I was twisting the dial on Halloween night, 1938, that I picked up on an American station, Orson Welles' *War of the Worlds*. It was a program which made many listeners hysterical as panic-stricken people ran for shelter, fully believing Martians had landed in New Jersey and were starting to destroy civilization. Then just under a year later, September 1939, a dramatic international thing happened. As I was twisting the dial the voice inside the radio said, "Germany has attacked Poland and World War 11 has begun."

Since my parents came from Poland in 1928, they too, soon began dial twisting to hear how the Nazi Death squads were executing Jews, my Catholic ancestors, and how the war was going.

Soon station twiddling became a contest between my mother and me. It was sort of an evening sport, not what station we could pick up, but how far from Selkirk, Manitoba where we lived. As one looks on a map they will notice that Selkirk is just north of Winnipeg and Winnipeg is near the centre of North America, so we could pick up many distant stations, especially after sunset during winter.

I remember saying to my mother while she was knitting, "Hey, Mom! I picked up WLW Cincinnati, WBBM Chicago, KDA Pittsburgh and KOA Denver."
"That's nothing, Joe," my mother replied. "Last night I picked up KFAB Omaha, Nebraska; KPO San Francisco, KNX Los Angeles and KSL Salt Lake City."

Later that night, I picked up and wrote in my logbook KFBK Sacramento, WWL New Orleans and clear channel, XRE Del Rio, Texas. XRE fascinated me because the station advertised almost everything imaginable. When I ordered a Children's Picture *Bible* I discovered that the powerful station was located in Mexico.
Soon in our home, there was radio mania and a significant means of expression.

The biggest change in radio broadcasting from my point of view as a young boy was the formation of networks feeding formatted programs to smaller stations. There was the CBC in Canada and NBC, CBS and the Mutual networks in United States, which influenced us daily. I'd come home from school and listen to Blackstone the Magician and Last of Mohicans. The programs were only fifteen minutes long but exciting. I'd plant myself in front of the radio, arms clasped around the knees, and escape into a different world. Early evenings I would listen to the Lone Ranger and Cisco Kid. As I got older I would listen to Inner Sanctum, The Whistler and The Shadow.

Sometimes I became so terrified that I had difficulty falling asleep.

Saturday afternoon we'd listen to Texaco's Metropolitan Opera of the Air hosted by Milton Cross. This was followed by Share the Wealth and then Foster Hewitt doing the Toronto Maple Leaf hockey broadcasts and I would emulate. Every Sunday night we'd listen to Jack Benny as he tried to cope with humiliation visited by violin teachers and an endless array of dim wits. Later we laughed at the antics of Charlie McCarthy, the wooden puppet who always had insults on his ventriloquist, Edgar Bergen, and guests like W. C. Fields who threatened to feed Charlie to the woodpecker. There were other American programs we enjoyed too: Fibber McGee and Molly, Our Miss Brooks, Fred Allen, Ozzie and Harriet, Amos n Andy, Green Hornet and Lux Radio Theatre.

Radio was a social phenomenon just as today everyone watching a screen on television or the computer for entertainment or news. At our home, CBC news was a must, especially the 9:00 p. m. news read by Lorne Greene. We also enjoyed the BBC news carried by the Canadian network.

In between bulletins, the radio station we listened to most often kept grinding out stories about the war. Words like *Hitler*, *Stalin*, *Vimy Ridge*, *Auschwitz* and *Nazi* became part of our vocabulary. Then there were grain prices, livestock quotations, who got married or buried, who were in the hospital, who had a baby, important messages to travelers, what price eggs were selling at the Co-Op and the specials at Marshall Wells Hardware Store.

My father, aside from listening to news bulletins, also liked the weather forecasts because they told him if a cold Arctic air mass was coming from the north, and if I could go fishing for catfish along the Red River and he do summer fallow without wearing a buffalo coat.

There were also hockey and baseball scores and police bulletins describing criminals who escaped from a jail after committing a murder or robbing a bank. As far as I was concerned, however, the most interesting program to listen to was the *Search for Talent Show* on the CBC, which my mother encouraged to enter. Since I didn't want to be a farmer but someone like announcer Lorne Greene, I agreed. But what was my talent? I didn't know how to play a musical instrument, tap dance, sing or yodel like Wilf Carter.

"Why don't you recite a poem?" Mom suggested.

"An excellent idea," I said and the following day memorized *The Cremation of Sam McGee* by Robert Service. It was a poem I enjoyed when my teacher read it in class while I was attending Selkirk Elementary School. I was eleven years old at the time. The year was 1941 and World War 2 was in its third year, a time I listened to the news each day and to the talent program each Saturday morning, originating at a different town from the stage of a local theatre.

"And here's an application form," my mother said while handing me a sheet of paper to fill out. "The Search for Talent Show will originate from Selkirk a month from today."

When my father heard my mother, he said, "Don't be silly. Joe will make a fool out of himself."

"That's all right," my mother replied. "Even if Joe doesn't win, it will be good for him later in life. It's not the prize that is important but an opportunity for Joe to speak in front of a live audience."

The first prize was an all-expense paid trip for the winner and his/her parents to the Okanagan Valley of British Columbia. The sponsor of the prize was Sun-Rype Fruit and Juices. The second prize was a weekend stay, including meals, at the Fort Gary Hotel in Winnipeg. The third prize was a set of luggage.

"But you'll have to go door to door begging for pledges," my father protested.

Mom corrected him, "No. He won't. But if Joe wants to sell tickets for the show, I'm certain it would be appreciated by the show organizers."

I enjoyed eating Okanagan Valley fruit, especially peaches and apples, so a trip to British Columbia appealed to me. If I did win, I could see what different fruit trees looked like and if Ogopogo, the Okanagan Lake monster, was real. Somehow I found myself riding my bicycle up and down our neighborhood and then the town of Selkirk itself, knocking on people's doors explaining what the tickets were for. I don't know why I did it; perhaps it was the same reason I was constantly listening to the radio, dialing to different stations. It could have also been that I enjoyed Mom's apple pies whose fillings came from Penticton.

When my father found out that I was selling tickets for the Search for Talent Show he took me aside and with Mom next to us said, "Look. There are already enough strangers hanging on doors every day trying to sell everything from vacuum cleaners, encyclopedia books to life insurance."

When I told my father that I had already sold all the tickets I could, he quieted down and wished me luck in reciting my poem, which he thought was a bit upscale for me.

In the process of selling tickets I discovered that a neighbor of ours had entered the contest too. Henny Field's mother, Lorna, was a piano teacher and when I visited their home, I found the living room, where the piano stood, like an Amazon jungle. There were tropical plants of all sorts, an aquarium filled with tiny fish and cages hanging from the ceiling with colorful birds, including a talking parrot with a metronome by one of its wings.

After I recited several verses of *The Cremation of Sam McGee,* Henny, who was ten at the time, said that she was going to play Beethoven's *Piano Concerto No. 4, Allegro Minderato* but that she really didn't want to be a pianist, like her mother wanted her to be, but an actress or a nurse. Henny also told me something else. "Joe," she said, "After hearing you recite your poem I think you need elocution lessons if you expect to win a prize."

I took Hinny's advice seriously and asked mother to find me an elocutionist. She did, Rose Bunchy, a septuagenarian with gray hair and wrinkles along her forehead and face.

Each day I walked a mile to Mrs. Bunchy's home for my lessons and the road I walked on, was a gravel one with many potholes. When a pickup truck, a car or a tractor came from either direction I was left in a cloud of dust making my throat so dry I had difficulty speaking. Before I could present myself for a lesson, I had to pass a hog farm whose stench was overwhelming. And then when I finally did reach Mrs. Bunchy's driveway, I shook my head at the house she lived in. On the outside, the white paint was peeling and shutters hung at odd angles.

I looked up to the eaves, expecting to see pigeons roosting when a galvanized gutter fell to the ground killing a gopher. Then I had to contend with three dogs: Fido, Rex and Venus the Meanest.

Fido was a huge mongrel who knocked me to the ground when he stood on his hind legs and tried to lick my face. Rex thought my right foot was a fire hydrant and Venus the Meanest was like the name implied, kept barking, snarling and grinding his teeth at me until Mrs. Bunchy opened the front door and said, "Please come inside, Joe."

While I found the Field's living room resembling a jungle, the one Mrs. Bunchy used to give me elocution lessons, reminded me of a museum. Mrs. Bunchy was into genealogy and on each wall hung photographs of her family tree whose roots went back in history as far as the Red River Settlement and Assiniboine Cree Indians were the principal group inhabiting the area.

As soon as I made myself comfortable Mrs. Bunchy said, "Okay, Joe, Let's start our lesson with a breathing exercise.

Stand next to me, stretch out your hands and breathe in, one, two, and three. Now exhale, one, two and three."
This part of lesson lasted five minutes and then Mrs. Bunchy said, "Joe, you must use your diaphragm in order to breathe properly."

After doing several mouth and tongue exercises Mrs. Bunchy then said, "Our next exercise will help you with your diction. Repeat after me enunciating the following phrases ten times. Let's start with *How now brown cow.*"
I repeated 'How now brown cow,' ten times and then proceeded with other phrases which included:

- Leath police realeaseth us and thus sufficeth us
- Peter Piper picked a peck of pickled peppers
- Ninety-nine naughty nuns in a nunnery
- Read leather, yellow leather. Red leather, yellow leather
- Shut the shutters and sit in the shop

With the latter I had difficulty. "Joe, you are sibilant and have trouble with your S's," Mrs. Bunchy said.
I knew what she meant. When I came to the word *sit* it came out as *shit* but instead I said, "I certainly do have trouble with my S. Can I use your bathroom please?"
"Go ahead," Mrs. Bunchy said and gave me directions how to get there.
When I returned Mrs. Bunchy showed me how to use a pause for dramatic purposes and to emphasize words correctly. As an illustration she used the phrase *What am I doing?* with emphasis on each different word.

What am I doing?
What *Am* I doing?
What am *I* doing?
What am I *doing?*
I found the exercise amusing and when I went to school next day I had my classmates say *What am I doing?* four different ways. I would get them to do the exercise ten times and then I would say, "I know what you are doing?"
They inevitably would say, "What?"
I would burst out with laughter and say, "You are making a fool out of yourself."

I thought Mrs. Bunchy was an excellent teacher. Besides being into genealogy she knew a lot about elocution, vowels, constanants, digraphs, diphthongs and inflections. She said it might be a worthwhile expenditure of energy for me to in my every day speech make my words eloquent and my grammar beyond reproach. As I was a fast-learning student I completed her lessons in time for my mother to say, "The Search for Talent Show goes on the air at eleven tomorrow morning."

It was a time when Henny Field sat at one end of the front row of the theatre and participating contestants and I sat in the third behind her. In between, there were musicians, singers, dancers and comedians. Some wore costumes while others looked like Maximum Security Guards from the Stony Plain Prison.
I kept licking my lips and stretching my mouth and jaw muscles at the same time wondering if I should go to the

bathroom one more time. Then I turned around and saw people entering the theatre. I was surprised that it was almost full.

I noticed that Mrs. Bunchy, Mrs. Livingstone and my parents were sitting a row behind me. Mrs. Bunchy wore a bright pink dress with a long yellow feather stuck in her white wide-brimmed hat. She reminded me of a cherry tree when it's covered all over with white blossoms in the spring. Mrs. Bunchy was busy reading the Search for Talent program that was given to everyone while entering the theatre. My mother wore a dark-colored skirt with a blouse which had a pattern of sunflowers on it. She was adjusting her hearing aid. My father who wore blue overalls with a multi-colored shirt that had its sleeves rolled up appeared uncomfortable as he twitched the ends of his mustache.

Henny's parents were sitting not far behind, although across the aisle, and as I looked towards them, Mrs. Field she winked at me, but when I turned towards Henny, she stuck out her tongue.

Several minutes later, Mom caught my attention and whispered, "Joe, stop staring at the audience. The Talent Show is about to begin."

A minute later, the theatre lights were dimmed and the master of ceremonies thanked everyone for coming. Next, he identified the contestants by name and made a remark that most of the contestants lived on a farm. To the right of the MC sat three judges.

The first contestant was a fifteen-year-old girl who sang *Tiptoe through the Tulips*. When her voice cracked in the middle of a high note, I thought I had a chance to win a prize.

The second contestant stepped up to the microphone but not before she missed a step leading to the stage and fell. After picking herself up the MC asked her several questions one of which was, "I understand you live on a farm, is that right?"

"I do," she graciously replied.

"So tell me, why are chickens in Selkirk such big eaters?"

The contestant hesitated and then said, "Because they eat a peck at a time."

While the audience was laughing the contestant did her version of *The Chicken Dance*.

The third contestant was a male standup comedy duo called Wimpy and Blimpy. I thought the names suited the couple because one was tall and skinny while his partner was short and stout.

Next, Henny Field walked onto the stage and performed Beethoven's *Piano Concerto No. 4, Allegro Minderato* on the piano and Henny, like Wimpy and Blimpy, received a hearty applause.

Then there were other contestants too. It appeared to me that each performer had a drive and juices flowing but as far as I was concerned after one sang *La Donna Mobile* and the other *Mi Chiamano Mimi* their faces reminded me of a pepperoni pizza.

Then it was my turn. I felt nervous when the MC called my name and when I reached the stage he said, "And you are Joe Rubeck?"

"That's me," I said and imagined thousands of people glued to their radios. I imagined also that I was heard beyond Winnipeg. Since CBW was a 50,000 watt station I probably could be heard as far away as Chicago where my favorite aunt, Pauline, lived.

"So you live on a farm?" the MC continued with his questions.

"Yes."

"So tell me, where do farmers leave their pigs when they come to town?"

I was going to say stockyard but instead said, "At porking meters."

The audience burst out with laughter and laughed even louder when I began reciting *The Cremation of Sam McGee* and in the opening line because of my sibilants, said, "There are sshtrange things done in the midnight sshun."

By the time I finished my poem, I fluffed the lines, five times and could have, there on the stage, before a live and radio audience, died of humiliation. I was about to make a quick dash for the nearest exit when I saw my parents, Mrs. Bunchy and Mrs. Livingstone in the aisle so I walked up to them and apologized. "I'm sorry," I said. "As you may have noticed I had trouble with my S's."

"Don't be," my mother intervened. "You did your best and that's what counts."

"That's all right. It's a good start if you want to be a radio announcer," Mrs. Bunchy said.

Mrs. Livingstone gave me a pat on the back and said, "Keep on reading books and eventually you'll reach the top of your chosen profession."

What my father said was, "You did a good job, son, but thank goodness it's over."

Several minutes later, the theatre lights were dimmed and the MC announced that according to the judges, Henny Field placed first. The Wimpy and Blimpy comedy team placed second, and the boy who sang *La Donna Mobile*, placed third. I placed last.

As soon as the winners were announced and the Search for Talent Show was over, my father took me, mother, Mrs. Bunchy and Mrs. Livingstone for an ice cream treat, but when we arrived home that afternoon, I shut myself in the bedroom, took Mrs. Livingston's suggestion seriously, and tried to read a comic book. I underestimated my instinct, however, and turned on the radio when on the Six O'clock News the announcer said that although Henny Field had won first prize, she had no intention of being a pianist.

The announcer said, "In fact I understand that Henny Field, after she returns from the Okanagan Valley will tell her parents that she will never touch a piano again. As far as I know, Miss Field wants to be either an actress or a nurse, and when she gets older, live in British Columbia."

CHAPTER 2

During 1950, when World War 2 ended five years earlier, and there was peace throughout the world, except for minor and cold wars, economic conditions improved in Canada. That's when my parents sold their farm near Selkirk and bought the thirty two-unit Patricia Motel in Penticton, British Columbia.

Penticton, aside from its fruit, is famous for its sun, fun, beaches, Ogopogo and spectacular natural scenery. The city of 25,000 is cradled with tree trimmed mountain slopes, dramatic cliffs, enjoyed a desert-like climate and bordered by two pristine lakes, Okanagan and Skaha. I was twenty at the time and had graduated from college. It was time when my father said, "What now, son?" and I said to him that I could imitate Lorne Greene and Foster Hewitt better than anyone I knew, and that I passionately wanted to be a radio announcer and nothing else.

Well, my father nearly had a bird. He was disappointed and it was only with my mother's intervention that I was able to attend Lorne Greene's Academy of Radio and

Television Arts in Toronto. My father thought that being the only child, I would eventually inherit the motel, and until then, I should be an accountant and help him keep the motel books straight.

But my mother at the time said, "No way, Joe Rubeck has a voice which shouldn't be wasted."

At the Academy, the curriculum included: announcing, acting, writing, speech, production, news gathering and of all things, ballet dancing. I had no idea how ballet would help my career but the instructor, a middle aged female named Marjorie Leete, said, "By taking ballet lessons you'll gain poise and benefit when interviewing people." I must have hypnotized her with my graceful tippy-toeing the *Death of a Saskatchewan Gopher* because she then showed me how to give a strong handshake. "Don't stick out your hand like a dead fish," she said.

Ms. Leete also told me that when I apply for employment to look the interviewer straight in the eye and to wear clothes that fit. "Not those baggy pants you are presently wearing. Tuck your shirt in and don't wear a T-shirt with obscene writing of any kind. And hey, get rid of that ducktail haircut."

At the Academy, I studied with other students from across Canada, whose dream, like mine, was to carve a name for ourselves in the broadcast industry. One of these was Drew Canwin from Sudbury, Ontario. We became friends and Drew told me that his dream was to become a television producer with the Canadian Broadcasting Corporation.

After a year of studying at the Academy, Lorne Greene, my idol, during a graduation ceremony, presented me with a "special" award. It was an alarm clock, which on the back were inscribed the words: To Joe Rubeck—For Diligence and Progress while a student at the Academy of Radio and Television Arts—1952.

Drew Canwin was presented a similar award for radio and television production. Television was just beginning to get a foothold in Canada.

The inscription on the back of the leather-bound alarm clock made me feel proud of myself. "Cool, the former kid from Selkirk, Manitoba is doing okay for myself," I thought. "No more taking part in talent contests, shooting gophers, crows, magpies and mud hens with a slingshot, but from this day onward, entertaining and informing people."

I felt I was ready to take on the electronic communications industry. My vision was to be the most versatile and best radio announcer there is.

After graduating from the Academy, the first thing I did was to return to Penticton and phone the on duty announcer at CJOE who was on the midnight to 5:00 a. m. shift. Big Paul Mitchell suggested I drop by shortly after midnight and he would give me a tour of the station.

When I met Big Paul, I was surprised, almost as the time in 1939, when World War 11 began. Big Paul was not a gargantuan like his voice projected but a midget no taller than forty inches. His feet did not touch the floor as he sat in his chair in front of a microphone. He had shoulder-length hair and whiskers that were curled at each end. Big Paul was dressed in a white T-shirt and blue jeans, which had a hole at the knees. Following a tour of the station Big Paul's appearance made me think, "Here is one profession where appearance, size and looks did not matter like it did on television. What did, was one had to have an articulate voice and if it was resonant, that much the better."

The following day, I made an appointment with the station's manager about possible employment. Harry Fahlman was a legend in the field of British Columbia radio, a larger-than-lifetime figure whose flair for the dramatic was evident in his appearance as well as at work. He had a deep, grating voice, was six feet six inches tall, he literally towered over me. Fahlman wore a flamboyant necktie and I thought drank copious amounts of alcohol because the tip of his nose was reddish in color. Fahlman was a character in an industry of characters but mostly significantly he was a survivor, while a parade of announcers had come and gone during his ten years as manager of CJOE whose motto was *CJOE Good Music and News 24 Hours*.

Following a handshake and discussing an announcer's salary, which was meager, Fahlman's first question was, "Have you any experience?"
"No," I said while handing him my resume.
And then while Fahlman glanced through my data and noticing that I was an Academy of Radio and Television Arts graduate, said, "Come, let's audition you."

I followed Fahlman to the News Room where he ripped off several items from a teletype. Next we walked to the Continuity Department where he picked up several copies of commercials. Then we entered an empty studio where I sat in front of a microphone and read out loud while Fahlman sat on a chair, picked his nose and listened.

Naturally I was nervous and fluffed my lines several times. I also mispronounced the words: genuine, mischievous, and comparable and sub judice. I had no trouble with my sibilance this time.

"Now let's see about your spelling," Fahlman said. "Can you please spell the word *scissors*?"

"S-I-S-0-R-S," I said.

"Wrong! How about the word *diarrhea*?"

"D-I-E-R-E-E-A."

"Wrong!" Fahlman said again. "How about the word *millennium*?"

"M-I-L-L-E-N-I-U-M."

'Wrong! Let's see if you can spell the word *criticize*?"

"C-R-I-T-I-C-S-I-Z-E."

"Wrong!" Fahlman said for the last time. "You can't spell words but do you want to know something?"

Curious to know I said, "What?"

"You have a voice that is pleasant, resonant and different. You are hired as a member of the station's announcing staff and do the midnight shift beginning Monday."

It was a Friday.

"But I misspelled all those words," I exclaimed.

"Listen," Fahlman said. "Most announcers can't spell. It is important, however, that one is careful about pronunciation of words and happy or sad, frustrated or euphoric, a radio announcer must follow a middle course. Whether you are talking to one person or a million, you must show sympathy, enthusiasm, and a willingness to listen, especially to people with a different background than yours."

Fahlman then handed me a *Pronunciation Guide* book to Most Mispronounced Words and said, "Study each word phonically.

I said I would and was delighted that I was hired to do the night shift, but on the other hand, wondered what had happened to Big Paul Mitchell. "Has Big Paul quit or is he moving to another station?" I asked.

"No," Fahlman replied. "Working the graveyard shift has finally got to Big Paul. He's under temporary leave as recommended by a psychiatrist."

Next, Fahlman introduced me to the Program Director and Chief Announcer, Happy Buck Milton, who in turn introduced me to the staff members and then, as a means of introduction to CJOE listeners, I took questions live on the air. The last caller identified herself as Louise Bohn and we chatted about when I was a boy in Selkirk and minor hockey league coaches weren't paid, how I helped my father clear land with an axe, drove a team of horses, fed chop to hogs and why all my life I wanted to be a radio announcer.

As soon as we were off the air, our conversation continued and Mrs. Bohn invited me to her home as she put it, "Share a home-cooked meal with me."

Since my mother was out of town and father, like me, didn't know how to cook, I accepted the invitation and at the appointed time, the following evening, knocked on her door several times.

As soon as Mrs. Bohn opened the front door to acknowledge my presence, I noticed that she was in her fifties, had her hair dyed blond and rather badly cut. She was wearing nondescript trousers with a gray polo-necked jersey. The only clue to her community status was a shiny ring on her left hand, and let me tell you, the diamond on it was huge, really huge.

Mrs. Bohn greeted me with surprise when she said, "Joe Rubeck! I'm amazed! What a surprise! Your voice on the radio doesn't match your figure. I thought you were much older and taller. Strange, isn't it, how a voice can be deceiving?"

"I'm sorry that my voice doesn't match my figure," I apologized.

"Don't be sorry. Please come in," Mrs. Bohn said as she stretched out her hand to shake mine.

As soon as I entered the home, I noticed above standards were applied but in need of repair. The dining room crystal chandelier was falling apart and held together with duct tape. The antique oak table in the dining room needed a new coat of varnish. The two French doors which led to the living room overlooking Okanagan Lake, needed fixing. Even the Venetian blinds pulled down as the autumn sunshine still flooded the home and all the plants within, needed watering.

Despite the condition of the interior of the home I casually said, "Mrs., Bohn, life for you must be a bowl of cherries?"

"But with dangers."

"What do you mean?"

"Well, as I was driving my Caddy last night, I had a flat tire. The car went out of control and I almost landed in Okanagan Lake."

"I'm sorry to hear that. On the other hand you may have forgotten to give your Caddy a regular inspection."

"You may be right about that," Mrs. Bohn said. "Besides having a pleasant voice on the radio you seem to have good judgment. Please come into the living room and sit down on the chesterfield. You'll be more comfortable than standing in the hallway."

I entered the living room and while we kept talking Mrs. Bohn went to the liquor cabinet and while leaning over said, "Shall we have a drink before we enjoy our dinner? What will you have: scotch, rye, rum, some wine perhaps?"

"Wine will do," I said, so Mrs. Bohn went to the basement wine cellar. When she returned, poured each a glassful, placed the bottle in the refrigerator and sat next to me. Holding her glass upward Mrs. Bohn said, "I want you to guess what it is?"

I took a sip of the wine. "It's either California or Italian."

"Neither. Guess again."

I took another sip. "Maybe it's French. Whatever it is the flavor and aroma is rich."

"They are. Aren't they? The wine was vinted by my husband, Tellex, before he died."

As soon as Mrs. Bohn and I finished our glass of wine, she poured another, and then we sat at the table to enjoy our meal, pot roast and Yorkshire pudding.

As we were enjoying our meal Mrs. Bohn said, "Like with wine age does matter." She then asked about my background and when I gave it, I asked about hers.

Mrs. Bohn said she was widow and that her husband had died two years ago. She also said that she had a sister in Zurich, Switzerland and that Mr. And Mrs. Bohn had immigrated to Canada from Switzerland in 1928.

"That's the same year my parents emigrated from Poland," I said.

Looking at a portrait of her husband hanging above the fireplace mantle Mrs. Bohn continued, "I loved Tellex but my love could not save him from a heart attack."

"And how about your health?" I asked.

"Well," she said, "My doctor says I have a tired heart which must be given prescription pills."

Further into our conversation, Mrs. Bohn said that she was a friend of Harry Fahlman who was divorced and living with his teenage daughter, and that because Mrs. Bohn wasn't feeling well, he was her guardian, "Of sorts." Mrs. Bohn also said that one should never judge a plant by its leaves or a radio announcer by his voice alone. "When I heard you on the radio I thought you were about my age, six-foot, and two-hundred pounds. What a surprise."

When I was about to leave, I thanked Mrs. Bohn for her company and the meal she cooked.

"How about having another with me tomorrow?" she asked.

"Not tomorrow."

"Why?"

"Because I have to get orientated to my new job as an announcer and furthermore, I have a blind date with a clerk at City Hall, which one the other CJOE announcers has arranged."

"And where are you going to take your date?"

"To a charity ball, which I understand, is a fund-raising event with proceeds going towards a hospital in Iraq,"

"Joe, before you leave can you please do me a favor?"

"Certainly. What is it that you want me to do?"

"Vacuum my swimming pool, if you don't mind."

I threw myself to work immediately and while vacuuming. I noticed Mrs. Bohn watching me. After I finished vacuuming, she asked me to help with the dishes.

"Sure thing," I said and while wiping a plate went on, "Mrs. Bohn, I'm no handyman but your home does need a lot of work done. If you wish, on Tuesday, I'll come and help you do some fixing."

"If you do, I'll remember you in my will," Mrs. Bohn said but I thought the comment was a flippant one.

Saturday evening, the Peach Bowl ballroom was filled with dancing couples. A large red and blue banner hanging from the ceiling read: *Thank You Penticton for Supporting the Construction of a Hospital in Erbil, Iraq.*

People in Penticton agreed that the annual Fund Raising Ball was the prime social event of the year. Crowning Miss Penticton during the Peach Festival pageant was second, and the annual Square Dance Jamboree was third.

My bubbly blind date was a City Hall receptionist who had more than curves than dimples. Tara Bell, wore a figure-hugging red sequined cocktail dress gathering appreciative stares from male patrons as she was six feet tall and I was five-eight. Despite the difference in our height, I thought Tara was a ravishing beauty. After we were formally introduced to each other by Happy Buck Milton, CJOE's chief announcer, I said to Tara in jest, "Bell, so you are a ding-dong?"

Tara burst out with laughter. "That's a new one. My previous blind date said I was a bit ringy-dingy."

Minutes later, we looked foolish whirling around the dance floor, not because of our feet but because of Tara's head. It was four inches above mine. As we were dancing, I said the name *Bell* was used by Charlotte and Emily Bronte as a pseudonym when they had their novels *Jane Eyre* and *Wuthering Heights* published.

Tara responded with a smile, "I'm not into classic literature but I do enjoy Italian pasta."

Halfway through the event, the MC interrupted proceedings when he stepped up to a microphone and said, "Attention please. The Iraqi consul to British Columbia wishes to say a few words."

The consul walked up to the microphone and began, "Ladies and gentlemen. On behalf of the Iraqi government I want to thank Penticton for its participation in the construction of a hospital in Erbil. What Penticton is doing is a humanitarian act which my government appreciates."

The consul concluded his speech by saying. "Pentictonites should see Iraq for themselves before making judgments on the country's human-rights record. The best way for the West is to keep informed what is going on in Iraq and as a philosopher once said, 'Prejudice is even further away from the truth than ignorance.' I seldom see objective reporting in Canada when it comes to our conflict with the rebellious Kurds."

Tara and I danced until 1:00 a. m. and in that time, discussed the state of Planet Earth, our height, the dinner Mrs. Bohn cooked and that neither of us enjoyed cooking our meals. As soon as the fund raising event came to an end, I walked Tara home under a quiet moonlit sky and asked, "Tara, how about a date Sunday evening?"
Tara agreed.

All day Sunday I agonized what to wear, something not frumpy but not sexy either. Finally I decided to wear a pair of gray pants and a blue blazer like I saw real estate salesmen wear. I always thought that if I didn't succeed as a radio announcer as a career I would become a real estate salesman.
This Sunday evening was going to be an event of monumental proportions and when it did arrive, I took Tara, no, not dancing but to the movie *The Last Picture Show*.
Following the movie we were inside Venghi's Restaurant, which was known for its cuisine and Penticton's most celebrated chef, Renato Venghi. Penticton had several popular restaurants but none as popular as Venghi's.
The lights were dim, candles burning, as soon as the hostess led us to our table. The master chef, Renato Venghi, came along too and we chatted. Renato began

by saying, "Welcome to Venghi's Restaurant. How are you?"

"Fine. Thank you," Tara and I replied simultaneously and then the waitress took our orders. Tara ordered a pasta dinner and me, a salad with a lot of oysters. Following some front-talk I asked Renato, "How is business?"

"Terrific," Renato said, "Especially during the tourist season. In the last three months we have had numerous requests for our recipes including one from *Gourmet Magazine* and another from *Bon Appetite*. I'm also exploring the possibilities of publishing a cook book featuring our favorite recipes."

When the waitress returned to pour the wine, Tara and I ordered, Renato said, "Ah, good food without wine is like a day without sunshine."

"And most of the joy of good food comes from the company one shares with you," I said.

"Right," Renato replied and then exchanged pleasantries with Tara only, which I did not mind.

When the food arrived and Tara had a taste of her pasta, she said, "Delicious. I wish I could cook like that."

"It would be my pleasure to show you," Renato said.

Tara felt pleased as Renato continued, "You know, in professional cuisine one doesn't prepare meals for his own taste. It's like art. I may like Renoir and you may prefer Picasso."

"You are absolutely right," Tara said. "Variety is the spice of life."

"But one thing is certain," Renato continued.

"Besides death and taxes, what?"

"In life, the two most important things are food and love, like the French say, realte de vie."

I then joined the conversation and said, "Renato, if you were to have just one meal in your lifetime, what would it be?"

This time Renato thought for a moment and after his thoughts crystallized, said, "I would go out in style. It would have to be around November so I could have fresh white truffler from Italy.

Then a little fois gras, so fresh it's still warm, soutered quickly. And then, a little Calvados over the top of some Belgian endive with it."

"Next, a baby wild boar, stuffed with chestnuts roasted over a fire. The skin would be so crisp, the flesh so tender. No dessert for this meal. I would rather continue with the wine.

A Brunello, maybe a '46 vintage. After that a little cognac, something on the rougher side, like Courvoisier. Finally, the best Havana cigar. Then I would be happy."

"Another question," I said. "Of all the restaurants in the world, if you were going to choose one for an evening, aside from your own, which would it be?"

"There are fine restaurants in Paris, Montreal, Casablanca and New York but I must draw on my own experience," Renato said. "It's not only the food but the service that counts. I'm no restaurant critic but I would choose the Twin Viking in Bangkok, Thailand."

"Since your restaurant is so popular in Penticton, did you ever consider opening other restaurants and franchising them like McDonalds?" Tara asked.

"Not franchising, but Montreal and New York are possibilities, I also thought of opening a restaurant in Zurich and Paris."

"What are the risks involved in opening a restaurant like yours in Penticton, especially if you plan to open so many?" Tara continued.

"The secret is not to spend millions on the dining room and pack it with many tables so you end up with nothing in the kitchen. There is another thing too."

"What is it?" I said.

'To have the right reservation manager. You may not know it but there are many rude customers. His or her job is to eliminate the riff-raff, if you know what I mean."

"Hey, I'd like a job like that," Tara said.

"Then why don't you apply?" Venghi said.

After Renato was through chatting with us, he returned to the kitchen, and Tara and I to our homes. As we walked along Lakeshore Drive, I asked Tara for another date but she declined. "No way, Jose," she said. "I'm going to apply to become a reservation manager at Venghi's Restaurant, and once I get it, there will be no time for dating."

If you could have witnessed my first Monday night in broadcasting, you would have bet I wouldn't succeed as a professional radio announcer. All day I had been hanging around the station being orientated in the world of radio. As the Patricia Motel was near the radio station, I kept watching the disc jockeys, newscasters, sports announcers. I was shown how to fill-in a log, pick music from the library, prepare a newscast and kept rehearsing what I would say during my opening program. I didn't sleep well the entire weekend. I was a basket case.

Picture me coming two hours before I was to sign on and then at the stroke of midnight, sitting alone in the control room surrounded by turntables, records, albums, tapes, a clock and a telephone. The program director, Happy Buck Milton, wished me luck and then I was on my own and went on the air.

I signed on with the theme *Midnight Now Is the Hour* by Eddie Calvert cued up. Thirty seconds later I faded the record so I can talk but nothing comes out.

My mouth was drier than southern Saskatchewan during the Dirty Thirties Depression. My hands shook as I brought up the music and fade it again.

Still no words came from my mouth. The only thing my listeners were hearing was a record going up and down in volume.

After a third time trying to say something, I became exasperated.

Finally I was able to tell my listeners in a squeaky voice about the predicament I was in, and that gave me confidence to continue. The rest of the show, as well as my career, went fine but I didn't date anyone for the next while as I spent much of my free time helping Mrs. Bohn renovate her kitchen.

CHAPTER 3

A delinquent young god shooting invisible arrows. A doctor in ancient times helping the sick for free. Love notes left in an urn for some unknown blind date. All are among the folklore of what has become Penticton High School's fest of the year—the annual Valentine dance.

Happy Buck Milton assigned me to cover the Friday night event for CJOE radio and since there was no live broadcast, I had an opportunity to dance with several of the girls, some graduating in June and growing into adulthood.

Among the girls I danced with was pretty Trixy Fahlman, who was incredibly sexy wearing high heels and a red mini-skirt. The musky smell of her perfume did not bother me as we danced a slow tempo tune and she pressed her breasts against my chest. As the night progressed, Trixy and I danced a second time and I accidentally stepped on her toes and apologized with, "I'm sorry."

"That's all right," Trixy said. "But do you want to know something?"

Curious, I said, "What?"

"I listen to your show each night on the radio and you should have a moniker. What if my friends and I call you Daddio Joe from now on?"

"Daddio Joe on the radio? Hey, that sounds poetic. That suits me fine," I said and then, as a five-piece band played, I led Trixy through intricate steps as she hummed to the tune we were dancing. "Daddio Joe on the radio. One, two, three. Daddio Joe on the radio. One, two, three."

When Trixy and I danced the third time, we thought we'd have some fun so we did Valentine four-liners. As we danced I said the first three lines and she filled in the blank so as I said Roses are red. Violets are blue. When I reach fifty."

Trixy filled in the blank with, "I'll still love you."

Next I said, "Trixy, I love you little. I love you a lot."

Trixy filled the blank with, "Your valentine, I'm not."

"Okay, let's try this one," I said. "You are my love. And all my life. How lucky I'll be."

Trixy filled in the blank with, "If I'm not your wife."

Finally I said, "I love you little. I love you big. I love you like . . .

Trixy responded with, "A little pig."

As soon as the dance ended, Trixy squeezed my hand and said, "Daddio Joe. I'm a fan of yours. I can't imagine why we haven't met before since my father is the manager of the radio station where you work."

"Your father is the Harry Fahlman at CJOE?" I said.

"That's my father and I don't know why we haven't met before."

"I don't know why either. Maybe that's a question you should ask your father."

"I'll do that."

I thought Trixy was a charming young lady so I said, "So what's after graduation? Are you going to enter the Miss Penticton pageant?"

"I'm afraid not. My father wants me to go to a finishing school in Switzerland but I'd like to be a rock n roll disc jockey."

"There you go. Mine wanted me to be an accountant."

As soon as the Valentine party was over Trixy went to her home, and I to the radio station where I taped a short account of the High School Valentine party and at the same time, wondering why I hadn't touched Trixy's lips since it was Valentine's Day.

On Monday afternoon, I was called into Fahlman's office and when I sat at a desk in front of him. I thought his anger was close to the surface, so much so, that his head might explode if he held the anger any longer.

"There's something I want to discuss with you, young man!" Fahlman roared.

I was startled by Fahlman's voice. As far as I was concerned everything seemed fine as far as my employment went.

"Over the weekend, I heard people talking about you," Fahlman continued. "And what I heard, as far as I'm concerned as a parent, is more revolting than seeing a snake with diarrhea."

"I don't know what that's supposed to mean," I apologized.

"It means while you and Trixy were dancing at the High School Friday night, you were rubbing your chest against her breasts. And she says she's a fan of yours."

"And that bothers you."

"It certainly does."

"Why?"

"Because I want Trixy to be a doctor and not a radio personality. That's why she'll be going to a finishing school in Switzerland. Your pursuit for her affection must stop immediately."

I said the situation between Trixy and me was *unfair* and *ridiculous* and I thought she was a lovely young woman, which many a man would pursue to be his wife.

"Listen. As you say Trixy is a lovely young lady and I want her to remain that way," Fahlman said while gesticulating with his hands.

What could I say except, "OK, Mr. Fahlman, Daddio Joe on the Radio says so."

"Daddio Joe? What is that supposed to mean?"

"Trixy suggests that should be my radio nick-name."

"I beg your pardon? Trixy gave you that name?"

"It was her idea."

"Glory hallelujah! I'll have to speak to her about that. The name sounds like an acne medication."

This was a time in history when the Broadway show tune sound was waning and rhythm and blues and progenitors of rock n roll were starting to flex their muscles colliding with the polished pristine gentility of those in the pop music power. It was a time too when radio announcers, especially disc jockeys, were using monikers like: Wolfman, Big Daddy, Hound Dog, Sam the Record Man and Daddio Joe, which I inherited accidentally while dancing with Trixy Fahlman.

After a year on Night Shift spinning records, answering phone calls, playing dedications and reading news, sports, weather reports, lost and found items and personal messages I was beginning to realize why Big Paul Mitchell needed psychiatric help. When it came to personal messages I'd read as many as I could, like: "Jesse in Osoyoos would like Winnie in Peachland to know that Grandma's cold is getting better. Thank you for the bananas."
Granted, much was left unsaid and I never did find out if Grandma was feeling better because of the bananas or Jessie kept poisoning Grandma.

One night, I was playing a record but halfway it began to skip. Before I could react, the needle scraped across the entire song leaving me with dead-air silence. Seeing the embarrassing moment I was in, I opened the microphone and said live on the air, "All right which one of you listeners at home just bumped your radio and made the record skip?"
After my face saving joke, I played another song. A few minutes later I received three phone calls apologizing for what they had done.

One night I got bored talking to a microphone so I decided to ask listeners to phone me so I knew I wasn't alone on Planet Earth. Five phone calls later, one of which was from my mother, I told my listeners that unless I got more calls they would hear a grown up woman cry on the air. A call came as I started playing another record. When I answered the phone, a friendly male voice said, "You are going to be thrilled to death. Daddio Joe, you have forty listeners here."

After I expressed my delight the listener said, "Yup, I've got the radio on in the barn for my cows."

A week later I received a letter.

"Please let me know as soon as possible the title of a song you played last week. I'm not sure whether it was Tuesday or Thursday. Perhaps it was Wednesday. It was a polka or a waltz but it may have been a fox trot. The lyrics were wonderful, although I can't remember what they said. I'm sorry I didn't catch the name of the composer nor the singer. On second thought, I'm not sure if it was your station, but give me the information anyway since I want to buy the record."

One female, although she never sent personal messages or wrote letters, tormented me regularly but refused to give her name. She seemed friendly, however, and underneath sounded like a respectable woman I would like to meet. During one conversation she asked if I'd like to come to her apartment which was less than a block away from the station so I said, "Okay, I'll come as soon as my shift is over?"

"No," she replied. "I'm a nurse and will be leaving for work soon. How about, right now?"

"Right now?" I looked up at a clock in front of me. It read 3:37 a. m. I debated with myself if I should take the risk of meeting someone I didn't know but eventually said, "I'll be over in a shake, as soon as I slap on Hank Snow's *Four Square* album on the air." One side of the album took twenty minutes to play.

While the album was playing on the air, I rushed to the caller's apartment, and when she let me inside and introduced herself as Henny Field I got excited and said, "What a surprise! Oh my, oh me, it's nice to see you again, Henny."

My heart began fluttering and adrenalin flowing. Henny was the most ravishing woman I had met thus far and I didn't need an educated flea to figure out her age. Since I was twenty three and Henny was a year younger during the Talent Show in Selkirk, that made her twenty two and from what I gathered still unmarried.

Following a brief reaquaintance Henny asked if I wanted to have fun with her. I thought she meant playing the piano but it was not so. It ran through my mind that Henny might appear to be a nice girl but who knows what's going on in her mind. Still I said, "Okay, Henny, I'll play with you."

As soon as I said that I would play with her, Henny hurried to her bedroom and brought out a checkerboard. For the next ten minutes I kept jumping Henny, with Kings, that's all.

Fifteen minutes had passed and by now I had to hurry back to the station. Hank Snow's album would end soon. Henny turned on the radio and monitored Hank Snow singing *A Fool Such As I*, I then realized that I had less than three minutes to race to the station or else I would be in trouble. I apologized to Henny that I could not stay longer but possibly we could date the following day. As soon as Henny said, "That's an excellent idea." I hurried back to the station control room like *Secretariat*.

Up a flight of stairs and around a corner I dashed into the CJOE control room where upon my arrival I was astonished that the needle got stuck in one of the grooves in the final cut of the album and was repeating itself over and over *"I Love You Because, I Love You because, I Love You Because."*

The phones were ringing and my head began spinning. I lifted the playback arm on the first turntable and slapped a Harry Bellefonte album on the second. At that precise moment I wished CJOE had no listeners but that did not happen because Fahlman had just returned from a meeting with the absentee owner in Vancouver. Before retiring he turned on the radio. As Bellefonte's album was on the air I picked up the telephone and said, "Good morning. CJOE. Can I help you?"
'You certainly can?" Fahlman said blowing a gasket. "Where have you been Daddio Joe? And don't say in the washroom! For the past three minutes all I could hear on the radio was Hank Snow repeating over and over, *I Love*

You Because, I Love You Because, I Love You Because. What's your explanation?"

What could I say? I told the truth and was lucky I didn't get fired.

I wasn't so lucky the following year, however, when on my midnight shift I introduced a wild new sound on CJOE and played *Laudy Miss Claudy* by Lloyd Price and *Hey, Miss Fannie* by the Clovers, which launched the rock n roll craze that dominated the decade.

At this point of my employment I felt CJOE programming wasn't keeping pace with the changing times, but a week earlier Fahlman got all the announcers together and said to them, "Rock n roll is nothing but country and western music with Afro-American rhythm and blues. The performers introducing the new sound strike most adults as being callow, pimply faced boys with ducktail haircuts and untrained voices, emitting mindless and frequently repulsive grunts."

With that assessment Fahlman may have been right. The rhythm of rock, seemed overpowering, and monotonous, the volume deafening, and the movements made by the performers, scandalous.

"Even more scandalous are some of the lyrics," Fahlman said at the time. "Take for instance, *Make me feel real loose, like a long necked-goose. Oh, Baby, that's what I like.* In fact the term Rock n Roll coined by New York disc jockey Allan Freed, was inspired by a raunchy old blues lyric *My Baby Rocks Me With A Steady Roll.* My conclusion is that Rock n Roll is unfit for a family audience and won't last long. We are a station of high standards and good taste."

Yet the new genre was clearly irresistible by teenage listeners like Trixy Fahlman and they phoned me every night for Rock n Roll requests. They wanted the guitar thumpers instead of Eddie Fisher, Dinah Shore or even Frank Sinatra.

It was in 1954 that I played *Rock Around the Clock* by Bill Haley and the Comets as the song rocked and rolled its way to the top of the charts selling 15-million copies worldwide.

Haley was the first White interpreter of a sound established by Black musicians several years earlier. This was the beginning of a huge shift as teenagers as a movement, were involved in the social phenomenon. They jived to the music and buying everything thrown at them: milkshakes and hamburgers, blue jeans and hair grease.

The following morning I was shakin', rockin' n rollin' when Fahlman called me into his office and said I had been fired but with two weeks notice.

'Fired! Why?" I wanted to know.

"Young man," Fahlman said, (Fahlman often referred to me as 'Young Man') "Because you have broken station policy. Rock n Roll music is deemed to salacious for polite society. I told you that, but you did not listen."

Coping with the trauma of being fired involved talking it out, working it out, and going on to recognize the skills I had to offer. "Losing my job because I, like many, enjoy Rock n Roll isn't a shameful event," I thought and I recovered quickly from the shock of being bounced by CJOE management. Since I was young, I felt no anger towards Fahlman, hurt or embarrassment, although I did feel pain and in the process walked about as if I was on top of an eggshell wondering what my next step would be.

I thought CJOE was a radio station where I could hang my hat for a while. But you can't dwell on it and be sad about it. You have to move on, because we all have bills to pay. But instead of moving on I decided my challenge would be to convince Fahlman that CJOE needed a new music format, if it was to compete with television, which by now was the in-form of entertainment.

In a small city like Penticton, rumors spread faster than one can spit out a cherry pit. Several days after I had been fired I confirmed on the air that my dismissal was because I played rock n roll music, which was against station policy and said casually, "If I have offended a listener, I'm sorry. However, I feel the rock era is here. The generation gap is splitting like the San Andreas Fault, but my station management fails to realize this."

Many listeners upon hearing my comment agreed, and started a petition collecting names in schools, shopping malls and street corners. Teenagers, housewives and even Henny, Trixy and Father Tim Brophy of St. Anne's Catholic parish signed it. The petition in part read: *We The Undersigned Want Daddio Joe To Remain With CJOE. In Our Opinion Daddio Joe Is Playing Our Type Of Music.* There were two thousand names on the petition within a week and then the pages were stapled to the front door of Fahlman's residence on Montreal Street. The petition was followed by protesters' taking turns and phoning the radio station every two minutes lighting up the switchboard

Soon the whole of Penticton got caught up in my firing and the relationship I had with Harry Fahlman. Even the local newspaper, *Herald*, did an article about the firing and followed it with a survey if I should remain with CJOE or not. I was surprised with the survey results which showed 60% of those interviewed wanted the station to have me back on the air, 25% hadn't heard of Daddio Joe and 15% had no opinion because they either watched television or at listened to out of town radio stations. Penticton was a one-station city at the time.

Fahlman must have been impressed with the *Herald* survey, because the following day he called me back into his office again and said, "Okay, Daddio Joe, I now agree CJOE's music policy must change, if we are to increase our audience rating and compete with television. You can have your job back but tell me, in your opinion, how our present format should change."

"To begin I suggest the station discard opera, symphonies and all long-hair music we are presently playing. You have to be as good as what is on television. People aren't going to listen to CJOE because we are a local station."

"Well, what do you suggest?"

"I suggest that our programming would be more meaningful if we catered to those under thirty-five. I would fill the airwaves with the top 100 rock, soul, doo-wop and country and western hits of the day. In the programming format, I would insert a previous million seller, an instrumental and play tunes from albums. I would call the program Penticton A. M. Penticton Noon, and Penticton P. M. depending on the time of day."

I also pointed out that Talk-Shows were gaining popularity and so were trivia quizzes and suggested that obituary notices, which the station carried regularly following the 12:30 News, should be left to the newspapers. There should be no religious or foreign language programming. I also suggested CJOE inaugurate a For Sale/Wanted to Buy and a Community Calendar feature and name it, Flea Market.

It was my opinion that the station should place more emphasis on local news and sports and the news staff increase from two to four.

Next I suggested CJOE do some public relations of its own by giving away T-shirts and baseball caps with the station's logo and JOE staff challenge community groups and service clubs to various games with proceeds going to charity.

"An excellent idea," Fahlman said. "Imagine, if you can, the radio station staff playing the firemen in a game of hockey. What a riot that we be, especially since I can't skate."

"Playing hockey against the local firemen and you unable to skate, could be a riot of course, but the first team the station should play is members of the local detachment of the RCMP.

"Why the RCMP?"

"A million dollars worth of publicity and automatically CJOE staff will become the underdog. The public knows Mounties always get their man; the point is how they are going to do it. They may catch a woman instead."

After discussing my format proposals Fahlman said, "Well, Daddio Joe, you can have your announcing job back on the radio. I'll implement some of the changes you recommend, but I'm taking you off the midnight shift."

I wondered why.

"Because Big Paul Mitchell has undergone psychiatric therapy and ready to go back to work."

I was surprised about Big Paul's recovery and the surprise increased when Fahlman backtracked and added a caveat as a condition of my employment.

"What's the caveat?" I said.

"That you not socialize with Henny Field for the next six months."

"Six months?" I roared. "What kind of punishment is that? Its outrages! Why six months?"

"It's because of your discipline. In order to be a versatile announcer one has to have discipline. As far as I'm concerned you have shown very little."

"What? I come to work on time. I finish my assignments. What else do you want me do?"

"Stop hanging around bars and chasing women."

"Why should I to satisfy a passing whim of yours?" I protested.

"Because, bars are unhealthy, even sleazy, where disreputable types hang out."

"On the contrary," I said, "Bars are where friends gather to gossip, joke, exchange views, get leads and other matters, doing no harm to anybody. It reduces complaints about low pay. And hey, have you ever seen me drunk?"

"Never," Fahlman said and then gave me an ultimatum. "Take it or leave it, Daddio Joe."

The thought of not seeing Henny for six months placed me in a dilemma. Should I continue my relationship with her and move to another station? What if Henny didn't want to move? Penticton is a wonderful place to live in with its lakes, beaches, mountains and unpolluted air. Its orchards and vineyards are everywhere. After some thought I chose to stay with CJOE and told Henny the crises I was in. Surprisingly her response at the time was, "That's okay, Daddio Joe. Maybe it was meant to be that way."

The following Monday, I began my shift starting at 6:00 p. m. until midnight and soon discovered the audience was different compared to the midnight shift. There were still lonely listeners, shut-in's, truck drivers, men and women working in factories and hospitals, unidentified objects flying in space, and there were also students doing homework. I knew they were students by their requests to play records with dedications to one another and in the process the questions they asked. Questions like: "Why do I always dream when I do homework?" "How many shopping days are there until Christmas?" "Why did I get zero in my last exam?" and, "Why should I make my bed and clean my room each day?"

When it came to reading the weather forecast there were no satellites or maps available to explain weather patterns, instead when it was going to rain I cheerfully predicted, "Well, it's rain, rain and more rain. Just how much? Your guess is as good as mine. Goodnight, folks"

Another time I was thinking about Selkirk, Manitoba when I accidentally announced, "The current temperature in Selkirk is twenty degrees."
Recovering quickly I added, "What a coincidence? It's also twenty three, here in beautiful downtown Penticton."

A week following the format change, I was surprised by a commotion in front of the radio station. There was a group of about twenty senior citizens from the Retirement Centre gossiping, leaning on canes, pushing walkers and protesting. With various placards in hand they were parading back and forth by the Radio Building, shouting in unison and demanding the return to the old format.
"Back to the Music We Understand," one of the placards read.
"Rock n Roll Music Is Evil," read another.
It wasn't until Fahlman spoke to the group that it disappeared.

I was into my third month of the shift when Fahlman suggested I accept phone calls on the air from 10:15 p. m. until midnight. The program was called *Open Line* but it wasn't long before I wished it were titled *Comedy Time* instead.

One night, I said to my listeners that my parents came to Manitoba from Poland and when I attended school in Selkirk we were so poor that all I had for lunch was lard sandwiches, and at home we ate out of paper plates.

"That's nothing," a listener called, "When my parents came to Penticton from Norway we ate out of paper plates too."

"But not from the same ones," I said and went on, "I can remember also that we ate bread only because we were poor."

The listener snapped, "Our family too. Now, however, our family is poor because of the high price for a loaf of bread."

Another listener phoned to say that he was so unlucky that if he bought a carnation hot house, the government would cancel Mother's Day.

"I'm unlucky too," I said.

"What do you mean? You got your announcer's job back."

"True. But I met this good-looking chick but I'm unable to socialize with her for six months."

When I suggested to another listener, that inflation ruined everything he quipped, "You are right Daddio Joe. Although a dime can still be used, as a screw driver."

Then one evening when most of our conversation on *Open Line* dealt with the subject of real estate, I asked a realtor who identified himself as Peter Wong, what was the difference between present home purchasers compared to the time I was a child in Selkirk.

"They're still buying homes," Wong said. "Only now purchasers charge them on their credit card."

I felt realtor Wong was in a similar state of mind which had sent Big Paul Mitchell to see a psychiatrist when he said that whenever there was a downturn in Canada's economy, his sales drop forcing him to a diet made up mostly of grapes.

"So what?" I said, "The Okanagan Valley is vineyard country. Everyone enjoys grapes here."

Wong surprised me and I'm certain many of my listeners, when he said, "What? Off the kitchen wallpaper?"

The following week, I was not only surprised but also disappointed with an equal proportion. My six-month probationary period imposed by Fahlman had expired but when I phoned Henny and asked for a date, she rejected me. "You've had your chance," she said. "I'm presently going out with someone else."

Henny then hung up the receiver.

I was king or the airwaves between 6:00 p. m. and midnight but not Henny's boyfriend.

CHAPTER 4

Most of the staff at CJOE was made up of young people when I began working there and we use to play pranks on each other. Often the prank was to make the announcer crackup while either reading a newscast or a commercial while live on the air.

One thing the Academy taught me was not to take news reading lightly. I remember the instructor saying that the word NEWS was made from the first letters of north, east, west and south and had to be read with authority, even light-hearted items at the end known as the *kicker*.

One evening as I was reading the 8:00 p. m. news from the main control room Big Paul Mitchell thought he would make me laugh and interrupt a news item. The newscast included items about hardship, discomfort, misery, fire and an earthquake. Big Paul climbed on top of a table in the front of the glass window facing me, and began stripping naked and gesturing wildly. His challenge was to convince me that there is a measurable value in having fun in one's work. Big Paul always advocated guerrilla tactics when all else failed to get announcers to loosen up and have fun at their work place. The prank was going on for several minutes until I closed my microphone switch and there was dead air for several seconds. The silence was not the result of Big Paul trying to make me burst out with laughter but at that precise moment the night cleaning lady walked into the room catching Big Paul standing on a table, naked.

Big Paul's antics continued the following evening when he was reading a newscast and an item about an increase in the Income Tax. He hardly missed a dulcet-toned syllable when an errant fly flew into his mouth. He swallowed the intruder and then continued bravely reading the news.

When I asked Big Paul why he didn't spit the fly out he said, "I'm a vegetarian and the buzzing fly was the first piece of meat I have tasted in a long time. And do you want to know something?"

I said, "What?"

"I haven't got the taste for it now," he said wryly of the fly tartare.

Big Paul Mitchell and I were constantly playing jokes on each other. One time during a remote broadcast I was to gulp down a glassful of water only to discover that Big Paul changed glasses and the one I was to drink was filled with vodka. I spit it out and started coughing like crazy on live radio while Big Paul was laughing his head off.

Another time we were on duty together. I was in the main control room doing a program when suddenly I noticed my chair was missing.

"Aha," I said to myself. "Big Paul, you're in trouble."

As a record was on the turntable I snuck out of control room thinking he was in the hallway. I rushed out and snack-dab I ran into the cleaning lady, knocking her over.

A minute later Big Paul returned the chair again laughing incredulously.

My conclusion about radio announcing was that it's possible to deal with serious matters and the same time, have fun. Deep down, I believe, most people do care about their work. They, including Harry Fahlman, however, have forgotten how to find humor in their workplace.

I must tell you about another incident, which nearly took me for a loop. This time Big Paul was reading the news and I was spinning records. While Big Paul was reading I took a break and went to the music library with the on air monitor turned on. It was three minutes into the newscast when I heard a clatter much louder than Santa Claus on a rooftop, and then suddenly there was silence. I ran back to the control room as fast as I could and seeing Big Paul on the floor kicking and foaming at the mouth, I said to myself, "This is no joke but a serious matter."

I then turned off Big Paul's microphone switch, slapped on an album on the turntable and as it was playing on the air I looked down at Big Paul and realized he had a seizure of some sort, so I called for an ambulance.

What had happened a paramedic told me afterward, was that Big Paul had an epileptic seizure and didn't tell anyone at the station that he was a victim of the disorder. Big Paul was at work next day.

Another time I grabbed a news-wire story about an African leader who was assassinated. Realizing too late that I couldn't pronounce his name I sputtered, "His name is being withheld pending notification of next of kin."

Since I was interested in gathering news, Harry Fahlman, several days later, assigned me to do a documentary about prostitution in Penticton which became a heated topic of discussion for City Council. There was a charming brunette who I felt wasn't stupid or ditsy and had been calling me while I was on the Midnight Shift. I had to work fast because in radio deadlines are important so I phoned Jezebel Beaumaris and said to her, "Miss, excuse me for saying this but you must have an interesting job?"

"Don't give me that goody, goody, stuff," Jezebel said. "The job ain't much to brag about. I'm really a file clerk. And the boss is good to me because he wants to get next to me. You understand what I mean?"

"But that's nothing, Miss," I said. "I understand from some of your customers that you are pretty and there aren't many pretty girls in Penticton."

"Wise guy" she said. "I'm not like other girls. I'm going to let you on a little secret, however. Believe it or not, I earn more money in one night that you do in a week."

"I believe you," I said, "CJOE doesn't pay much. As a freelancer you must be doing commercials."

"No such luck. I'm a hustler, a part-time prostitute on Saturday night, if you get what I mean?"

"Please. But how can a respectable-looking chick like you stoop so low? You mean to tell me that an honest working girl works for five days a week and then sells herself on Saturdays?"

"Why not? It's easy money and if a cop grabs me I can always prove in court that I'm a respectable working girl with a steady job."

I was crushed, at the same time I wanted to learn more. I even went so far to ask for a date since Henny Field was out of my life, but Jezebel said, "No dice. I look for old geezers with money and not struggling radio announcers. No hard feelings."

Later, Jezebel said, "I'll tell you something, Daddio Joe. You can put everything I say on tape for your documentary if we have breakfast together Saturday morning."

It goes without saying I was excited and when Saturday morning arrived, I grabbed a tape recorder and met Jezebel at Venghi's Restaurant. We sat at a table near a corner so that our conversation would be in private. Jezebel, that sinful chippie, had breakfast at my expense but I didn't mind, because she came to spill her story and possibly I could win a news gathering award.

Jezebel began by how she lived in Vancouver but came to Penticton as a model to enter the Miss Penticton Pageant but lost out so she had to take on odd jobs to keep her body together. "Bread ain't cheap," she said

When I asked Jezebel how she came to enter the profession of selling sex she said, "It began when I picked up an acquaintance with a street walker on Lakeshore Drive and soon as the Miss Penticton Pageant was over. She let me in on all the secrets—how to pick up rich guys and avoid being caught by police. So I went to work. I had something to sell that was certain to bring handsome returns in spot cash, and I didn't have to pay income tax."

Next Jezebel said, "Now let me tell you how I go about my business. I follow a certain routine and during my street walking for two hours Saturdays from ten in the evening until midnight. My routine is to walk up and down Lakeshore Drive where most people hang out Saturday nights. I walk slowly like I'm window shopping and never have trouble picking up an old geezer from out of town with plenty of money."

What I thought about Jezebel at the moment I leave to your imagination. All I knew was that I was getting interesting comment on tape. I kept a straight face and then asked Jezebel to tell me the rest. She needed no coaxing and went on, "Don't think I'm cheap. A guy must never be a young buck but the kind who after several drinks invites me to his apartment or hotel suite."

This is where it really got interested so I asked Jezebel not to keep me in suspense but to tell me what she generally did after getting the *old geezer* to his apartment or hotel suite. Jezebel burst out with laughter. "You bad boy, Daddio Joe, for asking such a question," she said. "But I'm going to answer so that you have it on tape. It's like this. At first I permit the old guy a little petting and a little necking until he gets a little warmed up for the final pitch.

But before I allow him any closer contact, I tell him it costs $100 if he wants me to be his lovey-dovey. If he pays, you can bet your sweet life, that I give the old guy his money's worth."

I felt telling Jezebel she was a bit twisted and that she was too far gone to be reformed so I simply remarked, "A fair exchange isn't robbery. The old geezer gets what he wants to pay for. But tell me, it can't always be as easy as that. Suppose the guy starts of by telling you to take the pitch, even if he has no intention of paying for it. What then?"

"That's easy. When the guy tells me that he can't or won't pay, I simply scream for help and then walk out on him to look for another customer. That's how I work this racket. And it works like a charm, because I got the technique and physical attributes as you can see for yourself."

Jezebel had everything it takes to get what she wanted. I could only thank her for her charming company because by now I had run out of tape. I made an appointment for the following Saturday morning to discuss why City Council was so concerned about girls walking the streets particularly during the Peach Festival and Square Dance Jamboree, but Jezebel didn't show up and I never meet her until 1960 when we were involved in a motor vehicle accident. The information I had, however, was an interview, which won the Canadian News Award for the best community related news program. Not only had I won an important award but also when the interview was aired during *rating week*, and because the subject matter dealt with sex, CJOE had the highest listener rating ever.

While on the subject of ratings radio stations produce their finest programs during *rating week*. Four times a year, each winter, spring, summer and autumn, an independent survey agency surveys listeners in the area. In order to increase listenership so the station can charge more for commercial spots, some stations offer their audience money, gifts and trips to exotic places during the week that ratings take place

I recall when CJOE, in order to boost listenership, had an announcer say throughout the length of the promotion," Don't change that dial because you can win a trip to Disneyland!"

The object of the promotion was for listeners to guess the number of peas displayed in a glass barrel at the Cherry Lane Shopping Centre. Not only did the number of peas promotion encourage to shop in the mall but also listeners were encouraged to give their estimate on the air every hour. When an announcer accepted phone calls the switchboard lit up. During one particular day the announcer said to his audience, "What is your pea estimate?"

A listener phoned to say; "My answer is fifteen feet when I pee from the swimming pool diving board."

At any rate when the contest was over the winner of the trip to Disneyland was a retired pea farmer from Penticton with the name Bob Jackson. His estimate of 21,279 was the closest to the correct answer, 25,000. Bob shared the prize with his brother Jack, who like himself, when he retired took residence at the Penticton Retirement Centre, where the manager described the two brothers as, "Holy Terrors."

After Bob and Jack returned from Disneyland I interviewed them. My first question to Bob was, "While in Los Angeles did you take any side trips?"

"We did. We went to Knott's Berry farm, toured Universal Studios and traveled to Tijuana, Mexico."

"Tell me about your experience in Tijuana," I said.

"Well, it began as soon as Jack and I crossed the U. S.—Mexican border and a young boy, about ten, in tattered clothing walked up to us and said, 'Senor, do you want to buy some chewing gum?'"

When we said we didn't, the boy was persistent and asked if we wanted to make love to his sister, and when we didn't, the kid said his sister was a virgin. When we didn't believe him he asked if we wanted a date with his mother who was a virgin also. That set the tone for our trip to Tijuana."

Another promotion CJOE had was a Love-At-First-Sight contest, which got blindsided. The promotion began when a couple was married at the station one afternoon and in exchange won an all-expense paid golfing trip to Vancouver. It was supposed to be a love at first sight wedding with the bride picking her hubby from five strangers whose ages ranged from twenty seven to sixty six, hailed from as far afield as Kelowna and Osoyoos and had called the radio station. The bride chose Mr. Right after a brief interview at the station next day.

"It's fun." the prospective groom said at the time and thought his date was *gorgeous*. "On the way out I said to Libby 'I guess I should get your phone number'." But word dribbled out several days later that the couple had dated for a long time, worked together at a restaurant and would do anything to go golfing outside Penticton.

The couple declined to be interviewed but the *Herald* in an editorial wrote, "It doesn't look good for a radio station if a station doesn't control its contests."

"Who is complaining about protecting radio's integrity?" Fahlman shot back. "This wouldn't be the same newspaper that gave away a free skiing trip to Denver and it turned out to be New Denver in the West Kootenay of British Columbia?"

Fahlman said CJOE did not know the newlyweds were not new to each other and had them keep the golfing trip to Vancouver. "The wedding stands," Fahlman said.

I do want to tell you about another interview I conducted during my early days in radio. It was with dramatic soprano, Nina Tikova, when she came to Penticton to give a concert at the High School Auditorium. Ms. Tikova was sponsored by a group of high society people who did not enjoy rock n roll and called themselves The Penticton Society for Better Music. Ms. Tikova's performance date had been announced as the most significant cultural event in Penticton in recent years.

Blessed with a powerful voice and an extraordinary range Ms. Tikova achieved stardom in Europe. Her voice was of enormous proportions ranging from G to D and her personality was suited to dramatic soprano roles in Verdi and Wagner.

One could say that Ms. Tikova was a prima donna wearing furs, jewelry and a fancy hat, which had red feathers sticking out on one side. Besides having a great voice Ms. Tikova had a great fondness of apricots. After I made her comfortable in a studio I brought her a basketful to enjoy.

During my interview we talked about Ms. Tikova's role in *Tannhaueser, Tosca, Aida* and *Madame Butterfly.* In between bits of conversation I played her most popular arias. I'm glad that our librarian at Selkirk, Manitoba, Catherine Livingstone encouraged me to read books, all types of books, including books about music. I was now reaping the benefits and had a good background on music terminology. At any rate at about the middle of my interview Ms. Tikova popped an apricot into her mouth at the same time that a huge transport truck passed by the station causing the building to vibrate. The vibrations were so strong that they made a ceiling tile come loose, striking Ms. Tikova on the head which in turn made the apricot she was enjoying, stuck in her throat.

Ms, Tikova coughed and coughed and when she finally swallowed the apricot let out a scream that could be heard as far as Rridgedale Avenue. Her voice was so loud that it tipped the volume indicator, knocking the transmitter off the air.

During Ms. Tikova's concert that night, there were many applauses and, "Bravos."

I know there were, because Big Paul Mitchell and I were sitting in the back row applauding with the rest of the audience.

It was while we were attending Ms. Tikova's concert I discovered that although Big Paul Mitchell enjoyed classical music and a relentless practical joker, there was something in his life like in mine, missing—a female companion.

A day after the concert, I had Big Paul stop at the Patricia Motel and introduced him to Jane Gordon, the motel receptionist. According to Jane's resume she stopped growing when she was ten, was thirty-six inches in height, and weighed thirty-six pounds, a beautiful dark-haired lady. No one knew Jane was a midget when she answered phone calls, unless they saw her in person.

The following day at the radio station Big Paul said to me, "Daddio Joe, Jane is the most charming little lady I ever met. I believe she's what my psychiatrist prescribed to be my wife. Will you put a good word on my behalf?"
When I reneged Big Paul continued, "Daddio Joe, look, you have been my friend for a long time. I feel I must marry this young lady, she's a gorgeous, perfect woman."

Big Paul became so obsessed with Jane that he couldn't think about anything else. He was ready for domestic bliss and unusually excited, so I urged him to calm down and proceed with caution as he could hardly expect Miss Gordon's affection overnight. "And one more thing," I said.
"What?"

That is when I revealed that if Big Paul was going to pursue Jane's affection, that he had a rival for the young lady's heart.

"Who?"

"Another midget who works for the Federal Government in the Income Tax Department, and although he's a midget, he's muscular and larger than you."

"What's his name?"

"Gregory Kastner."

"Gregory Kastner, I know him. I'll fight him if necessary."

I found a way to turn a delicate situation into an advantage by inviting Big Paul and Jane to a barbecue at the Patricia Motel where, when they came, my mother said, "Oh my, what a tiny but a well-matched couple."

As the hamburgers were prepared the conversation between Big Paul Mitchell and Jane Gordon led to Miss Gordon to say, "Call me Jane instead of Miss Gordon."

"And you may call me Big Paul."

As the barbecue progressed, Big Paul sat by Jane's side. And as the barbecue ended, it was pitch-dark outside and they were talking, laughing and flirting until the fireflies came and that was the only source of light they had.

Following the barbecue every time Big Paul came to Patricia Motel he would never fail to bring Jane a red rose but Gregory Kastner was not indifferent to Big Paul's presence. Whenever he saw Big Paul approaching the motel he would strut like a bantam rooster spitting out unkind words.

One afternoon Big Paul and Gregory got into a scuffle. The heavier Gregory was actually a peaceful man while Big Paul on the other hand had taken Korean martial arts for self-defense. Before Gregory could say, "You'll never take Miss Gordon away from me," he had been thrown on his back and given a whack across his head. In future meetings Gregory was careful to keep his distance and Big Paul kept wooing Jane.

Fearful that his parents would not approve of his plans to marry Jane, Big Paul was eager to have them meet under favorable circumstances. After they had met Big Paul's parents gave their only son their approval.

The following night Big Paul met Jane again at the Patricia Motel swimming pool, and this time they talked about a trip Jane was about to take to Ottawa.

"I wish I was going with you," Big Paul said.

"I thought you had remarked that you didn't enjoy traveling," Jane said

"That depends upon my company."

"You may find my company not agreeable."

"I would be glad to take the risk," Big Paul said and then slipped an arm around Jane's waste.

That's when she said, "Big Paul, of course I would like you to accompany me."

Big Paul's arm clasped Jane's little waist closer and said with trepidation, "Well, don't you think it would be pleasanter if we were husband and wife?"

"That!" Jane said to her suitor, was no way to joke.

"The matter" Big Paul continued, was much too serious to joke about and went on, "The moment I saw you at the Patricia Motel I felt you were recommended by a guardian angel to be my wife."

"Well, I think I love you well enough, but I would never marry without my parents consent," Jane said.

"Is that so? Then I will ask them."

"Go ahead and make sure you bring along a bottle of whiskey for my father."

"Your father?"

"Yes my father; but I warn you he's a retired Army Sergeant and not very pretty to look at, so be careful."

That night Big Paul phoned Jane's parents but her father told him he was busy so they made an appointment for the following weekend, taking full advantage.

"Nothing like some time to ponder one's fate," Jane's father said to his wife.

When the appointed time came, Jane's father opened the door and waited. Big Paul walked up trying to appear in full control and promptly fell while up the stairs dropping the whiskey bottle he was carrying. Once he got a hold of himself Big Paul and Jane's father went into a den. After they talked about everything under the sun, Big Paul finally got around asking about marrying Jane.

Having talked to Big Paul's parents' the day before Jane's father said, "There are three points that have to be cleared up before you can marry Jane. First, I'm concerned that my future grandchildren will become bald permanently since you appear to loosing your hair."

Big Paul's eyes got as big as plates. Big Paul replied that all his family had his or her hair and no one, absolutely no one, was bald.

"I need this confirmed," Jane's father said. "Would you please call your father so I can talk to him?"

Big Paul barely could dial a number but he did. After a brief conversation with his father Jane's father said, "The second point is that I have heard you were married once before."

Big Paul's eyes got huge again and he swore that he was never married before.

"I need this confirmed also," Jane's father said and handed him a piece of paper with a lady's name and phone number on it that he found in the phone book. The phone call didn't last long because eventually she hung up on him.

Big Paul thought it was all over until Jane's father said, "Before I give you permission to marry our daughter I need to see your Income tax returns for the last three years."

Big Paul's jaw drooped to the floor. He started to go and get them. When he reached the door Jane's father stuck out his hand, shook Big Paul's and said, "Yes, you can marry Jane. Welcome to the family."

Big Paul didn't know how to address his future father-in-law.

"Just call me *sir*," Jane's father said.

Relieved, to celebrate their consent Big Paul thought it would be nice to enjoy a beautiful evening and take Jane on a stroll along Okanagan Lake, with a bottle of champagne, of course. As they strolled along Lakeshore

Drive Big Paul became restless and wanted to find a bench to sit on and when he finally found one fit for a proposal, he opened a small blue silk-covered box that he had pulled out of his pocket. Jane was amazed to find a sparkling solitaire diamond ring inside.

News of the approaching wedding set CJOE staff and rest of Penticton on its ears. When Fahlman suggested that the wedding take place in October, a time when most of the fruit in the Okanagan Valley was already picked and vacationers had gone home, Big Paul protested, "Not for $100,000. We will get married during the month of June."

The bride-to-be nodded her approval.

On June 17th at St. Anne's Catholic Church Big Paul Mitchell took Jane Gordon as his bride when Father Brophy intoned, "I pronounce you, Big Paul Mitchell and you Jane Gordon, husband and wife."

During the mass Father Brophy said that both Big Paul and Jane were "Warm and wonderful people" and reflected on the couple's love story and what they treasured most in each other.

For the marriage ceremony, Jane wore a sleeveless silk organza gown with embroidered flowers, beads and pearls, accompanied by a tiara and finger-length veil. And Jane's sister Monica, maid of honor, chose a celadon-green A-line dress.

Big Paul and I, as best man, wore matching three-button tuxedos. Big Paul also chose a white pique shirt and a silver vest to accent his outfit.

One hundred guests were invited to the reception at the Penticton Inn. The bride and groom stood on top of a table in the Harvest Room as they welcomed guests and received gifts which included a totem pole from the local Indian Band, carved especially for the occasion.

The simple and yet delicious five tiers of the wedding cake filled with lemon curd and vanilla butter cream, was forty inches in height, the same as the groom and his weight. Fresh flowers matching the table centerpieces delicately graced each layer in deep jewel tones.

Interest in the wedding was so intense that it pushed news of a brawl between Quebec fruit pickers and a local gang of hippies off the front page of the *Herald*.

For their honeymoon Mr. and Mrs. Mitchell changed into casual clothing and headed eastward in a rented car that had been adjusted to their height. The first stop was Banff, then Calgary, Regina, Winnipeg, Sudbury and then Ottawa where they were invited to the Governor General's residence where the Queen's representative and his wife gave a reception in the couple's honor.

Fashion editor, Amanda Grace, who was among the guests, wrote in the Toronto *Globe and Mail*, "Mr. and Mrs. Mitchell looked like a couple from Fairyland."

As soon as Mr. and Mrs. Mitchell returned to Penticton from their honeymoon, I interviewed them on the radio. My first question was, "What is it like to be a midget?"

"We exist in a world that is to big for us. We have needs of an adult but our bodies are that of a child. Everything around us: houses, furniture, automobiles and even microphones, are made for people normal size," Big Paul said.

"And for little people it's an alien world, a world of inconvenience." Jane continued.

Then I asked Jane, "Are beds a problem?"

"They are," Jane said. "Climbing in and out of a bed requires care. Tables and chairs are not the right size. When I go to a hairdresser, I have to sit on an auxiliary chair. Things are too big to handle comfortably. Knives, forks and spoons weren't made for small people to hold. Telephones are awkward to pick up and their weight imposes strain. Combs, hairbrushes and razors seem oversized and getting in and out of a bathtub need planning."

As the interview progressed another question I asked was, "What else bothers little people?"

This time Big Paul took over, "Little peop;e have trouble with their clothes and if I want to open a window or turn on the light I may have to reach my arm out in full length or get up on a stool. Turning a doorknob or pressing a button to ring may be impossible if you are small."

Near the end of the interview Big Paul said, "Do you want to know something else, Daddio Joe?"

I said, "What?"

"Harry Fahlman always jokes about my size."

"What does he say?"

"He says his daughter Trixy was taller than me when she was born."

"I wouldn't worry about such a comment," I said. "The comment may have been made in jest."

A day after I interviewed Mr. and Mrs. Mitchell I was called into Fahlman's office where he congratulated me on a *splendid* interview I had conducted about small people. After discussing the interview in detail Fahlman said, "Daddio Joe, how would you like to report on Penticton's participation in the construction of a hospital in Erbil, Iraq?"

"And determine if the funds Pentictonites provided are spent wisely?" I said.

"Exactly."

"You mean to say you want me to go to Iraq?"

"And once you get there, interview hospital authorities and report back to CJOE."

Although I was afraid of flying I thought Fahlman's assignment was interesting so I said, "Why not? I'll go."

I had already written stories for CJOE programming which dealt with the rise of Fidel Castro, the formation of the European Common Market and the Banking system in Switzerland and interviewed a prostitute, an opera singer and two midgets one of which was my co-worker.

My latest assignment was to report on the joint Canadian/American construction of a hospital in Erbil, a 5000 year-old ancient community near the Turkish border and not far from the Lagross Mountains.

Fahlman said that I was to be accompanied by an American correspondent representing the ABC network, Cal Argue, where in London we would finalize our journey.

Once our journey was finalized Cal Argue and I were on a lonely stretch of road between Baghdad and Erbil driving a four-wheel when our vehicle sputtered and suddenly stopped. Cal and I were bent over the stalled engine of a Nissan when I said, "It's the sparkplugs causing the trouble."

"The Japanese make computers and fuel efficient vehicles but know little about sparkplugs," Cal said.

Cal and I were discussing our problem when a White Land Rover with three men inside pulled up on the other side of the stalled Nissan. The men wore turbans and spoke English.

I thought the trio had stopped t help but one pointed a gun towards me and said, "Okay, mister, into the back of the Land Rover."

He motioned to Cal to follow. We complied and thus began a frightful ambush of Daddio Joe Rubeck and Cal Argue, at the hands of Kurdish rebels, Arayan dissidents who had struggled for territorial autonomy for centuries.

One of the rebels took the Nissan and the other two, now each pointing a gun, drove Cal and me across semi-arid hills eastward into the Lagross Mountains. It was fifteen minutes later that the driver issued an order, "Both of you lie face down in the back of the Land Rover," he said while the other handcuffed us.

Each time we tried to explain the purpose of our trip, to do a story on the hospital in Erbil, we got slapped on the face.

"Terrorists," I whispered to Cal when the slapping stopped. "I wonder how many millions of dollars they're after."

"We are not terrorists," the driver retorted. He was the one who spoke fluent English and had blond hair. "We are Sunni Moslems and have been fighting for our territory since the Ottoman Empire. We support the Communists in their fight against the right-wing Arab kingdom of Iraq."

"Which drops American-made bombs on Kurdish villages and draws oil from the areas we call homeland," the second rebel said and while giving us stern look continued, "We have taken thirty hostages this year. You are numbers thirty one and thirty two. And I must warn you if you are Americans you could find yourself dead if you try to escape."

"But I'm Canadian and my partner is an American," I said.

"Then we will not harm you, sir, but with the American I'm not so certain. Both of you can sit now that we have established your nationality."

Then the rebel who was driving, and seemed more relaxed, pulled out a package of cigarettes. "Have one," he said and was surprised that neither of us smoked.

The sun was still shining as we reached the mountainous region controlled by the rebel guerillas. Four times we stopped at Kurdish villages comprising of stone and mud huts built into the mountainsides. The captors seemed to be on speaking terms with the villagers and laughed and joked in their native tongue before we were fed yogurt, black beans and rice. Along the way more rebels were picked up and began to chatter and then one said, "You have been captured by the Socialist faction."

"So where are you taking us?" Cal asked. "Our employers in America and Canada should know about this."

"We are taking you across the border to Iran."

"And then what?"

"We will set you free."

"Thank Allah for that," I said. "And when we are released we can do a report on the Canadian/American construction of the hospital in Erbil?"

The Kurd shook his head. "Sorry, you can't."

That evening while the caravan stopped to rest, the rebels abandoned their vehicles and continued at night under darkness on horseback and foot to avoid detection by Iraqi patrols. It took ten nights to travel the high mountainous altitude, 100 miles to the Kurdish base of Doletu.

Cal and I were concerned what was happening but we tried not to show our anger. Our home for the next while was a 10 x 12 foot hut with foam rubber for bedding. Our meals were the same: yogurt, rice and pieces of chicken thrown in at suppertime. This is what the rebels ate and boredom soon set in.

Back in London, Washington and Ottawa a Crises Centre was formed as soon as word reached that Cal and I were kidnapped while on our way to cover a hospital story in Erbil.

John Roberts, the ABC radio network supervisor in the London bureau, was put in charge of operations at

Broadcast headquarters. A large map of the Person Gulf was stapled to the wall which included Iraq, Turkey and Iran. Conference phones and telex machines were installed as Roberts scrutinized the situation of the kidnapped reporters.

Roberts also reviewed our spec sheets and learned our strong disposition. Both Cal and I were young men, single and enjoyed outdoor sports.

Roberts felt there was no need for rash decisions as Kurds were not known to be nasty to their captives but did phone Fahlman in Penticton and said, "Joe Rubeck and Cal Argue must be rescued."

Meanwhile radio stations in Canada, particularly CJOE in Penticton, kept listeners informed about the kidnapping. ". . . Still no word on Joe Rubeck and Cal Argue." CJOE bulletins repeated daily.

It was April 1955 when at 2:09 p. m. the first break came. A long distance caller asked for a "Mr. Fahlman" in London.

When Fahlman picked up the receiver the caller said in broken English, "Your are Mr. Fahlman?"

"Speaking."

There was crackling on the line so Fahlman said, "Who is this?"

"I'm one of the Kurds authorized to deal with the capture of Joe Rubeck and Cal Argue."

"Yes, go on," Fahlman said as those near him closed in and listened quietly.

"For more information meet me in London tomorrow," the Kurd said and then gave the time and location. The brief conversation ended with a "clique."

"Hello, hello," Fahlman continued but the line was dead.

Fahlman immediately called my parents in Penticton and the ABC radio network in New York.

On a crowded subway station in London, Fahlman rendezvoused with an anonymous Kurd who handed Fahlman a letter. It took a day for the Canadian embassy in London to translate it. The translation in part read: "The brave Kurdish commandos have captured two Western reporters despite warnings not give publicity to a hospital built by Canadians and Americans in Erbil. Iraq is our enemy."

The letter outlined a demand, which included a halt in Iraq's bombing of Kurdish villages, a cessation of political prisoner taking and publicity for the Kurdish cause. The letter demanded also a response within three days but didn't provide a return address.

In Doletu Cal and I were sinking into a routine so I said to Cal, "Adjusting to the drudgery is the hardest. Imagine if we were married and had to worry about a wife and family."

Cal agreed and said, "Every day we rise at 5:30 so as to be ready in case the Iraqi start bombing the natives."

The following day the Kurd negotiator, who identified himself only as Mohammed, contacted the Crises Centre in London and spoke with Fahlman.

"A ransom but no money. I don't understand," Fahlman said referring to the original note the Kurd handed him. The phone call was from Iran.

"Lives are more important than money. That is why Iraq must stop bombing our villages and you must give us free publicity," the Kurd negotiator said.

"We have studied your demands and they are quite simple. There is a condition, however."

"What's the condition?" the Kurd said.

"That Joe Rubeck and Cal Argue be released first.

"Another trick by the Westerners."

"That's not true. We'll do anything possible."

"Then why do reporters Rubeck and Argue want to give coverage to a hospital in Iraq?"

"It's only a humanitarian mission. For the Canadian part, Penticton had a fund-raising drive and residents want to know if the funds were well spent or wasted."

"How about publicity for the Kurdish cause?"

"Your cause? We'll call a press conference and try to get you on Voice of America." Fahlman said.

Minutes later, the Kurdish negotiator agreed to release Cal and me to a group of Iranians who were attempting to overthrow the Shah as their leader.

"That's like jumping from a frying pan into a fire," Fahlman said. "At any rate praise Allah. Canada and America appreciate that you are going to release Joe and Cal to the Iranians.

Cal and I were kept in an abandoned hotel in Tehran, which had a french window. To pass the time away we read

Time and a summary of *Two World Wars* while officials of the Canadian, American and Iranian embassies continued negotiating with Iran rebels who were plotting a coup against the evils of Shah Mohammad Reza Pahlavi's regime.

Negotiations became difficult but after three days I was released by the Iranian rebels and a free man. I immediately picked up the phone at the embassy and phoned Penticton and Fahlman in London.

"Where are you calling from?" was the first question Fahlman asked.

"From the Canadian embassy in Tehran."

"Are you all right?" was the second.

"I'm fine. The Canadian ambassador used his influence and convinced the Iranian rebels to free me as humanitarian gesture."

"And how about Cal Argue?" was the third question.

This is where I had difficulty speaking and after brushing a tear from a cheek I said, "Cal tried to escape so Iranian rebels shot him."

"Why did they do that?"

"Because Cal was an American."

As soon as Fahlman and I returned to Penticton, Fahlman thanked me for my efforts to cover the Erbil hospital story and asked if I'd like to return the following week and try again.

"I'm not going to cover the Erbil hospital story in the next while," I said. "The world needs foreign correspondents but being one is a deadly business, especially when there's a civil war and undisciplined people running around with guns. Say, how about not returning to Erbil until after I get married? Hopefully that will take place soon."

"Why wait until you are married?" Fahlman persisted.

"Because, Erbil is where my bride and I will spend our honeymoon."

Despite having failed to cover the Erbil hospital story in Iraq, I felt a gust of exhilaration about a possible marriage until I asked Fahlman for an advance on my salary so I could buy a vehicle and he replied, 'Sorry Daddio Joe I tried to get an advance for Big Paul Mitchell but the absentee owner refused to give one."

"In that case I'll approach Mrs. Bohn for one?'

"You are a bit late," Fahlman said.

"Why?"

"Because she has left Penticton to visit with her sister in Switzerland."

"Then I have an idea."

"What is it?"

"Although radio announcing is my labor love lost, I need to boost my income in order to survive. Do you mind if I try selling real estate part time as a sideline?"

"Provided it doesn't interfere with your work at CJOE. Go ahead."

CHAPTER 5

As soon as I received my real estate license I rushed to see the agent at Best Realty, George Best. I had just finished a shift at CJOE and was still out of breath when Mr. Best said to me, "Daddio Joe. People don't buy real estate on logic. They buy on emotion 75% of the time. If you want to make yourself a bundle of money I suggest you advertise in the *World Arab News*."

I was lucky because a week after I placed an ad in the newspaper Sheik Ami Hamblatt phoned me from Zurich, and said, "Mr. Rubeck. Will you represent me as an agent in purchasing property in Penticton, British Columbia? That's where you live. Isn't it?"
I confirmed that aside being employed by CJOE I was a Penticton realtor and wanted to know what type of property the Sheik wished to buy.
"Lakeshore land that will turn Penticton into an international resort," Hamblatt said.
"Like Club Med?"

"Larger. I want you to scout lakeshore property and bring photographs where I can build a casino and space where a corporate jet can land."

"Do you know that that will cost you? Land in Penticton isn't cheap."

"Never mind what the land will cost, sir. Just think of the commission you will earn."

Following still more conversation Hamblatt's last words were, "I want you to fly to Zurich. May I make a reservation for you at the Dolder Grand Hotel?"

Despite of my fright of flying I said, "Go ahead," The date and time of the appointment were set.

As I had holiday days coming I took a leave of absence from CJOE and then a flight to Zurich, where I met Hamblatt in his foreign office. As I was showing photographs of three potential sites for a casino, I felt the Sheik was vague about the sources of financing he had. At times Hamblatt claimed he made his fortune selling scrap metal during World War 11 and at other times attributing his wealth to being a relative of the Royal Family in Saudi Arabia.

I had doubts Hamblatt had the means to make good on his proposed investment unless he sold armaments to the Kurds and other revolutionary groups, but when he said he had studied in Harvard and won a Rhodes scholarship to study jurisprudence and civil law at Oxford University my attitude changed.

Sheik Hamblatt was unlike any other CEO I had met. He wore jeans with a shirt open at the neck.

The thobe, the traditional Arab garment and headdress, was tied in a haphazard manner. Between this thumb and forefinger on his left hand was the Mohammedan tattoo indicating that he had made a pilgrimage to Mecca.

Hamblatt himself sported a beard and strolled casually as he spoke and walked back and forth behind his desk. "I will make what ever sacrifices are necessary to put Penticton on the International recreation map," he said.

The Sheik reminded me of a miniature King Farouk of Egypt and only the mayor of Penticton, Les Day, a gargantuan, was larger, stouter and more muscle bound.

"I will make offer on the twenty acre site." the Sheik said after he examined the photographs.

"Why that particular site?" I asked.

"Because, it's lakeshore property with a southern exposure and where I can also build an office for Islamic Studies.

"But there are only a handful of Muslims in Penticton," I reminded the Arab.

"I respect your judgment on real estate values but when it comes to religion leave that me," Hamblatt said.

Following several transatlantic phone calls there were only the normal legal details of the solicitors to work out and the Sheik himself flying to Penticton to view the property he was interested in. The Sheik was also anxious to meet Mayor Day.

Once our meeting concluded I returned to the hotel where at the registration desk the clerk said, "Mr. Rubeck, there has been a phone call for you during your absence. The caller seemed anxious to speak to you."

The clerk handed me a piece of paper with a message on it. The message was that I call Jean Nadeau at the Swiss Union Bank.

When I arrived at the bank, a friendly banker with a French accent greeted me. "Monsieur Rubeck. My name is Jean Nadeau," the young-looking banker said. His hair hung down to his shoulder that was so thick, so matted that if a fly or a beetle had been caught in his hair it would never find its way out.

"The bank has been trying to reach you for several days. How coincidental that you should be in Zurich, "Monsieur Nadeau then said.

"Delighted to be here," I said while shaking the banker's hand.

"I have special instructions for you, sir," Monsieur Nadeau continued.

"What do you mean?" I immediately thought the special instructions were from Sheik Hamblatt with whom I had just met. I noticed that the banker was speaking in a quiet voice so I said, "You are talking to me as if it's a secret."

"You may say that. My instructions from the bank are very explicit and one of the rules is that I must talk to you in private."

"I looked at the banker with alarm. "What's this all about?"

"You are Joe Rubeck, I presume."

"Yes, I'm him."

"But can you prove it?"

I showed him my passport, birth certificate, credit card and driver's license with my photograph on it.

"If I may be permitted," the banker continued in a softer voice still, "Our instructions are to notify you that a Louise Bohn has died and that she has a safety deposit box with us."

"I was surprised. "Mrs. Bohn has died? When and where?"

"Last week at her sister's residence."

The banker handed me a copy of the instructions Mrs. Bohn had left with the bank and asked me to sign the paper."

As I was about to sign the document I asked the banker what was the cause of Mrs. Bohn's death.

"Her sister says it was a stroke."

"Well, do I have to sign?"

"Only if you want to have Mrs. Bohn's safety deposit box opened."

"Do I have access if there's money inside the safety box?"

"If its money that's in there you may do whatever you want."

I read the instructions again confirming that Fahlman had a key.

"The key. Does the bank have a duplicate copy?" I said.

"Because of the confidentiality of Swiss banks, I'm not permitted to divulge additional information."

"And if Fahlman hasn't got the key, what then?"

"If it's an issue involving inheritance you will have to file a claim with the Probate Court of Switzerland."

"And that could take a long, long time?"

The banker was apologetic, "In some cases."

"At least can you tell me the contents of Mrs. Bohn's safety deposit box?"

"I'm afraid not. It's part of the confidentiality we talked about earlier. What a client puts into his or her safety deposit box in Switzerland is strictly their business."

"I'll sign the papers but let's get this straight, in order to open the safety deposit box I'll have to return to Penticton and ask Fahlman if he has a key?"

"That's right, and so long as your signature confirms Mrs. Bohn's wishes, and no Swiss banking laws are violated."

I signed the papers, kept one copy and while returning the other to the banker I said, "Tell me monsieur Nadeau, is it as violation of Swiss banking laws to invite you to dinner?"

"That is permitted but I'm sorry to accept your invitation due to a previous commitment. But tell me, sir, I know Canada is a large country, but just the same, you may have heard of her, like you, she's from Penticton, studying in Switzerland."

"What's her name?"

"Trixy Fahlman."

"Trixy Fahlman. I think I know her."

"Her father is manager of a radio station."

"Then I definitely know her."

"Then why don't you join us? I'm certain Miss Fahlman will be delighted to see you.

As a matter of fact I insist that you come. I'll call Venghi's Restaurant to change our reservation from two to three."

"Did I hear you correctly, you said Venghi's Restaurant, in Zurich?" I said.

"And originally in Canada. Renato Venghi has carved quite a name for himself. There's also a Venghi in Paris."

The banker and I arranged to meet at 8:00 p. m. and when we did Trixy and I exchanged greetings. When the hostess greeted the three of us in a waiting room she said, "For how many?"

The banker said that he had made a reservation for three and went on to say pointing to Trixy and me, "These people are from Canada."

"How do you do" the tall hostess said, "What part of Canada are you from?"

"We are from Penticton," Trixy said.

After a brief conversation I realized that we were speaking with Tara Bell who had ditched me.

"Tara Bell, what are you doing in Zurich?" I said.

"I married RenatoVenghi shortly after you and I dated. I'm the reservation manager and eliminate the riff raff that may want to dine here."

"And Renato, where is he?'

"Opening a restaurant in Rome."

For a moment, Tara and I stood in silence embracing each other and then she led us to a candle lit table.

After we had eaten our meal and socialized Jean and Trixy left but I stayed until the restaurant closed for the night and Tara and I were by ourselves. By candle light we reminisced about Penticton and what we had been doing since we split. And then I said to Tara, "How has your marriage to Renato been?"

"It has its up's and down's but there is one consolation."

"What is that?"

"I don't have to do my own cooking."

Next Tara asked why I was in Zurich.

"I believe I'm about to close a humongous real estate deal with a Sheik," I said. "He has made an offer on Okanagan Lake shore property where he wants to build a casino and says he wants to make Penticton an International trouist centre which would rival Las Vegas."

Then I went on to say that offer was made on an acreage, which belonged to a German baron who is an heir to Mercedes Benz. The house on this acreage is 15,000 square feet with a bowling alley in the basement. In the dining room there's a chandelier imported from France that's worth at least $100,000. There's also an escalator, which brought one from the house to the beach and airstrip nearby.

Then I asked Tara if she ever heard of Sheik Ami Hamblatt.

"I have," Tara said. "He eats here often and I understand he owns boutiques, art galleries and antique shops around the lakefront and Bellvue Platz in Zurich. What else he owns I don't know but he must be worth a bundle of money. He seems to be into everything."

"I've never dealt with an Arab before. From your experience, what are they like?" I said.

Tara was quick to say, "They do not erect images and altar gods but they do offer sacrifices to the Supreme God on top of high mountains. Birthdays are celebrated with a feast, they are moderate eaters as far as I can tell when they eat at Venghi's, and have a rule that man isn't bound by any arrangement that they have made when drinking, unless one confirms in the morning when sober again."

"Well, Sheik Hamblatt appeared to be sober when he signed the offer on the land in Penticton," I said and asked, "What else?"

"They are proud of their large families; they consider it disgraceful to tell a lie and are fair in their dealings."

By now it was almost dawn and the early morning traffic in Zurich began to stir. The wine bottle in front of Tara and me was empty and the candles almost at an end. It was like it use to be in Venghi's in Penticton only this time Tara was part-owner, if not my heart, at least Venghi's Restaurant.

Before parting Tara and I faced each other and that's when I said, "I must return to Canada now. The plane leaves in two hours which gives me just enough time to pickup my suitcase at the Dolder Grand Hotel and get to the airport." I gave Tara a peck on the cheek and it was now my turn to say, "Auf wiedersehen sweetheart."

As soon as I returned to Penticton, Fahlman confirmed that Mrs. Bohn left a spare key to her safety deposit box with him. "And do you want to know something else?" he said.

"What?"

"You must have done a lot of fixing at her home."

"What makes you say that?"

"Because she left you $5000 in her will."

"Whoopee!" I said. "At last I'll be able to myself a vehicle. No more selling real estate in order to supplement my income. I'll be a full time radio announcer again."

Sheik Hamblatt arrived in Penticton in his own private jet and registered at the Penticton Inn. The Sheik was delighted when on the following day I introduced him to Mayor Les Day who was famous in his own right by having bet Fidel Castro to a cane-cutting contest in Cuba, wrestled with alligators in Florida, with a grizzly bear in the Yukon and on a bet, ran through the streets of Moscow almost naked in the dead of winter.

In some parts of the world the Mayor of Penticton was more famous than the legendary Okanagan Lake monster, Ogopogo.

Following the introduction and discussing the possibility of a license for a casino the Mayor challenged the Sheik to a foot race from Penticton to Naramata but the Sheik laughed at the thought because of his size and weight couldn't run fast.

"Let's pull wrists instead and the loser donates $1000 to the hospital in Erbil, Iraq," Sheik Hamblatt said.

"You heard about the project?" the Mayor asked.

"Of course. I'm one of the patrons."

"It's a deal," the Mayor said and both shook hands. Date, time and location were agreed.

News of the challenge spread quickly and became the talk of Penticton. There was so much interest in the *Twist of the Century* that Fahlman assigned me to describe the contest on the radio.

As soon as the contest was over, Sheik Hamblat was declared the winner and personally wrote a cheque matching the $1000 figure. Pentictonites were impressed with the Sheik's generosity but some began wondering about his casino and the financing schemes, which defied conventional explanations.

As soon as Hamblatt's plans became public knowledge, townsfolk began protesting by writing letters to the *Herald* and phoning *CJOE* wondering the effect gambling would have on society. That's when Sheik Hamblatt suddenly disappeared.

I did not know how to get in touch with the Sheik because when I called his office in Zurich, it was closed. When I called Best Realty agent George Best he said the Sheik's cheque was NSF. When I called the hospital in Erbil, no one had heard of him.
Then a bailiff got in touch with me and wanted to know how I could get in touch with the Sheik. All I could say is, "I wish I knew."
The bailiff said that the Sheik neglected to pay his bill at the Hotel before he fled.

My introduction into selling real estate wasn't a good one but just the same I was in a happy mood next day when Peach City Service Station had its grand opening and I was assigned to do a remote promoting it.

Why was I in such a good mood? Because several days earlier I received in the mail Mrs. Bohn inheritance and bought a new MGA sports car. It was a convertible, English racing white in color with red upholstery.

In the course of the broadcast a teenage employee of the service station assisted me in handing out prizes to customers who came to fill up with gas or have a lube job done. As soon as I said something to the effect, that the first car driven by a nurse would win a free thankful of gasoline, who should pull up to the pumps in a red Volkswagen Beatle but Henny Field.

After the attendant filled her gas tank I asked Henny for a date but she declined the invitation.

"No chance," she said. "You had your opportunity but blew it. I have a steady boyfriend, Shantz. Shantz and I have leading parts in the Penticton Little Theatre production of *Arsenic and Old Lace* that's on tonight. You may come and watch us but don't feel hurt.

My feelings were hurt; however, as Henny reminded me of a Hollywood starlet, she looked so beautiful. The sight of her, even the smell of her sent my heart a fluttering. But what could I say. I had an opportunity to be her boyfriend but because of Fahlman's demand that I not socialize with Henny, I let the opportunity slip away.

The hurt escalated the following day when I went to the Patricia Motel parking lot and found that my MGA sports car was missing. I immediately phoned the cops but they initially thought I was joking but two days later, phoned and said the car was found abandoned near Hope on the rugged Hope-Princeton Highway and the youth who had stolen it, had been charged with theft. I eventually found that the youth was the young man who was assisting me during the service station remote broadcast.

"What condition is it in?" I asked and was told everything seemed all right but the keys were missing.

"I have spare set," I said and the following day took a bus to Hope. When I arrived at the police station to pick up my car, I was delighted it wasn't damaged although out of gas and like the cop said earlier, keys missing. Fortunately I had another set and within an hour was driving back home pleased at the same time listening to the radio and Hank Williams singing *Your Cheating Heart*. It was raining at the time.

I drove past towering monarchs of Western Red Cedar, Douglas fir and Western Hemlock creating a magical blend of light and shadow. By the Skagit River I saw Dogwood growing in dense thickets, their roots saturated with water, their foliage providing cover and nesting sites from the Warbler to other small birds.

Under the foot of jackpine I saw rhondendrun growing in profusion and as I kept driving eastward there were mountain bluffs, rivers and bridges to cross. The rain and fog I was driving through soon changed to heavy clouds and snow. A distinct change occurred not only in the weather but in plant and bird life too. Cedar, balsam and hemlock gave way to lodgepole, pine, juniper and aspen. Englishmen's spruce was rapidly replaced by Sitka spruce. Coast shrubs such as devils club, false azaleas, mountain ash and vine maple now disappeared and were replaced by a smattering of shrubs and open ground.

I drove past Manning Park and Lightning Lake where storm clouds were gathering around the top of mountain peaks. There were lightning flashes and cannonades. Seeing and hearing these, I pressed the gas pedal to the floor until I had a view of Copper Mountain across the deep gorge of the Similkameen River which runs parallel to the Hope-Princeton Highway.

Although Copper Mountain was the site of one of the world's largest copper mines from 1920 until 1957, there was a sight of a different kind as soon as I passed an eighteen-wheeler and fifty meters later, while negotiating a sharp downhill curve, struck an ice patch plummeting the car into the Similkameen River. I don't member anything else only that I was in the arms of Henny Field in the Penticton Regional Hospital.

When I regained consciousness I asked Henny what had happened and she said that I arrived in the Emergency room by ambulance and that my sports car had been demolished.

Henny's uniform evoked classic responses and when I asked her why she had taken up nursing instead of becoming a concert pianist she said, "Because I always wanted to help people. Nursing gives me that opportunity."

Then I asked Henny about her boyfriend, Shantz, and was surprised when her answer was, "Shantz and I have parted company."

"What happened?"

"He's serving time."

"Sorry."

"Don't be. We weren't close anyway."

This is where it really got interested so I said, "What happened?"

"He didn't like playing checkers and I didn't go for his drinking, drugs and the police scanner."

Soon Henny and I were shedding tears. Henny because she had lost a boyfriend and me my sports car. I saw emptiness in her eyes and she must have seen some in mine. Suddenly the tears we fought disappeared and we were holding each other tightly. Finally the moment came when I said, "Henny, about a date?"

"I thought you'd never ask because the way I treated you. Sure thing," Henny said. "How about tonight? As soon as I'm through my shift, I'll spend time with you while you recuperate."

I spent one month in the hospital and enjoyed every moments of it.

Three months after I was released from the hospital, Henny and I were sunbathing at Okanagan Beach. This particular day the beach was crowded, the temperature near 100F and tossing the frisbee was the rage.

"Let's move," Henny said impatiently after an errant frisbee struck her in the shoulder. "Let's move to another part of the beach where it's private and I want to tell you something," I said.

We moved to a secluded spot behind a barkless log where Henny laid a blanket on the sand and asked me to put suntan lotion on her back. I pressed the tube between the palms of my hand and spread the lotion on her back and shoulder, then her legs and asked her to turn over. Then I lay down beside her.

While the sun was blazing and Okanagan Lake was tranquil and placid Henny turned towards me and said, "Daddio Joe, I've been to see a doctor."

"You see doctors almost every day," I said.

"But this is different."

In jest I said, "You lost your rhythm?"

Henny chuckled. "Joe, you know I'm not Catholic."

"What are you then?"

"I don't know what I am but I do know, that I love you."

I kissed Henny, she returned the kiss and then we ran our tongues in each other's mouths. While in our ecstasy I asked Henny to marry me.

"I'm happy you asked," Henny said. "Yes, I would like to be your wife."

"This means you'll have to take religious instructions."

"I don't mind."

"Then we better call your parents in Manitoba.'

"We will."

"If that is the case, close your eyes and show me your hand."

That's when I slipped on Henny's finger an engagement ring. More kisses followed and then I said, "Henny you are going to be a beautiful bride."

"I hope so. Joe, I want you to be proud of me for ever."

Following further exchange of pleasantries, including secret goals and bank account balances, Henny picked herself off the blanket and said, "I'm not certain where the wedding should take place, Selkirk or Penticton. I'm afraid because you are Catholic my parents will not accept you as my husband."

As I was putting my clothes back on, Henny said, "I know what I'll do."

"What?"

"I'll call Father Brophy and my parents later. At any rate the wedding should take place in September, don't you think?"

"September is one of my favorite months. Let's go for it," I said.

As soon as Henny returned to her apartment I stood by her while she spoke with her mother on the telephone in Selkirk. When Henny told her mother that her and I were getting married her mother suggested, "Your father and I have talked about mixed-marriages many times and there is one point we agree on."

"What is that?"

"That a couple should not have sex before they get married. That's one thing we like about the Catholic Church."

"What does it matter if Joe is Catholic, Jewish or Hindu, for heaven's sake Mom, it will be me sleeping with him and not you?"

"I don't need to remind you that mixed-marriages don't last," Henny's mother then said.

"Mom, this is not a mixed marriage. I plan to turn Catholic."

Her mother continued, "It takes a long time to know what a man is really like."

"In the days of the dinosaurs, perhaps. There are couples that now get married after a short courtship and others, well, I didn't want to say this Mom but they just shack up. You wouldn't want me to do that, would you?"

"Certainly not. There are many fish in the ocean and men are common as dirt, but the secret is to find one who is supportive, cares and you can trust."

Henny's mother's voice then softened. "Knowing you as a child, Henny, a man like Daddio Joe may be difficult to find so go ahead, get married if you think you are going to spend the rest of your life with him."

Henny then went on to say how wonderful I was and how much she loved me and I her. "Although Joe doesn't like to cook his own meals he is kind, generous, my best friend. I want to spend the rest of my life with him. Joe is also patient, understanding, one I can trust and love. He also has a sense of humor."

"But remember one thing, dear," Henny's mother said.

"What?"

"Don't give up your nursing career. You may need it as a backup. And one more thing."

"Henny said "What?" again

"The wedding should take place in Penticton and I'm happy you are not marrying a farmer, fisherman or a policeman. By the way are you pregnant per chance?"

Henny said she was, "But not by Shantz but by Daddio Joe."

"One more thing," Henny's mother continued. "Where are you going to go on your honeymoon?"

"To tell you the truth, I'm not certain, but where ever it is, Joe says it's an ancient town in northern Iraq which is a travel centre linked by roads to Turkey, Syria and Iran. Joe says Erbil is one of the oldest continuously inhabited towns in the world and dates back to 2500 B. C. Imagine!"

"Times have changed," Henny's mother sighed. "When your father and I got married we couldn't afford a trip to Winnipeg. Now honeymooners travel to exotic places like Erbil. At any rate we'll see you in Penticton on your wedding day."

"Great," Henny said. "Joe and I will have the wedding banns read as soon as he tries to avert a strike at Okanagan Lumber."

"In Penticton there's growing anger that union members have not received their fair share of the pie and the promise of profit-sharing has not materialized. I'm so mad. I'm ticked off that we have to stand and fight for what we already have. I'll whine. I'll scream. I'll stamp my feet. I'll have a temper taciturn if that's what it takes to get a better deal from Okanagan Lumber Inc." a listener phoned Open Line, which I was, the host of the popular program.

"What else bothers you?" I said to the caller as Okanagan Lumber Inc. and the International Woodworker's union was in the process of negotiating a new contract.

"What else? Well, it's going to be devastating. If a strike takes place there will be a serious impact on Penticton. There's going to be little money spent. It looks like a long, hot summer on the picket line. Corporate Big Shots insist they have to keep labor costs low to remain competitive.

How come, then they have given themselves such high salaries and bonuses?"

Okanagan Lumber, a secondary industry in Penticton, and the International Woodworker's Union representative continued negotiations but as the strike deadline approached nothing happened. It was when the company ordered guard dogs to watch the plant because its own employees wouldn't, that I called company and union officials for an interview on the Open Line program. I encouraged phone calls from employees and their wives. "The union local president is a trouble maker?" an irate wife said as the calls began pouring in. "The union, like its local president, doesn't know what it's doing. If there's going to be a strike, I don't want my old man hanging around the house drinking beer and watching television."

When I pushed a different button and said, "Line two, you are on the air." Another wife disagreed with the comments by the earlier caller. She said, "Those management slobs who live in a posh subdivision, sit on their ass all day. They don't care about the ordinary worker who doesn't make enough wages to feed his family adequately."

Next' a caller phoned in and said, "Hey, I don't know if the company, in the event of a strike, plans to bring in replacement workers. At any rate Okanagan Lumber Inc. is a subsidiary of an American giant. I think it's up to the company to make the next move."

Phone calls kept pouring in and appeared evenly divided as to the public perception of the employer and its employees.

The following evening, the Open Line topic was the same—the possibility of a strike at Okanagan Lumber Inc. Negotiations continued and strategy by both sides was planned in the interim. Company negotiators met Union counterparts. Two days later the employees met in the Peach Bowl to hear the latest company offer.

The meeting room in the Peach Bowl was a bedlam of noise and confusion as the president of the union local pounded on the table with a gavel and said, "Attention please. Brothers and Sisters. The meeting will now come to order and we discuss the company's latest offer."

The noise subsided to a murmur as the local president then said, "A vote on the latest offer, which the Bargaining Committee recommends acceptance, will take place by secret ballot tomorrow."

Members of the bargaining Committee then explained the company offer in detail and how it would benefit its employees.

Next day, the vote was taken and ballots counted. The company offer of a 5% wage increase plus health and vacation benefits, was accepted.

The following day I was sent a joint letter from the union and the company thanking me for my interest and intervention, bringing the controversial issues into open on the radio, which eventually helped both parties in reaching a settlement.

With the Okanagan Lumber Inc. strike settled, I felt the company stock was going to double within a year. I was excited too, because the following month I was about to make the greatest investment of my life—marrying Henny Field.

CHAPTER 6

Since Henny was living in a bachelor apartment and I with my parents, the search for a one-bedroom apartment began by Henny and I driving from one end of Penticton to another, checking the units out. It was on the second day that we drove through a neighborhood where we thought we would like to live and stopped at Hillview Manor where the landlord greeted us, we filled out an application form and gave a security deposit.

The landlord said that she would have our application reviewed and an answer forthcoming the following day if we were successful or not as, she had to phone the previous landlord for a reference and our place of employment. These two steps she said were important to ensure we were still working and not evicted for non-payment, damage or noise, from our current residence. Then a credit check would have to be done before we would be accepted.

Hillview Manor was an older type six story, fifty unit complex with a panoramic view of Okanagan Lake and the mountains behind it. On the minus side, however, as soon as we moved in, we discovered that elevator didn't always work properly. This occurred when we were packing wedding supplies to the 6th floor and the elevator got stuck between the sixth and fifth.

I banged on the elevator side with a can of tomato soup and fortunately fifteen minutes later, another tenant heard the noise, called the landlord, who in turn called the elevator company. Henny and I remained calm but the elevator mechanic did not arrive until three hours later because on his way he was involved in a motor vehicle accident. It took another hour before we were rescued and believe me it was no fun to be victims of a faulty elevator.

One week before the wedding, and a time in history when Elvis Presley was becoming popular, teenagers were dancing on the streets of Penticton and rioting in parking lots, employees of Venghi's Restaurant which was supposed to do the wedding catering, went on strike for better wages.

Henny and I then made arrangements with the Peach Bowl and organized a meal which included three suckling pigs to be barbecued and then picked up during the ceremony by friends.

My mother made four types of salads and cabbage rolls. Watermelon shells were hallowed out and filled with various melon balls, a task assigned to Henny's parents.

On the wedding day, Henny and I beamed at each other as Father Brophy announced that we were man and wife and then we went to the sacristy to sign the register. We emerged from the church arm in arm as, well wishers, many of them my listeners; some were Henny's friends from the hospital and the Little Theatre.

For better or worse, Henny's wedding dress was perfect for the bride. The ruffled voile dress cost two hundred dollar, rather expensive for that time. The bodice was re-embroidered Alencon lace. The dress came with an oversize stole that duplicated the ruffles of the skirt. The stole could be worn as a jacket or as a cover-up.
Henny's headpiece was French lace-and-flower confections wrapped with open Swiss veiling, an original design by Francesca of Penticton. Henny also had three stems of red roses to complete her bridal look. The gloves and shoes matched her wedding dress.

Following the congratulatory hand shaking in front of the church Henny and I disappeared in my new convertible Ford, which I had purchased after receiving an insurance payment for my demolished MGA. The best man, Happy Buck Milton, drove us to a photo studio, where we had portraits taken, and then to the Peach Bowl for the reception. I was surprised that there wasn't a reception line when going to the bathroom. Anyway, I noted with great enthusiasm, that there appeared to be a sacred Polish custom associated with most *reception lines*, the specifics of which were performed with great reverence by both men and women upon entering the hall. It consisted of drinking a shot of whiskey and chasing it with a beer. No one seemed to notice that as soon as I had my shot, I stopped breathing. I was having great difficulty in controlling my bowels, and water was dripping out of my nose. As an after-thought, I still can't remember what happened to the glass. I may have swallowed it as well.

Halfway through the reception, our MC, Harry Fahlman, asked Father Brophy to say something. He did, by reminding Henny and me that we were, "Two bright, intelligent people bonded by holy matrimony."

Father Brophy then quoted the *Bible* and talked about King Saul's jealousy because David killed more Philistines than he did and how Saul tricked David to be his brother-in-law, only privately wanting to kill him with a javelin. And then Father Brophy said, "Later David married another man's wife by the name of Bethsheba and the Lord did not like what David did. David, a one time hero, judged himself as a sinner and the Lord punished him and Bethsheba by making their first child dead."

Having said this, Father Brophy continued, "It happened during the time of the *Bible* I know but it seems to me things haven't changed twenty one centuries later."

Father Brophy urged us to share as husband and wife and to communicate with each other our feelings. "Marriage is no guarantee for security, health and wealth, particularly when society attitudes are changing so rapidly and that includes in music."

Father Brophy then asked everyone to stand and join him in proposing a toast to the bride and groom. He lifted his glass of wine to his lips and said, "God bless Henny and Daddio Joe. May their marriage be a lasting one."

As soon as Father Brophy finished speaking, everyone applauded and banged their plates with cutlery implying that Henny and I should stand up and kiss, which we did, again and again.

With the meal over, tables cleared, and the bar opened, dancing began. This wasn't a Legion Hall party celebrating VE-Day, when swing was prevalent, but rather a party celebrating our marriage and rock n roll music was popular.

Henny and I danced a waltz and then rock n roll took over. During that time Big Paul Mitchell sat at a stool and on the piano played several Fats Domino tunes.

The following day, we opened wedding gifts in our apartment bedroom. Henny's and my parents each gave us an 1846 Roger Bros. Sterlingware set. We also received place settings of matching china, electrical appliances and enough linen and towels as Henny put it, "To last a lifetime."

The following day, we were on our honeymoon. The first leg of our flight took us to Montreal where we boarded a jet which stopped to pick up additional passengers in New York, and then it was clear soaring over the Atlantic to Baghdad and then a bus to Erbil, population 350,000. Picture this after a long flight, a bus ride, an interesting conversation with the cab driver we finally managed to get to the hotel where our eyes caught a sign that read: *If this is you first visit to Erbil, you are welcome to it.*

After registering, the first thing Henny noticed was the enormous size of our room. Then she turned on the hot water faucet in the bathroom and there was a rattling. "rattta ta ta ta" tune which shook, if not the entire building, at least our room.

That's when I said, "Pardon me Henny but I forgot something."

I picked Henny up and carried her back to the hallway and then back into our room where I said, "The threshold. My bride must enter the room with honor."

As I said those words, I dropped Henny on the bed, kissed her several times and lay besides her running my hand across her stomach.

"A baby Rubeck in the basket," I said and then asked if anyone at the wedding noticed that she was pregnant.

"I doubt it," Henny said. "And Mom wasn't upset as I thought she would be. Mom felt it was going to be our baby and we knew how to handle the situation."

Following a shower and a snack, Henny and I walked to the registration desk to discuss a car rental. After discussing one with the hostess she handed me a key to a Renault.

Henny and I then cruised the Islamic city of Erbil, capital of Kurdistan, and initially were disappointed what we saw: billboards, rusty abandoned cars and sidewalk cafes. As we kept driving, however, the scenery suddenly became different. We were in a world as if in *National Geographic*, filled with a barren desert and bazaars.

There was a constant procession of men robed in turbans and veiled woman, walking in and out of the hospital which I came to investigate.

Nearby, there were ragged children, herds of sheep and goats, pack animals laden with goods and on occasion a water cart. It opened me up to more learning. By volunteering myself to such a different environment and culture was like being mentally naked.

"You know you are in a different world here," Henny said as we were in an area of Erbil filled with noise, smells and crowds. After we parked the car near an old mosque, and did a walk-about of the hospital without anyone knowing who we were, we mixed with people outside and asked for their impression of the hospital.

On the whole reaction was favorable. Then as we walked further I said, "Henny, look.

Arabs, Christians, Berbers, Oriental Jews and nomadic Blue men, sure is different from any thing we see in Penticton."

A short distance further still we saw the Erbil Castle, Choly Minaret, health offices, doctors' clinics and pharmacies. Because of the ancient architecture it was instant exotica. And then we watched urchins on top of a monkey and Arabs sitting on leather hassocks eating without cutlery.

When we returned to the hotel, I filed my report to CJOE and then while entering the restaurant were met by veiled women wiggling and a waiter who to me appeared to be a comedian and gay, both at the same time. Once Henny and I were seated we enjoyed a five-course dinner, although spicy, it was tasty despite the high cholesterol.

The following morning, we drove to the Erbil hospital again and were told that the administrator was absent due to a pilgrimage to Mecca. "Dr. Azziz will be back in two days," the acting administrator said.

I interviewed the acting administrator, and then doctors, nurses, cleaning staff and patients. I found there was no corruption of any kind and the funds which arrived from Penticton were used to purchase state of the art medical equipment from United States.

Two days later, as I was interviewing other people, the administrator appeared from nowhere and confirmed a report I had sent to CJOE that he had been on a pilgrimage to Mecca.

Dr. Azziz reminded me that it was a duty required by all able-bodied Muslims to do the hajj at least once in their lifetime, if they could afford it. Dr. Azziz said that many Muslims, however, were unable to take part in the journey because as he phrased it, "They lack money."

"Money?" I said and then asked, if any of the funds sent by Pentictonites could have been used to subsidize a journey, He looked at me sternly and said adamantly, "No," and reminded me that a pilgrimage to Mecca is an once-in-a-lifetime experience. "For a Muslim it's an important day to remember."

After I finished interviewing Dr. Azziz, Henny and I returned to our hotel and on the way saw Arabs riding camels, and then by contrast, with his caftan flowing, a man sweating from the dry dusty dessert riding a gas-fueled scooter.

In the midst of a festival that was taking place Erbil had a charm of its own as we drove through streets enjoying our honeymoon. There were orchards of olive trees and dates were everywhere. Other streets were lined with trees and the gardens were filled with bougainvilleas and flowering jasmine. Nearby, we spotted a merchant hollering in English, "Slippers, painted toe! Each pair for three American dollars!"

"I'll give you one," Henny said as we stopped our car and approached the merchant.

"Three," he replied

"Two."

"Two and one-half."

"No. Two, take it or leave it."

The merchant finally said, "Sold!"

Besides Henny and men there were other tourists in Erbil as well, mostly from Europe. There were also Kif smoking hippies, Kurds in town from the mountains, and wandering tribesmen in indigo blue robes rubbing shoulders with everyone while ogling merchandise, food and street performances. This is where Henny reminded me to watch my wallet while she did the same with hers. Then she said, "Hey, look over there!" and pointed towards a water vendor ringing a bell. He was wearing a tartan but there were no bagpipes. The water seller was clad with a goatskin around his back and a necklace of brass cups dangling from his neck. The strange looking Arab said he made his living by posing for pictures so Henny and I posed with him, while a tourist snapped us and I in turned the tourist the favor.

In time, Henny and I discovered that Erbil was in the middle of a mousem, an Arab institution, and like its counterpart, weekly souks or markets, it was a festive occasion and for centuries Erbil was a meeting place of caravans, a haven for travelers.

It was late afternoon by now as Arabs converged to sell their wares and some of the vendors were: acrobats, dancers, snake charmers, jugglers, magicians, acupuncturists and story tellers sitting cross-legged, spinning tales out of *Thousand and One Nights.*

Henny and I stayed in Erbil for two weeks, and in that time, made side trips to Baghdad and, I at least a hundred trips to Henny's lips discussing our future. At one point I said, "Henny, if it's a boy we'll call him Lorne, after Lorne Greene."

"And if it's a girl?"

"Have your pick."

"I'd like her to be named Lorna, after my mother."

"And then we'll have more Lorne's and Lorna's."

Henny smiled with approval and it was time to fly back to Canada.

On the first day after returning home from our honeymoon, and minutes before I returned to work at the radio station, I said to Henny, "Goodbye, my hollyhock."

As soon as I left Henny grabbed a seed catalogue to try to understand what the casual remark meant. The catalogue read: "Colorful and beautiful."

Henny immediately phoned her mother in Selkirk and told her about our honeymoon in Erbil and the lovely comment I gave her. Her mother, however, was suspicious about my kind words and suggested Henny look up the word *hollyhock* in the dictionary. So after she finished speaking with her mother Henny picked up a dictionary and looked up the word hollyhock, which the dictionary said, "Rather common. Does best along fences, and barns. Poor in beds."

That evening, as Henny and I were enjoying a cup of coffee, she made announcement that she was giving up her career as a nurse to raise a family. I didn't mind Henny's decision because I too wanted to have children right away but not before we purchased a home. The apartment we were living at Hillview Manor was large enough to keep Henny away from her mother and small enough to keep her mother from coming to our place for a visit. When her mother did come, however, she said to Henny, "The landlord must ask a lot for rent?"

"He does," Henny said. "Last month he asked for his rent three times."

It so happened that our apartment was on the sixth floor and the following day, Henny phoned the landlord to say, "I'm afraid to look down."

"Because of the height?" the landlord said.

"No. Because of the cockroaches."

As soon as it was confirmed that Henny was pregnant we decided to buy a home. To assist us in the purchase I called on realtor Peter Wong who phoned me frequently on Open Line. Wong used a mixture of astrology, numerology and age-old Chinese customs as to where Henny and I were suited to live in relation to water and blowing of the wind. After checking out several houses we decided to make an offer on one in the Sage Mesa subdivision. It was an older type three-bedroom bungalow near a creek, on the edge of a cliff and had a panoramic view of Okanagan Lake.

Our first visitors were the neighbors, Dr. Abe and Nancy Hoffman. It was Dr. Hoffman who said, "Despite the poor condition of your home you have an excellent view of Okanagan Lake"

"Maybe so," Henny said. "But if you had to renovate and paint it, like we must, pay taxes on the property, which doesn't have running water or connected to a sewer line, you wouldn't say it was such a beautiful place."

A month after we moved into our home, there were things that weren't working. The first thing to go was the hot water tank that burst and had to be replaced. The sliding glass door to the balcony got stuck each time we went to enjoy the view and fresh air and nearby creek needed unplugging because two beavers built a dam above.

Speaking of the Hoffman's, talk about an unlikely couple. Nancy was a statuesque blond, body sculpted by the gods and Dr. Abe? I thought Nancy and Abe were overmatched—at least as their looks and height, were concerned. He was short. She was tall. Understand, I'm not saying Abe looked like a troll under a bridge. It was his huge nose, pigeon toes and the unorthodox black clothes he wore. Still the Rubeck's and Hoffman's became friends and we often took advice from them.

One advice we took, was to install a new septic tank after it developed a habit of backing up at most inopportune times. On Christmas Day while Henny was busy rushing around preparing dinner, I was out in the back yard, with a bucket bailing away in the snow. But what could I say? Our lives were a continuous process of gradual unfolding and learning. That's why we accepted the Hoffman's not only as friends but also as mentors.

I thought why Nancy married Dr. Hoffman was because he's a gynecologist who practices at the Penticton General Hospital. So Nancy latched on to him for his dough he was making and now she's laughing all the way to the bank. But then, after doing some research I discovered that Nancy wasn't exactly rooting through a Goodwill bin for sweaters or jeans before she met Dr. Abe Hoffman. After winning the Miss Penticton Peach Festival Pageant, she became a top model commanding an imposing salary in six figures. Sometimes I don't know what attracts people to each other.

Ever since Henny and I purchased our home, I was moved from the 6:00 p. m. to midnight shift to one that air-time ran from 1:00 until 6:00 p. m. Mind you I did other things too: sweep floors, run errands, carried out the garbage and worked eighty hours a week but I couldn't now because I worked about sixty-five and required at least eight hours of sleep at night.

At any rate from 1:05 until 4:00 I was assigned as host of a program titled *Problem Corner* that catered to CJOE's women audience. On Problem Corner I encouraged phone participation and in the event there weren't any phone calls I would play Country and Western music. *Problem Corner* was as much fun doing as it was to listen to it. This wasn't a swap-shop or a preformatted program you hear today. It was honest, live radio that often went over the edge. Problem Corner was my brainchild and was part of a homespun package to overtake rival TV ratings. It was completely different kind of radio. There was joking, banter and sarcasm. It was really the forerunner of the goofy radio-talk shows we hear today.

During my first month on *Problem Corner* I had some many phone calls that I could write a book about kitty litter, how to remove oil stains from bricks and concrete. I would have chapters on table salt used to brush teeth instead of toothpaste. How to take away an itch caused by pure wool garments. Why rhubarb is good for you if you can't digest food.

Cycles of the moon affect bacon in the frying pan. Not to clean carpets with cornmeal because if you do and spill water on it, stalks of corn will appear on the living room floor.

I was told that there is no angel in angel cake, no horse in horseradish and no butter inside a butterfly's stomach. Boron-rich foods: apples, peas, broccoli and carrots increase alertness. How to create compost on the fourth floor balcony and who put the bomp in the bomp-da-bomp-da-bomp. Listeners also told me that water, detergent and patience was needed in order to kill fairy rings on the front lawn.

Because the program was heard throughout the southern half of the Okanagan Valley, I signed off with, "This is you host who loves you the most. I'm Daddio Joe Rubeck. Keep those cards and letters coming."

And they did come. Listeners wanted to know about my personal life. Was I married? If I preferred the Beatles to the Rolling Stones. What I thought about City Council, the provincial and federal governments. One listener even wanted a loan so she could send her daughter to university. Still another wanted to know which alphabetical letter F or X is more often used in one's daily vocabulary.

I was embarrassed, however, when on *Problem Corner* I had to deal with a problem of my own making. It was an extremely warm August afternoon when I asked my audience, "What shall we have for lunch this afternoon?"

One listener called and on the air casually said, "At our home we are having chicken shit sandwiches."

In disbelief I said, "You are what?"

"We are having chicken shit sandwiches," the listener repeated and hung up the receiver

I also remember receiving a phone call enquiring about the best way to kill wasps. Since no one phoned with an answer I said, "Hanging a fish head or any piece of meat over a bucket of water will attract wasps that will gorge themselves on food and then fall into the bucket drowning themselves."

Seconds later a member of Green Peace phoned and objected to my reference on how to get rid of wasps.

"Wasps like seals and whales are part of Mother Nature and should not be destroyed," the caller said.

During another *Problem Corner* program, I did a survey to determine just how alert my listeners were, so I solicited a *yes* or *no* answer to the question. "If you knew the Mayor of Penticton was a heterosexual, would you vote for him or her?"

Eight out of ten calls said they wouldn't.

Shortly after we moved into our Sage Mesa home, there wasn't a day that went by that we weren't threatened by forces from the city: salesmen who wanted to put new siding on our home, Girl Guide cookie pushers, Amway distributors, insurance and vacuum cleaning salesmen, among others.

There's nothing more humble that being sucked in by a vacuum cleaner salesman who says he is working his way through college.

Henny and I had no idea of his intention until an acquaintance of mine, Al Tropack, opened a gigantic box and pulled out an assortment of attachments, from a back massager to a wood-sander to something that blows up a mattress.

"We are going to give you something for nothing," Tropack said and by the time we figured out what was going on he was completely inside the house, shoes off, using our sink to get hot water for a shampoo demonstration and insisting, "May I see your old vacuum cleaner?"

Henny dragged the old vacuum cleaner from the closet.

"Does the beater bar on you machine ever turn?" Tropack continued while demonstrating. "What happens if you rub glass into your skin?"

Henny and I remained silent.

"Your skin bleeds. And that's what's happening to your carpet. Your carpet is bleeding from having dirt rub into fibers."

By now the machine had sucked a mountain of sand from our carpet, which we intended to replace later.

"You are proud of your new home, aren't you? You want to look its best, right?" Tropack persisted.

Henny and I were reluctant to say "Yes" to this question because we knew this paved the way to other questions eventually, "May I have your credit card, please?"

Mr. Tropack, next spoke about the multi-purpose use of the vacuum cleaner and tried to convince us that we weren't buying a vacuum cleaner but a hair dryer/handyman/plastic baby sitter.

"This vacuum cleaner will not only message your scalp but paint your furniture and blow guck out of the kitchen drain. As well kids can sword-fight with the wands as they won't break. This vacuum cleaner will shampoo your fridge if you want and suck out wasps from their nest."

But the clincher was the "Mattress Myth", a classic tale of horror to buckle your knees and leave you begging for this life-saving appliance. Tropack said, "Mr. And Mrs.

Rubeck, every twenty seven days we shed a layer of skin. Guess where one-third of it goes?"

Where?" Henny asked.

"Into your mattress, where it combines with other body secretion to leave body ash. This body ash feeds on bed mites, forty thousand bed mites can feed of body ash. Your entire mattress is teeming with bed mites and I know a Vancouver lady who once had part of her nose eaten away by these little pests while she slept."

When Henny doubted the myth Tropack went on, "It's true, I wouldn't lie to you. And this vacuum cleaner will suck these mites screaming from their home in your mattress."

Henny and I refused Tropack to let our mattress to be examined for bed mites, so he said, "Would you like to buy the vacuum cleaner any way?"

"No, thank you," Henny said.

"What if it's half price for the next fifteen minutes?"

Again Henny said, "No thank you."

"But I'm on the verge of winning a contest."

"No, thank you."

Tropack was understandably disappointed and took an excruitiating amount of time to pack his vacuum cleaner.

As soon as Tropack left, Minor Soccer kids were knocking on the door selling raffle tickets. When one of the kids found out that I use to play the game he politely asked, "Mr., can you please coach the Sage Mesa Rascals?"

When I hesitated he pleaded, "Please, pretty please."
When I asked what happened to the previous coach the kid
said, "He quit because parents' weren't cooperating."

As soon as we had a telephone installed, it rang constantly
with community groups requesting donations, for pledges,
and if we could spare time as volunteers at the Crises
Centre. There were also phone solicitors who were doing
surveys as to what chewing gum we enjoyed the most,
which political party we thought would win the next
election, and what we thought of the local RCMP and the
controversial method they used when it came to dealing
with Quebec fruit pickers who inundated the Okanagan
Valley each summer.

CHAPTER 7

When we lived in the downtown Hillview apartment Halloween had become a night for little people and by *little* I don't mean midgets but those less than eight years old. They would dress up as witches, goblins, and canvass door to door with a parent by their side, wait to be identified before you dropped a Twinkie or a chocolate bar into their bags.

In Sage Mesa, Halloween wasn't a holiday but a full-scale invasion, not only by local kids but some as far away as Summerland. Greed stations were set up where the goodies would be emptied and they would start out "fresh" with another round of pounding on doors.

And the beggars themselves were so intimidating that if you didn't give them something they would spit in your face.

The small children came between 5:00 and 5:30 while it was still daylight. After that the beggars got bigger and bigger and the costumes less colorful and demands more aggressive. At 8:00 p. m. while opening the door I confronted a skinhead who was six feet tall and his partner was at least six inches taller. Both had tattoos, a crew cut and a face that gave them a look of a sunflower gone into seed. When I put an apple into their shopping bag they didn't thank me and went out mumbling something to the effect, "Mark our word, Daddio Joe, we'll get you one of these days."

Around eleven o'clock I turned the front door lights off and said to Henny, "From now on I refuse to answer the door."

"Afraid of the skinheads?"

"No."

"Why then?"

"Because we have run out of treats. Look. The refrigerator is empty and there are no snacks left."

As soon as I said those words Henny peaked through the curtain and saw a motorcycle gang approaching the driveway. When they turned into our yard, I turned the lights back on and I said, "Oh, dear, what will we give them?"

Henny suggested a potato.

That would be dangerous so to appease the gang Henny gave each member a 25 cent coin which she took out of the piggy bank.

As soon as the gang left and it was 11:30, I said, "Do we dare to turn off the front door light this time?"

"I don't think so," Henny said. "It's too risky. The Hoffman's turned off their lights early last Halloween and someone threw a rock into their swimming pool breaking the plastic liner."

Henny and I stayed up until dawn playing checkers. It was then that we discovered someone had knocked down our outhouse. Until it was put back into place we had to use the Hoffman bathroom.

In Sage Mesa pregnancy wasn't a condition or a status symbol. It was the current style and seemed that almost every woman under thirty-five was wearing a stomach in various stages of development, whether they looked good or not.

When Henny visited Dr. Hoffman's clinic for a routine checkup he confirmed that she was going to have twins. Then after Henny had left, the doc looked at a chart on his desk and said to the nurse, "On what day does Mrs. Rubeck expect her bundle of joy from heaven?"

"May 4th." the nurse replied.

"And the next lady?"

"May 4th also."

"And this one?"

"May 4th."

Dr. Hoffman was surprised that so many women were expecting to have a baby on the same day and it wasn't a full moon night. "What's going on here?" he thought but said, "What a coincidence? Don't tell me this other lady is expecting on May 4th.

"I don't know," the nurse said. "All I know is that she wasn't at the CJOE staff party."

During 1955, I was 25 years old when during the month of February Fahlman assigned me to cover the World

Hockey Championship games in Krefeld, Germany. Since the Penticton Vee's were representing Canada and I could emulate Foster Hewitt better than anyone I knew, even though it was a short notice, I jumped at the opportunity. In no time flat I kissed Henny goodbye, joined the hockey players and climbed aboard a jet at the same time wondering why every seat smelled like an Odor Eater soaked in dry cleaning chemicals. And even before the *Fasten Your Seat Belt* sign came on I had a headache.

From Penticton to Krefeld is a nine-hour flight. I was a high-risk traveler because since returning from Erbil and being held hostage, I became afraid of flying more than ever before. I was also allergic to day-old sandwiches, dry cabin air and afraid because one of the players I knew sitting next to me at one time had tuberculosis. Then as we were flying across the Atlantic I had a flashback the time I was a boy in Selkirk and witnessed a grisly plane crash in a wheat field which many people were killed and others horribly maimed. The crash made such an impression on me until this date and since our honeymoon, I refused to fly in an aircraft. I was afraid of flying but what was I to do? Not doing a hockey broadcast meant that I wouldn't improve by broadcasting skills as my personal challenge was to be the most versatile and best radio announcer there is.

Again, I felt as if I was falling through puffy gray clouds below and crashing into the ocean filled with sharks. After flying through a severe thunder and lightning storm

I felt so frightened that it drew the attention of a flight attendant who asked if I wanted a gravol.

"No, thank you," I said. "But I'll have a shot of whisky instead."

When the attendant came back she handed me a double scotch. I must have had an empty stomach because up there, 32,000 feet above the clouds, I got light-headed, and then fell asleep until I heard the pilot say, "Krefeld, Germany in sight. Please prepare for landing."

When the jet landed the hockey players and I checked into a hotel. but not before the pilot said, "Thank you for flying our airline. Best of luck Penticton, in search of the World Hockey Championship."

I enjoyed doing the hockey broadcasts, particularly the final game when the score was Soviet Union 4 and Canada 5 in the final seconds. I became excited and shouted, "The final score is Soviet Union 4, and Canada represented by the Penticton Vee's, five. Penticton Vee's are the new World Hockey champions!"

Back in Penticton fans were glued to their radio and as soon as I announced the final score the Mayor declared a public holiday.

I admit that during one of the earlier games I used a word on the air that normally isn't part of my vocabulary. Minutes prior to the game I was testing a feed line back to Penticton repeating over and over, "One, two, three, four. Can you hear me back at CJOE or do you want more volume?"

I became frustrated with the routine and said the word "shit" which went live on the air. Our times between Krefeld and Penticton obviously weren't synchronized to the split second.

When I returned to Penticton Fahlman called me into his office and ranted and raved, pointing to a stack of letters on his desk, complaining about my offensive language. I apologized and said, "Look. Even Lorne Greene had made mistakes. On the CBC news I heard him say one evening that farmers in Western Canada were expecting a bumper *crap* instead of *crop*.

The following week Fahlman called me into his office again and said, "Daddio Joe, when I say the words, hog line, broom and sweep, what game am I talking about?" "Clean the pig pen," I said. "When I was a child living on a farm near Selkirk my father made me do that each day."
"Wrong," Fahlman said, "It's time for the annual Penticton Curling Bonspiel and I assign you to describe the championship game on the radio.

"Although I'm not familiar with the game of curling, I'll give it my best shot," I said and when the time came, I did my best to describe the final game between rinks skipped by bank manager Robert Brown, and vacuum cleaner salesman Al Tropack. Tropack was the salesman who tried to sell Henny and me a vacuum cleaner but failed.

In the broadcast process I made many mistakes by saying something to the effect that curling was similar to bowling on ice and instead of using balls one used "rocks."

The bonspiel was a round robin affair and although it was spring, I said I did not see any robins yet. Instead of saying "In-turn" I said 'Right turn" and instead of saying there were four players on the team with a spare I said, "Each team enjoys a fifth." Instead of saying the skip was roaring I said the skip was "croaking."

Although the profile of curling was increasing in Penticton it wasn't because of me describing the game on CJOE. One of the things, which were interesting, wasn't the shot making but the friendships I made and the parties I attended and that there was no body checking or high sticking and the game ended with a handshake. The players were more approachable to do interviews compared to broomball, figure skating or snow-golf participants.

After describing the game to the best of my abilities, I felt the game of curling was more suited for television coverage than radio. Television left less to one's imagination. One participant even told me that curling was better than sex. "For one thing," he said. "In curling you don't have to fake it when you're having a good time, you can score up to ten times a night, don't regret a mistake nine months later and there are four positions to know but you have to be good at only one of them."

On May 4, 1957, as the nurse predicted and Buddy Holly and the Crickets were singing *That Will Be the Day* I was inside the Penticton Hospital walking the corridor back and forth. It was here that I spotted Al Tropack, the vacuum cleaner salesman, and during a brief conversation I said to him, "Why does it have to happen on our first day of vacation?"

"You should complain," Tropack replied. "My wife is expecting too and I have been waiting five hours already."

An hour later Henny gave birth to a set of twins and the following week Father Brophy baptized them *Lorne and Lorna.*

When Nancy Hoffman came to see the twins she said to Henny, "I hear twins are pretty rare."

Henny, while smiling said, "Rare? Dr. Hoffman tells me it's practically a miracle. Chances of having twins are once in a million."

"Good heavens," Nancy said. "When did you ever find time for your housework?"

Lorne and Lorna were a month old when insurance salesman, K. D. Hurdle, phoned and said, "As responsible parents you should buy the twins an insurance policy."

"Why don't you come to the house and we'll talk about it," I said and when Hirdle did come, he grabbed my hand and then Henny's, and while pumping Henny's, said, "Your face is familiar. Didn't we go to school together?'

"Not unless you lived in Selkirk, Manitoba."

"I did, and when you were a youngster watched you on the Search For Talent show. Do you still play the piano?"

"I don't," Henny said.

"But seriously folks," Hirdle continued, "I didn't come here to talk about the past, but to spell out a few facts of life."

I though Henny being a registered nurse knew more about the birds and bees than Hirdle did so I asked, "What kind of facts of life?"

"You have just moved to Sage Mesa and have two kids. You, Daddio Joe Rubeck, work as an announcer at CJOE and you, Mrs. Rubeck, are a nurse and now a full-time mama. You drive a Ford car. This far have I got the picture right?"

Henny and I said simultaneously, "Right." and I proceeded to ask what source did he use for our family background.

"The Welcome Wagon lady and as to the twins, the Birth column in the *Herald* newspaper."

Next Hirdle showed us a photograph of a family ravaged by an earthquake in Iran and an entire family was crying because they had lost their home and belongings. Pointing to the photograph Hirdle said, "Now what if this happened to you Mr. And Mrs. Rubeck, and Lorne and Lorna were the only survivors, the bank repossessed your home and car. Do you know what that means?"

"It means that we would have to declare bankruptcy and start again," I said.

"No," Hirdle corrected me, "It means Mummy and Daddy don' make plans?"

"That wouldn't be the first time," Henny said.

"Well, it's still not too late. Our company has a package, which includes life insurance, and insurance on your home and car. Tell me, how much insurance do you carry on yourself, Mr. Rubeck?"

"I don't know," I said and turned towards Henny.

"I have a policy but it's solely on my name and my Mom and Dad are the beneficiaries," Henny said.

"There you go. I would change that immediately."

"The policy you mentioned, how much will it cost?" Henny asked.

"You can have the policy which I described covering your lives, home, car and sickness and accident plus a no-frill-no-fault burial rider for $49 a month."

"Forty-nine dollars a month? Are you certain we won't be over-insured?" I asked.

"No, Daddio Joe. One needs all the protection one can get these days. There are so many surprises, fire, B and E's and especially highway accidents."

Henny and I each signed a policy contract and when Hirdle got up from his chair he casually said, "Mr. and Mrs. Rubeck, you are such bright people that I almost forgot. Can you put aside another twenty dollars a month for Lorne and Lorna's education?"

"We haven't thought about their education yet," Lorna said

"There you go again," Hirdle said and went on, "Do you know that a college degree can pay of with life-time earnings 40% higher than those of high school graduates?"

Henny and I shrugged our shoulders and then when Hirdle flashed a United Nations pamphlet that said,

"Mankind Owes to the Child the Best It Can Give" we signed another policy.

Finally Hirdle said, "Thank you for doing business with you. Welcome to Sage Mesa. Now, don't you feel better?"

As soon as Hirdle left the phone rang in the living room. I picked up the receiver after the third ring and said, "Hello." On the other end of the line was the president of the Penticton Minor Soccer League and said one of the players in the league hinted that I would be willing to coach a team. That's not exactly what I said to the kid but to the president, "I would be delighted to coach a team provided coaching did not interfere with my schedule at the radio station."

Win or lose, it's not easy leading kids under twelve years of age be it in soccer, baseball, hockey or football. Coaching the Sage Mesa Rascals reminded me of the time I entered the Search For Talent Contest while I was a kid in Selkirk, Manitoba. Like the contestants, some of my players were good, some fair, and some just awful but no matter who the kids were, their parents like my mother, wanted to see their son involved. Sometimes I thought I was a baby sitter as only a handful of parents came to watch their son play.

If my player was out of position I would tell him so but not criticize his skills, like my father did. I wouldn't say to him for example, that he should have dribbled the ball and passed it because he couldn't dribble and definitely could not kick. My mother did the same with me when I stood on the stage in front of a microphone and recited *The Cremation Of Sam McGee* but because of my sibilance I failed.

As the first game progressed the score was West Bench Marmots 6, Sage Mesa Rascals 3 and then I heard a kid, like I once did, say. "I've been in the game for a short time and was subbed off."

"I've been on only twice," said another

What I said pacing the sideline back and forth was, "Come on boys, you are playing well and deserve a pat on your shoulder."

Then one of our players scored and the scoreboard read: West Bench Marmots 6—Sage Mesa Rascals 4.

Minutes later the game was over and some of the players blamed the loss on the referee like I did on my sibilance. I did not say a word but took the kids for an ice cream treat at the Dairy Queen, at my own expense, of course. While the kids were enjoying their camaraderie I phoned the CJOE Sports Department with the score.

CHAPTER 8

Henny and I were having a fabulous spring skiing weekend at Apex Mountain Resort where we ran into many friends but spent most of the time alone. It was a perfect spring break while my parents looked after Lorne and Lorna. And I would have been more perfect if Henny hadn't begun to feel ill. She blamed the illness on the wind and the sunshine. She couldn't imagine anything else but when we returned to Penticton I insisted she see Dr. Hoffman and check her illness out, and when she did, Henny was ecstatic.

"Whoopee! I'm pregnant again!" she said.

I was thrilled about having a third child too and everyone at the radio station teased me this time. Even Fahlman said, "Daddio Joe. Can't you leave the poor girl alone long enough so that she can comb her hair?"

It was six months later that there were days that Henny began suffering with morning sickness and couldn't keep down water. Every time she sat on the toilet she would throw up.

Henny kept salted crackers beside our bed, and sometimes they were all she could bear to eat. The nausea was worse at night and didn't stop after the first trimester the way Dr. Hoffman said it would. Her morning sickness lasted until on a hot and humid day I paced nervously up and down the Penticton Regional Hospital corridor.

"Dr. Hoffman has been in the delivery room for a long time," I said impatiently to another expectant father who identified himself as Washington Ozzie, the hairiest man I had ever seen.

"Don't be afraid. Your wife will pull through," Ozzie said. His wife arrived at the hospital ten minutes earlier. When Ozzie said that his wife gave birth five minutes after her arrival, I became dejected and said, "Of all the luck. And I've been here nearly for two hours and your wife, gave birth in five minutes."

Earlier, when Dr. Hoffman appeared, he said that chances were fifty-fifty that both Henny and the baby would survive. I recalled riding next to Henny in an ambulance holding her arms in mine. The baby had shifted and Dr. Hoffman at the time said, there was pressure inside Henny and she was bleeding. A placenta privia had caused the hemorrhaging.

Quickly Henny was placed on a table and an orderly rushed her up to the operating room. Henny was gone through the OR door in a split second and I waited in the corridor.

"I've been here waiting two hours," I kept repeating and pacing the floor back and forth.

Ozzie, watching, tried to console me by saying, "She'll be all right Mr. Rubeck. I wouldn't worry."

Then I heard Dr. Hoffman's voice in the distance. I rushed towards him and asked, "How is Henny doing?"

"We just performed a Caesarean section. Henny is in considerable pain. Henny will pull through but I'm not so certain about your son."

"What do you mean, doctor?"

"The baby is four weeks premature and needs a blood replacement."

I then felt Dr. Hoffman's arm on my shoulder. "Let's go! He can have some of mine!" I said.

Dr. Hoffman shook his head. "I'm afraid your blood won't do Daddio Joe. There's the Rh factor involved and your blood would be incompatible. The type of blood we need only one in a thousand has it. I've put a call to the Red Cross already. It depends how fast we can get it here if your son lives or not. Do you know what an Rh factor means?"

I said I was uncertain as a sinking feeling came over me.

As soon as Dr. Hoffman explained what Rh factor mean Ozzie sprang to his feet. I did not know hairy men could speak so fast as he said, "You can have some of my blood!"

I thought besides being hairy, Ozzie was ugly looking with his protruding buckteeth so I said, "Then my child will look like a susquatch."

"He won't," Dr. Hoffman assured me. "But he may have a disorder of some kind for the rest of his life."

"What do you mean?"

"The genes. Your son may be different from the rest of your children. We'll have to wait and see."

"Doc, are you serious about the blood?" Ozzie continued. "My blood is B negative that you speak of."

Despair worked its way into my face. It was unusual for me to make derogatory comment about other people.

I'm sorry," I said to Ozzie for implying that he looked like half human and half animal.

Ozzie accepted my apology and then Dr. Hoffman said, "Come Mr. Ozzie with me and we'll see about your blood. Let's confirm that it's your type."

Ozzie and I followed Dr. Hoffman into a laboratory where a technician pricked Ozzie's finger, put a sample of the blood under a microscope and then said, "He's right, doctor. It is Rh B negative."

"How about a pintful?" Dr. Hoffman said to Ozzie. "We can only hope the other donors arrive on time."

"Okay. Let's hurry," Ozzie said and away they went.

An hour later, Dr. Hoffman returned looking tired and somber to where I was pacing the floor.

"Can I see Henny and my son, now?" I said as soon as Dr. Hoffman was within speaking distance.

"Only for a moment," Dr. Hoffman said. "Both are still weak."

Eventually when I got to see Henny and the child, I thought the baby looked cute so I said, "I think we will call our son Ozzie, after all it was Washington Ozzie that saved his life."

Exhausted, Henny said, "That's an excellent idea."

Then when Henny and I watched the baby in the Observation Room that evening I stood proudly looking down at the sleeping infant with a mixture of emotions: disbelief, doubt, delight, amazement, enchantment, skepticism. Touched by my unusual display and deep emotions it aroused, with eyes glistening Henny slipped her arms around me and said, "A penny for your thoughts."

"It's amazing!" I replied, "I just bought a crib for the child at a garage sale."

Both Henny and I were ecstatic, that is, until a dramatic thing happened in Sage Mesa that evening. While it was hot and humid during the daytime the weather suddenly changed into a torrential rain causing flash floods throughout the Okanagan Valley triggering washouts and mudslides. Four homes in Sage Mesa, including ours and Dr. Hoffman's, were swept from their foundations, tumbling down a cliff with parts landing on Highway 97.

When I returned to the radio station, chief announcer, Happy Buck Milton had already reported that the floodwaters had killed three people, four homes were destroyed and that Nancy Hoffman was missing and presumed dead.

When Happy Buck asked if I would do the announcing so that he could follow-up on the flood and interview authorities, I accepted and the first news item I read on the 8:00 p. m.

News was: "Late this evening a raging flood swept four homes of their foundation at Sage Mesa. Police report that three people have been killed and one is reported missing. Okanagan Lake is chocked with debris and so is the Okanagan River which empties into Skaha Lake."

Several hours later, Happy Buck Milton returned to the station and I, after making certain Lorne and Lorna were alive and at their grandparents', I paid Henny and Ozzie a quick visit at the hospital. Henny had already heard on the radio that our home was one of four destroyed because of the mudslide

"Thank goodness we have house insurance covering the damage," Henny said.

"Don't count on it."

"Why so? We pay $49 a month in premiums for the policy taken out with K. D. Hirdle."

"True, but Hirdle didn't say the coverage included acts of God."

"So what are we going to do?"

"The provincial government has issued a statement that it will likely help families who have been victims of the storm and not covered by conventional insurance."

When I returned to the station my, next newscast began, "Civil Defense Emergency says Highway 97, which runs parallel to Okanagan Lake and next to the clay banks in Sage Mesa, where most of the damage occurred, has been temporarily closed as bulldozers are clearing debris left by the storm."

"The Mayor of Penticton and members of council have just concluded a tour of the mudslide area and here is what he had to say." I punched a cartridge into the tape machine and what the audience heard on the air was the Mayor saying, "The 100-metre wide slide at Sage Mesa reminds me of a moonscape." Then I pushed another button after introducing an alderman. The alderman's voice clip said, "The washout in Sage Mesa rminds me of a ski hill under construction. I have never seen a mudslide like this before. What a waste of humanity. I hope we find Nancy Hoffman alive."

They did.

As soon word spread that Nancy Hoffman was found alive. I rushed with a tape recorder to the Penticton Regional Hospital where on the Women Medical floor is, she granted me an interview. She said, "I was in the bathtub when our home collapsed, because of a mudslide. The house tumbled down a cliff. As I was wept away out of the house, into Okanagan Lake and eventually into the Okanagan River, I hung on to a drifting log until the spot where the Okanagan River empties into Skaha Lake.

"As I can not swim I kept kicking my legs hanging onto the log for dear life. I called for help but because of darkness and the torrential rain no one heard or saw me. I drifted until the log got jammed at the bridge near Skaha Lake. Exhausted, I managed to struggle to shore but then I collapsed, and can't remember anything more except that I woke up in the hospital emergency ward."

In a separate interview I spoke to Dr. Hoffman who said, "It's a miracle Nancy is still alive. I spoke to her last at 5:00 p. m. before I had to make a delivery at the hospital and didn't know until later that our home was swept away and my wife missing."

When I returned to see Nancy again, I saw tears welling down her eyes. I could tell, however, that she had her senses, didn't seem confused but her hands and feet had lost Color, confirming she was in the water a long time. Nancy was listed in satisfactory condition suffering from scrapes and minor injuries.

As soon as Nancy, Henny and Ozzie were released from the hospital, our family lived with my parents at the Patricia Motel. Our first task was to find another home to live in. What we found and liked to make an offer on was a rustic two story wood-frame, four-bedroom house in the suburb of Naramata.

The Hoffman's bought themselves an enormous house in a gated golf community where nanny's wore Rolexes and you either had a royalty-type wedding or didn't get married at all. They also purchased a cottage near Peachland.

There are those who say there are four types of suburbanites: Those who talk how rich they're going to be and those who talk about how rich they used to be. Those whose yard smells like chlorine, for people who think they own a swimming pool but don't.

"And then there are those whose homes are further apart from each other but the mortgage payments are closer together. I'm afraid that's the category Henny and I found ourselves in when we went to a bank for a mortgage interview.

Inconsiderate bank customers may be their own enemies while dealing with banks, but I didn't think we were when we met with the branch manager, Larry Buckley, who was fashionably dressed, with blue eyes, a pug nose and known for his honesty.

Henny and I were seated in front of Buckley's desk and as he was filling out our application form, the first question he asked was "Can you give me a statement?'

"Certainly," I said. "How about, we have Canada Saving bonds in your bank worth five-thousand dollars."

I was certain *that* wasn't the statement Buckley wanted but he pressed on and his second question was, "Do you want your bond redeemed or converted?"

"Depends if you are a bank or a church," I said jokingly.

"That's funny," Buckley said so after noticing his sense of humor and relaxed manner, and our application was approved, I asked Buckley for a taped interview which I could play on the radio. I already had done a documentary on the Swiss banking system and wanted to know what irritated the banking staff the most in Canada.

"Good question," Buckley said. "Offhand I'd say dealing with customers who don't know their account number." Buckley then said the teller has to take time to look up the number, which contributes to slow-moving lineups".

"And the second most irritable complaint?"

"A customer who wants the teller to balance a cheque book."

Buckley elaborated on what he meant which involved a teller dealing with customers who at times are rude and use fowl language. "It's difficult for the staff member to bounce back and be completely relaxed and pleasant."

Buckley then said that some customers don't keep their cheque book up to date. "They expect us to tell them whenever a cheque arrives and there aren't sufficient funds in the account. Others expect us to know what cheques haven't cleared. This includes looking up entries for customers who have forgotten them or are lazy to record them."

Buckley also said a problem arises when a customer tries to cash a cheque made out to a third party or a cheque made to *Mr. and Mrs.* which doesn't have both signatures on the back. "Delays can occur, especially on busy days, when a customer wants a pass book updated for the first time in several months."

Near the end of my interview Buckley said, "And then there are the last minute customers, those who come into a bank three minutes before closing with an hour's worth of complex transactions and then want cash when everything is closed also drives the bank staff crazy."

"I can relate to that," I said. "I never mean to wait until the last minute to do my banking, but now and then I get tied up with my work at the radio station and make a dash into a bank just as an employee is about to close the door."

I always thought bank managers were stuffy grouches who appeared at a Rotary luncheon each week, but that wasn't the case with Larry Buckley. I did have concern, however, not with the interview but our mortgage payments. I thought they were excessive based on my and Henny's income.

Because of my interview with Buckley I learned a great deal about Canada's banking system and eventually hoped to do a documentary on the subject particularly at a time when banks were contemplating to merge and industrial giants were battling banks for a share of the plastic profits. Everyone from telephone companies, insurance carriers, and appliance makers had leaped into the credit card arena. And if that hadn't been enough for the banks, a Japanese credit card company also entered the race.

Our new home in Naramata was ten miles from downtown Penticton and the first thing we discovered was that we needed two vehicles. One day Henny opened the *Herald* and saw a reasonably priced camper truck advertised privately.

"Here's ideal transportation for you to go to work and haul your soccer team around," she said.

Within minutes after seeing the green three-quarter-tonne pickup with a camper on it, we bought it, and printed on one side the word *Ogopogo 2* with a serpentine-like figure next to it.

By the end of the first month, the thrill of driving a camper truck had worn off. I had transported the Sage Mesa Rascals to two soccer tournaments but hadn't won a game yet. In the second month I hauled manure in the pickup to fertilize our garden and that's when the players refused to ride with me, so did Henny, Lorne, Lorna, and Ozzie.

"You don't suppose you can get rid of the odor and have the truck vacuumed as well?" Henny said politely.

I did, by taking the vehicle to the Peach Tree Service Station in Penticton where an attendant gave Ogopogo 2 a wash, polish and a vacuuming job.

The road between Naramata and Penticton runs parallel to the east side of Okanagan Lake. It's narrow and winding with several hills. On my way back to Naramata I stopped for a red light when a car rear-ended me.

"Can't you see where you're going?" I said to the driver, only to discover she wasn't a fat slob but t a Zsa Sza Gabor look-alike.

"What do you mean I can't see? I hit you, didn't I?" the blond said.

Seeing there was little damage done to the pickup I didn't argue. As I was walking away from the rear bumper she said pointing her finger at me, "You are Daddio Joe Rubeck from the radio station. Aren't you?"

"I am."

"I can tell by your picture in the newspaper, and do you want to know something?"

"What?"

"You deserved to be hit."

"Why?"

"Because on your *Kitchen Corner* program I heard you say to a listener that it was okay to have chicken shit sandwiches for lunch on a hot day. Remember?"

I wasn't going to argue with a woman I felt a bit twisted so I climbed into Ogopogo 2 and began driving towards Naramata.

Halfway there I stopped to pickup a female hitchhiker who identified herself as Jezebel Beaumaris. I recalled the name but couldn't recall under what circumstances until she said I had done an interview with her and because of the interview; CJOE had the highest linstenership ever.

Jezebel and I were discussing the interview and the fact that she had moved to Vancouver but visiting Penticton. Soon I was coming down the Naramata Hill I and discovered that my brakes didn't work. My heart began missing a beat as I saw smoke belching out of the rear tires. People and cars were crossing the street but I avoided hitting them. I asked Jezebel to hold on tightly and seconds later Ogopogo 2 struck a power pole knocking out power for an hour. People gathered around Jezebel and me like flies. I saw some speaking to Jezebel as I opened the hood and then checked the brakes. As I was checking the brakes I heard Jezebel say, "I'm, all right. I'm not hurt."

Minutes later, I said to Jezebel that an accident report had to be made out but that I couldn't write because my hand was sore from checking the brakes. "If you help me I'll hand in the report to authorities that much sooner," I said

Without hesitation Jezebel filled out the report with our names and addresses as well as the time and place of the accident on two blank forms—one for me and the other for her.

By the time the report was done, power came back on, so I went to a corner drugstore and had first aid. When I got back to Ogopogo 2 and the site of the accident, Jezebel was gone. I had the camper-truck towed to have it repaired, There, from Bob's Towing Service, I called for a taxi to take me home. By now I knew Henny was anxiously waiting but the taxi driver taught me a lesson.

By nature, like most media people, I'm inquisitive and chatty. As the taxi pulled away, I verbally pounced on the driver commenting on my accident, the weather and the beautiful scenery. I made it abundantly clear that I had not taken a taxi for a long time. First we drove north then west and finally we turned south. At that point I said to myself. "Hey, what's happening here?"

Even though my sense of direction at times is non-existent I knew the driver had taken the scenic and not the shortest route. The cost for the trip was fifteen dollars instead of ten.

The lesson I learned from the experience is, if you ever ride a taxi, keep your mouth shut. Don't give any indication you don't know lay of the land or that it's your first visit to a certain place.

When I arrived home I asked Henny if anyone had called during my absence and she replied, "Yes" and on a piece of paper handed me a telephone number. When I dialed it, a male voice identified himself as Jezebel's lawyer Ace Whitmore and said, "Jezebel Beaumaris is suing you?"

I was surprised. "What? What for?"

"Ms Beaumaris was a passenger in a camper truck you were driving, was she not?"

"She was."

"And your truck struck a power pole?"

"That's correct also."

"Well, sir, she's suing you because she broke her right hand while riding with you."

"Fine, I guess I'll be seeing you and Jezebel in court," I said.

In the morning I brought a copy of the accident report to insurance agent D. K. Hirdle. I hoped he would have enough consideration to see that the accident wasn't my fault and that accidents are bound to happen, no matter what prevention one takes.

I kept waiting while Hirdle went over our insurance policy and then the accident report. After several minutes, though it seemed like hours, Hirdle stood up from his desk and said smiling, "Daddio Joe, so you let Jezebel Beaumaris make out the accident report. It's a lucky thing you did."

"How come?"

"It's as clear as you live in Naramata, Jezebel Beaumaris is a phony unless she's left handed. That lets you out."

"You mean to say Jezebel has no case at all?"

"None that will stand up in court of law. Leave everything to me, Daddio Joe, I'll have our lawyer call this case off."

CHAPTER 9

The most notable development in the world of radio and popular music in the first five years of the 1960's was the emergence of the Beatles. By 1964 there were many English British artists competing and often exceeding American Rock n Roll groups in popularity. Another development was the appearance of such troubadours as Bob Dylan, Peter, Paul and Mary and Joan Baez. It was a crazy world and not just funny or music crazy. I mean crazy in the literal sense of the word—insane, bonkers, cuckoo. It's people, many of them my listeners, who had lost touch with reality. Sure we're crazy. We just don't think we are. But a few crazy people do. Occasionally, however, one goes temporarily insane, only if for a moment or two, and sees the world for what it is. That's what happened to me one day as I was driving our Ogopogo 2 camper truck, on my way to work.

Inspired by a newscast Happy Buck Milton was reading I began thinking about some of the major issues of the day and the manner in which we as a society were dealing with them. Just for kicks I tried to listen as Happy Buck was reading a newscast as if I were an alien who just landed in Penticton and trying to come acquainted with society. That's when I decided the word *crazy* was clinically, legally insane. For example, we continue to choose up sides and argue over the right to bear machine guns.

We can choose from a variety of drugs that weren't heard of when I was a child in Selkirk. But none of them—not cocaine, LSD, angel dust or magic mushrooms—has been able to supplement the number (1) and (2) drugs of choice, both legal, alcohol and tobacco.

Every night thousands of homeless people sleep on benches covering themselves with newspapers with ads offering apartments and homes for rent or sale. As thousands of others starve, farmers are paid not to grow crops. And while our homeless wait, we send millions to other countries in foreign aid. Our *leaders* stress the importance of education, and then cut funds for education and universities raise tuition fees.

The same leaders tell us our population is decreasing and yet we allow abortion instead of promoting adoption. Anti-abortionists are known as *pro life* but every pro-lifer I have ever met has been a staunch defender of the death penalty.
The same government tells us smoking causes cancer, heart diseases and any number of other physical and economic ills but subsidizes the tobacco farmer. In other words we pay doctors to tell us smoking is tantamount to suicide, and then pay others to provide us with weapons. By any

measure, that's just plain crazy. Ironically, I thought all this while enjoying the most insane activity available in our society. It was our camper truck, Ogopogo 2, which I was driving.

Sure I realize that driving sounds like an ordinary enough activity, but as seen through the eyes of an alien, I was sitting in a metal box that was moving at sixty miles and hour with a few feet of other metal boxes moving at similar speeds. Some even faster as they were passing one another with reckless abandon.

Despite the fact that I heard almost daily on the radio about strangers who drive while drunk, stoned, pissed to the gills or otherwise physically incapable of operating such a vehicle, I was putting my life in their hands. What a maniac I am? After all, about 50,000 people a year die on the roads in the United States, that's twice the population of Penticton, and 5000 in Canada, we allow cars to be operated by sixteen year-olds. We also renew licenses of people whose reaction time is measured in minutes who can't read an eye chart without a magnifying glass. That's when I had a fall out with Fahlman. To coincide with the July 1st long holiday weekend CJOE held a promotional contest in conjunction with Harry's Pizza House on Government Street.

The listener who had proof of purchase of a pizza and the correct number of motorists killed on Canadian highways that weekend, won the number of pizzas that matched the number of people killed on the highways. Imagine!

When the contest was over, Harry's Pizza House sold over 5000 pizzas during the promotion. Of all the entries there were four hundred and eight seven with the correct answer, which was 67.

From the correct answers a draw was made and the winner was the vacuum cleaner salesman, Al Tropack.

It's a crazy world all right so be careful. I had to, when on the radio I said I had been gypped when I went to a movie and did not enjoy it. Penticton's Gypsy community protested to Fahlman and I had to give an apology. Gypped is a synonym for being cheated or swindled. Although Webster's dictionary says I used the word correctly, Penticton Gypsies didn't.

I did not receive a similar protest when our camper truck, Ogopogo 2, was damaged when I struck a pole or at the time I uttered the word *niggardly* when talking about a possible shortfall at the hospital in Erbil.

Another time a listener complained that I often began my sentences with contractions *And* and *But* at the beginning of sentences. There's a grammatical myth that such sentences are somehow wrong so I said to her, "But look at a chapter in the Gospel of Luke in the King James version of the *Bible* that reports the birth of Jesus. It starts *And it came to pass in those days.* If you check closely you'll find that 38 out of the 52 sentences in the chapter begin with the word *And.*"

I did, however, make a blunder when I was on the air and said something to the effect that, "I was a member of the fifth estate."

A listener did not hesitate to phone and say, "Hey, Daddio Joe, you mean fourth estate, don't you?"
Was my face red? You bet.

Desperate not to butcher any more words or skewer any more idioms, I decided to seek professional help that would improve my vocabulary. I didn't have time to read the great canon of literary works nor did I have the stamina to go to Night School. What I needed was a quick fix—a cure for the limp mind. My announcing career depended on it. That's when I stumbled upon a book titled *The Quick and Easy Guide to Sounding Smart and Cultured for Dummies*. It's an A to Z guide to literary expressions. Complete with phonetic spellings and on-the-nose explanations, it's the ultimate low-down on the highbrow.
One quick read of the pocket size primer and I was ready to join the cognoscenti and start spouting on the zeitgeist on my program. The book taught me never to use small words when I could use a big one, never to use an English word when I could use a foreign one, and finally the more the syllables the better.

In August I had a terrible experience as a radio announcer. No, Fahlman did not fire me another time but it was just as painful.

I was sitting alone in our Naramata home when there was a knock on the door. I opened and two skinheads who came to trick or treat when we lived in Sage Mesa grabbed me and beat me physically.

Later it occurred to me why they beat me was not because I gave them an apple instead of a Twinkie during Halloween but because when they entered our home I made fun at them because of their tattoos. The first had a tattoo that read Vilian instead of Villain so I said; "You should have a tattoo on your forehead that says *stupid* too."

The second had a tattoo on his bare back and it was a huge but spelled Harley-Davidson wrong. It was spelled Hairy Davison so I asked if that was his name. That's when our encounter began.

After I called police the two young men were arrested. Following plea-bargaining they pleaded guilty and each received a suspended sentence. That's why I detest plea-bargaining. I felt the two men should have received a substantial jail sentence.

When people meet me on the street they often ask, "As a radio announcer what do you think of television?" The subject also came up when we had Nancy and Dr. Hoffman for dinner and talk turned to television and belief that children watched too much of the media.

I glanced nervously over my shoulder into the family room where Lorne, Lorna and Ozzie were immersed in Walt Disney's *Robin Hood*. I had lured them there out of respect for our childless guests who probably wouldn't appreciate the joys of dining with kids who treat the butter dish as a finger bowl. The Hoffman's were talking about some people they knew who had given away their television in anticipation of their first child. There would be no fights over TV in the home because there would be no television.

"What do you think of that?" Dr. Hoffman asked me. "Does it sound a little excessive?"

It sounded excessive to me but I didn't say that. I didn't want to admit that I couldn't imagine raising Lorne, Lorna and Ozzie without a television set in our home.

"Well, it will be tough. They'll be buying a TV before the kid is three?" I said. "Funny, isn't it, how our view of television changed since our kids appeared on the scene?"

Henny and I had a lot of firm ideas about television and children before we had our own. We both had known kids whose solid contribution to an evening's visit would be the occasional grunt from the TV room, where they had been transferred in front of absolutely nothing, as long as the screen flickered. None of that for our kids we vowed. What kind of parents would let their children go with that we wondered? Now since we have children we know. We are often tired, frazzled parents who get angry if we don't get our break so we have turned to television to help us through.

Maybe we are wrong, maybe as we had read in an advice column, we should only allow our children to watch television when either parent can sit down and watch with them. This includes professional wrestling and hockey. Certainly no one wants kids who are TV junkies. But Henny and I took television the same way we took candy—it may not be good but a small amount won't hurt them. And chosen properly, they might actually get something out of the programs like I did, listening to the radio when I was a child.

Lorne, Lorna and Ozzie made their own choices like I had made. We draw the line of course; there is no excessive violence and fowl language. But that too seems to be hanging and difficult to supervise. For instance we received our power bill, which I thought was excessively high. I swore and cursed. A day later Lorna used the f*** word which is both a noun and a verb. It can also be an adverb as in "She's f***ing-well quit high school." Or it can be a pronoun. 'We can't afford a new car because f***head lost his money gambling."

"Aha, Lorna is parroting her father," Henny said when she heard Lorna use the distasteful word.

When I told Dr. Hoffman about Lorna's use of the f*** word he said, "Daddio Joe, swearing is nothing to get alarmed about. Children, like parents, utter choice words when for example, they get cut off on the highway, have a flat tire, their hockey team misses an empty net, and like yourself, get a high utility bill."

Dr. Hoffman also said the myth that only adults can swear is outdated and advised to stay calm when we hear one of our children swearing and to treat them gently. "Remember young children mimic what they hear. You use to mimic Lorne Greene and Foster Hewitt. Often they mimic without knowing the meaning of what they are saying. Cursing and swearing is used to express emotion ranging from to anger," he said.

Leaving swearing and cursing behind I then asked Dr. Hoffman to do a quick poll to see what young people thought about aging. Dr. Hoffman called the three children to come to the living room and to each posed the question: "What do you think about old people?"

Ozzie said he didn't want to get old because it meant being a cripple, gray hair and a face that's wrinkly and then added, "That's also when you and your teeth don't sleep together."

Lorna said, "It's kind of weird because I don't want to die. I want to stay healthy and marry a millionaire. You reach old age when you straighten out the wrinkles in your pantyhose and discover you aren't wearing any."

Lorne said, "When you get old you can't walk or drive a car, not like being a teenager, and you wake up looking like your driver's license picture."

I soon discovered that even preschoolers had negative attitude towards the elderly and that by age twelve to thirteen, children's ageist attitudes were difficult to change.

Is radio becoming different? I believe it is. We speak on the air about subjects which were unthinkable several decades before. There is less drama and records have subliminal meanings encouraging our teenagers to have premarital sex, use drugs to cure all ills and dress outlandishly. Ozzie for instance, has reached an age where he's into hard metal music and loves wearing Lorna's clothing. One day I even heard Ozzie saying, "Mom and Dad I would like a doll for Christmas."

And when the Christmas season came, Ozzie was disappointed that he did not get his doll but a board game instead.

Christmas season is, according to the famous song at least, the most wonderful time of the year. That is until we stuffed ourselves with eggnog, candy, pudding, turkey and all the trimmings. It was a stressful time to say the least.

At present the world of the teenager is changing so quickly that we have to run to keep pace, especially when it comes to the use of computers cell phones and the Internet. Mainstream kids have to grow faster than perhaps any other previous generation.

They have to be on top of technology that is sweeping the world, a divorce rate that has led to an increase of single-parent families; adjust to a shifting economy, and study harder to satisfy tough university and college admission requirements. Not to mention dealing with the usual teenage concerns: sex, drugs, alcohol, cars, part-time jobs, pimples and Saturday night dates. Their attitudes are changing as well. Their world is tougher compared to the time I was a teenager in Selkirk, Manitoba. As for our family we were fortunate thus far. Besides Ozzie wearing Lorna's clothing around the house and Lorna thinking

she's a Hollywood starlet, constantly wearing gucky makeup on her face, every time Henny and I turn around someone was shaking our hands and congratulating us
Just as I developed an appetite for being complimented on my achievements with the radio station Henny and I were getting compliments on achievements of our children. For example, Lorna was named musician of the year during her junior high school's final band concert. We were proud? You bet. I got the whole thing on video.

After the concert, friends, acquaintances, strangers too, took turns shaking mine and Henny's hands saying, "Congratulations, Lorna sure can play the cello."
I wasn't quite sure what to say. After all Lorna was the one who deserved the praise. Sure Henny and I encouraged her, paid for and drove her to and from lessons, dropped her at band practice and bought her the cello that cost more that we paid for the camper truck.

A week later, we received the same treatment after Lorne received a literary award for writing a book of poems entitled *Caustic and Roses*. The way people slapped Henny and me on he back one would think that I had written the poems. But Henny and I had done only our jobs by encouraging Lorne in the literary field.

And 0zzie too was given an award by the Chamber of Commerce for a contest promoting Penticton. He had painted a sketch of the best-known character in the Okanagan Valley that according to legend lives in and around Okanagan Lake. The pre-historic serpentine-like monster, Ogopogo, was well known in the valley long before Whitman arrived. The Indians worshiped Ogopogo and the story has persisted that the monster-like figure is still alive. In one ten-year period, twenty one sober and reputable citizens spotted Ogopogo in Okanagan Lake. The creature is reported to be twenty feet in length with a serpentine-like body and the head of a horse with four feet, a tail of a fish and green in color. Despite winning the contest Ozzie surprised Henny and me when while saying his prayers one night we overheard him say, "Dear God, when I wake up I hope I'll be a little girl."

The following week after Lorne, Lorna and Ozzie received their awards the *Herald* wanted to do a profile of me in an upcoming edition and left a blank form to fill out with Jane Mitchell, the receptionist, at the radio station. I filled it out the same day and read as follows:

Current Project	Paying of our mortgage
Background	Born in Selkirk, Manitoba. Use to shoot gophers, magpies and mud hens with a slingshot.
Family	Wife Henny is a nurse and enjoys acting as a hobby. Three children: Lorne, Lorna and Ozzie
Pets	None. Budgie bird killed by carpet cleaner

Why I got into radio	Curiosity. I wanted to be like Lorne Greene
Past Jobs	Farmhand, floor sweeper and garbage collector
Biggest Disappointment	(1) When I wrecked my sports car. (2) Failing to Win Search For talent Show contest while a youngster in Selkirk, Manitoba
Greatest Accomplishment	Henny becoming my wife and then 3 kids
Person I most admire	Henny
Hobbies	Volunteer soccer coach
Greatest fear	Lorna will get pregnant
Favorite Food	Roast beef—outside cut
Favorite way to spend money	Never had any
Pet peeve	Politicians and evangelists—hate them both
Funniest night	The night I went to meet Henny at 3:37 a. m. and an album groove got stuck while on the air
Fatherly advice	Before you borrow money from a friend, decide which you want more. Forgive your enemies— nothing annoys them more
Most often used cliché	"*Each and every one.*" I have eliminated the words *You know, ya,* and *okay* in my interviews

Recent knowledge	Only female mosquitoes are fitted for biting and blood sucking. The male mosquito is a vegetarian
Favorite book	None in particular
Favorite entertainment personality	Lorne Greene
Future ambition	Tour Canada
The most destructive habit	Worry
The greatest joy	Giving
The greatest loss	Loss of self respect
Most satisfying work	Helping others
Ugliest personality trait	Selfishness
The most endangered species	Dedicated leaders
Out greatest natural resource	Our youth
The greatest 'shot in the arm'	Encouragement
The most effective sleeping pill	Peace of mind
The most crippling failure disease	Excuses
The most powerful force in life	Love

The most dangerous pariah	A gossiper
The worst thing to be without	Hope
The deadliest weapon	The tongue
The greatest asset	Faith
Most worthless emotion	Self pity
Most beautiful attire	Smile
Most prized possession	Integrity
Most powerful communication	Prayer
Most contagious spirit	Enthusiasm
Favorite saint	St. Francis of Assisi

As Henny and I were discussing the possibility of touring Canada on a bone-chilling morning with snow drifting across the landscape, Penticton experienced its worst blizzard of the winter that year. Ten inches of snow had already fallen and CJOE weather advisory said another ten was to fall before the storm passed over. But already there were all sorts of problems: motor vehicle accidents, water pipes frozen and the apartment where Big Paul Mitchel and his wife, Jane, lived, caught on fire and the couple narrowly escaped death.

As Okanagan Manor was stone's throw from Patricia Motel my father rescued the couple before firemen arrived, but somehow Big Paul was never the same afterward. His health began to deteriorate and early one morning he suffered a stroke and died.

Except for being a midget Big Paul's life was fulfilling. Father Kobuk's words inside St. Anne's church and the crowd's emotional farewell outside perfectly captured the two sides of Big Paul—the quiet, fun-loving midget and Big Paul radio announcer who stirred his listener's passions.

In his brief eulogy Harry Fahlman spoke little about Big Paul's size and more about his announcing career.

The casket placed before the altar remained closed. There were no radio awards or mementos, nothing to suggest the enormity of Big Paul's impact on CJOE's audience.

Outside, a small crowd came to pay its respects, and when the hour-long funeral mass, which included Psalm 23, as well as readings from the Old and New testaments and singing of *Ave Maria* and *Amazing Grace*, ended; the hearse drove off to the Lakeview Cemetery. There were cries of 'Goodbye Big Paul" accompanied by respectful, spontaneous applause.

It was a dignified and private funeral, just as Big Paul wanted it and his parents were determined to follow his wishes. This meant including people like the manager of CJOE, Harry Fahlman, do the eulogy.

At the cemetery family members wept as the four-foot coffin was buried, and later, a shaft was raised over the grave. On it stood a life-size statue of Big Paul Mitchell, which he posed while he as holding on to a microphone when he was eighteen years of age and first employed by CJOE.

I visited Big Paul's gravesite a month after he was buried. There was a simple marker that read: BIG PAUL MITCHELL.

It was still so unbelievable that a midget friend of mine had died as I saw pots of flowers lay beside the grave, placed by his admirers. I brought my own tribute to Big Paul. From my pocket I took a photograph and placed it on the grave. It was a picture I had taken when we first met at CJOE and he gave me a tour of the radio station.

Big Paul had been in the grave only several months when Jane, aside from being a receptionist at the Patricia Motel, devoted her spare time to the promotion of better access to public buildings for small people.

At City Hall, for instance, she met with the Mayor and said; "City Council has helped those with wheelchairs by slating curbs on corner sidewalks but nothing about the placement of telephones in public buildings. A midget has to stand on a stool or an empty apple box to pick up the receiver, which is large for little hands to hold."

Following the meeting with the Mayor, Jane's life generally changed and was against having a totem pole, which the Penticton Indian Band presented to her and Big Paul as a wedding gift, and placed at the Okanagan Manor entrance. Jane phoned me on *Speakup*, please which I hosted at the time and said something to the effect that

163

she hated totem poles with a passion. "Faces of birds, fish and animals stacked one on top of the other, I hate with a passion. It's sorcery. It's witchcraft. The totem pole is evil," she said.

But many listeners, and especially the tenants of Okanagan Manor, thought differently and suggested Jane back off attacking Indian culture, which she did. Rather than propagate a controversy Jane wrote her husband's biography and reminisced about his hardships and triumphs as a radio announcer. She recalled how being a midget wasn't an easy life. In one chapter she wrote: "If nature endowed Big Paul with a wonderful voice it was comparatively small compensation for the inconvenience, troubles and annoyance imposed on his diminutive stature."

A month after Big Paul's biography was completed, Jane died. While it is known that midgets have lived until their nineties, Jane and Big Paul Mitchell died at an early age. Her headstone next to her husband's read with four words:

BIG PAUL MITCHELL'S WIFE.

CHAPTER 10

Throughout most of my broadcasting career I spoke about social issues on various programs. Over a cup of coffee one day Fahlman said to me, "Daddio Joe, you always speak about irrelevant, trivial things nobody cares about. How about saying something about women issues that will shake society?"

"Alright," I said and in subsequent programs dealt with why few women are interested in becoming firefighters, about a female auctioneer making her way in a male dominated trade, female hockey gaining popularity and why female employees don't earn as much as a man.

Aside from writing and reading women issues I also MC's a program called *New Record Jury* where an invited panel of guests talked about new record releases. Because of the program I was named in a lawsuit. I told the panel at the time, "I want all of you to close your eyes and tell me what color shirt or blouse you are wearing."

Unfortunately a listener was visiting Penticton from Vancouver and while driving on Naramata Road, closed her eyes too and wrapped her car and herself around a telephone pole. The next day listeners lawyer entered suit but eventually it was thrown out of court and I spoke less and less about women's issues and more and more about the soaring hydro rates, shortage of doctors, spiraling education costs and the plight of the elderly. It was during a program aimed at people age fifty and over, that a listener won an AM/FM radio. Several days later that lady wrote me a letter that I read with great interest but not on the air. She wrote:

Dear Mr. Rubeck:
God bless you for the beautiful radio I won recently on your program. I'm eighty four years old and live at the municipal home for the aged. All the people I have known are gone. It's nice to know that someone thinks of me. God bless you for your kindness to an old forgotten soul.

My roommate is ninety five and always had her own radio, but would never let me listen to it, no matter how often or sweetly I asked. The other day her radio fell and broke into a lot of pieces. It was awful. She was very upset.
She then asked if she could listen to mine, and I said, "Sorry."

Sincerely,

Edna Johnson

Another time I MC'd a quiz show where if the contestant spelled the word *spelunking* (the exploration and study of caves) correctly, he/she would win a $100 prize. When a plump housewife won I asked, "What is the first thing you're going to do with the money"? she replied, "Count it."

The most dramatic interview I ever conducted but not on the radio was when Police Chief Robinson called me shortly after one midnight and said, "Daddio Joe, we have problems in a hostage taking and wonder if you can help us?"

"Sure," I said and wanted more information.

The Chief said that a drunken husband with a butcher knife had taken hostage an estranged wife. "He wants to speak to the premier of British Columbia or Daddio Joe on the radio. We can't get a hold of the premier so we called you."

What followed was a tense all-night negotiation between the husband and myself. I will never forget the scene: the husband brandishing a butcher knife at his wife's throat. Her wrists were twisted behind her back and bound with copper wire. From her wrists, the wire ran around her neck. The husband held one end of the wire and jerked it every so often making it cut into his ex-wife's flesh.

It was the most chilling interview I ever conducted. Miracously after six hours I convinced the husband to release his wife and when it was over, I spent the following hour on the air broadcasting the tapes I had made.

But the hostage taking incidents wasn't as horrific as the time a caller who identified himself as James Purdy phoned me one afternoon at the radio station and said in an agitated voice, "Daddio Joe, why don't you come to my house and watch me kill a police officer. Since I seem to know you I promise not to harm you. I have two rifles beside me and I'm not afraid to use them. Quickly come down to my house as fast as you can."

"Oh yah," I said.

"That's the truth. I'll only aim at the cops who I believe have been tracking me for years."

Well, I thought this person was a basket case so I notified the RCMP about the unusual call I had. By the time I arrived at the home a RCMP Emergency Response Team arrived at the scene and escorted Purdy's wife away. The area was cordoned off and neighbors were told to leave or stay in their basements. Police negotiators called Purdy on the phone and said he wanted to leave the house. Spike belts were deployed around his blue truck. After a six-hour standoff Purdy bolted from the house and headed for the truck where Corporal James Corley, held a standard-issue Smith & Wesson 9 mm pistol in his hand. Seconds later there was a barrage of shots and the cop was shot dead. A hail of bullets then immediately felled Purdy. Both, thirty-one year old Purdy and Corley, a 25-year veteran of the force, died at the scene.

After I had given news reports of the incident I closed my final report by saying, "With the best training in the world, the best equipment in the world and the best technology in the world, sometimes things go horribly wrong."

I felt my interest in major crime heightened my profile in Penticton and since then I dropped the moniker Daddio

Joe. I had grown into adulthood. My taste for music was changing too in the radio announcing game. From now onward listeners were referring to me as not Daddio Joe but Mr. Rubeck, the announcer on the radio.

As a radio announcer/writer for CJOE I had by now covered many crimes, community and charity events, civic affairs, debates and functions. One of these was the unveiling of a fountain/sculpture at City Hall. The outrage that accompanied the first public viewing surpassed even the anger over the corruption and cost of overruns during the construction of a new City Hall itself.

Created by a University of British Columbia architecture professor and selected by City Council, the bronze sculpture was meant to depict a stylized flock of Canada geese and officially called *The Migrants*. But I promptly renamed it on the air, *The Spaghetti Tree* and then wrote a song about the fountain with the chorus "The spaghetti tree! The spaghetti tree! What a horrible site to see!'

I observed that while its designer considered the fountain a work of art, many of my listeners did not agree.

The professor defended the creation during an interview with me and said that the work was *interpative* and the abstract intended to show nine geese, with the water spraying out of each of their bills. As soon as the fountain was put into operation it was discovered too late that even a very slight breeze resulted in the drenching of people trying to enter the main doors to City Hall

One soaked citizen labeled the fountain as *Abstract Atrocity* while another argued that the fountain/sculpture should be taken to the city's junkyard. Another said, "I refuse to pay my taxes and utility bills if I have to pass near the fountain."

Despite such opposition the *Spaghetti Tree* survived in front of City Hall and what I had to say at the time was that, "Pentictonites are being goosed."

Eventually city council agreed that the fountain/sculpture was indeed a work of art, and art was part of culture, and Canada geese messing up parks, beaches and sidewalks with their droppings was part of culture.

Another part of Penticton's culture is the legendary serpentine-like Okanagan Lake monster, Ogopogo. To promote Penticton's culture and Okanagan tourism CJOE offered its listeners a $5000 reward for an authentic picture of the prehistoric creature to be taken during the tourist season. A University of British Columbia zoology professor would verify the picture and more importantly, Lloyds of London, the insurer who underwrote the contest, would evaluate the professor's finding before a cheque would be written.

Naturally the contest raised the ire of staunch Ogopogo believers as well as those who thought the monster was a hoax. Soon Greenepeace entered the controversy, pleaded for the monster's safety and a spokesperson said, "We don't want any harm done to Ogopogo's sought after hide. In the chance that Ogopogo does exist let's treat him better than we treat our wolves and whales."

The first reported sighting of Ogopogo took place in 1872 but mention of the creature can be found in Indian legends when it was known as N'ha-n-tik. Later it is said Ogopogo appeared to witness a baptismal service in Okanagan Lake and during an immersion, the pastor was attracted by the appearance what he thought was a super giant muskrat swimming swiftly to shore. But the head was raised a foot above the water and along the back of the head appeared to be eighteen inches in length. Seeing the monster those who were submerged jumped out of the water and later changed religion.

Later still another observer said he saw Ogopogo racing from one end of Okanagan Lake to the other, "As if he was preparing for the summer Olympics."

Announcement of the photograph contest, aside from drunken tourists, the long list of Ogopogo spotters included international media, businessmen and museum curators.

Among the first international contestant to arrive to see if he could spot Ogopogo was a scientist from the Soviet Union who after seeing an unusual object swimming in Okanagan Lake claimed Ogopogo was between ten and twenty feet in length but unable to prove it.

A researcher from England explained how prehistoric eggs could have been preserved at the bottom of the lake until there was an earthquake and it released the eggs into the water where Ogopogo was hatched.

A Big Foot enthusiast from Australia believed in the Susquatch but wasn't ready to accept the anthropology professors theory from England of eggs being shaken by an earthquake creating Ogopogo, so he didn't enter the contest. With his binoculars he sat on various beaches and clay banks and watched others looking for the creature and getting a snapshot of him.

A scientific team from New York, after doing preliminary research, called for a full-scale white paper investigation of Okanagan Lake that in places is over 1000 feet deep. They too, however did not snap a picture of the beast but a reporter from Montreal claimed he saw Ogopogo 200 yards out into the lake as it moved slowly, then submerged into the water but as he was taking a picture the camera dropped damaging the lens.

A tourist from Spain was fishing from his boat and reported that Ogopogo created waves nearly upsetting his boat. The waves were so large that they swept away the camera.

An investor reported another sighting from a German who was making an offer on an orchard near the bedroom community of Naramata. "Ogopogo rolled over in the water and then descended below the surface," the German said.

During the three-month contest there were other sightings of Ogopogo as well. "Ogopogo put on a high speed performance which left me gasping." An eminent visitor from Switzerland said, "Unfortunately when I snapped the picture the camera was without film."

A contest participant from France said, "While I was water skiing I saw big waves. There was no other boat in sight. There was no wind and the lake was as smooth as a glass of French champagne. I became hysterical, however, dropping my rope and when the boat driver came to pick me up we saw Ogopogo dive twice, about two minutes and 500 yards apart. To bad we didn't have our camera ready otherwise I'm certain we would have won the $1000 prize."

A contest participant from Poland took an oath but could not confirm by way of a photograph that he saw Ogopogo lunge out the water, grab a squawking seagull, ten feet above the water, and ate the bird for lunch.

A visitor from Scotland denied that anyone in his group had seen Ogopogo but confirmed that he had seen the Lochness Monster in a lake in Scotland.

A die-hard fisherman from Penticton said that kokanee fish spawn in a creek emptying into Okanagan Lake, and this is supposed to provide food for Ogopogo. "The kokanee are never seen in the lake. They appear only at spawning time," the Pentictonite said.

A contestant from Greece said he had taken a photograph what he thought was Ogopogo but when the film was developed the photograph was that of an upset houseboat.

A researcher from Japan used a device called *Side Scan Sonar* and picked up a hit in 500 feet of water that registered twenty feet in length. When he went over the area a second time, the object disappeared, and was picked up in another location. A chunk of bait was lowered and when it returned to the surface it had been bitten in half.

Still others who came to Penticton said they had a photograph of Ogopogo but the quality wasn't good enough to enter because Highway 97, from where the picture was taken, ran 1000 feet above Okanagan Lake.

At any rate excitement in Penticton mounted during the length of the contest. Unfortunately there was no winner because the photographs that were turned in did not have the signature of the University of British Columbia department of zoology professor.

Although there were no winners the promotion did, if anything else, spark worldwide interest in Ogopogo and put Penticton and Ogopogo on a map in Albania and Zimbabwe.

All in all a goodtime was had by everyone and personally it was even better for my family when the following September the Penticton Indian band in a ceremony on the reserve named me *Honorary Chief* and Henny, Lorne. Lorna and Ozzie, honorary *Ravens*.

We sat at the edge of a circle with Ozzie in Henny's arms and Lorne and Lorna at our feet.

Chief Yellowhorn then placed a feather headdress on my head and said, "From this moment onward Joe Rubeck shall be known as Chief Raven Announcer."

I appreciated the gesture that the local Natives bestowed on me.

After my initiation to the tribe Chief Yellowhorn came over to Henny and said, "I now make you, Henny Rubeck, *a sister* of the raven and Lorne, Lorna and Ozzie *children* of the raven."

As soon as Chief Yellowhorn said those words drums thundered, chants echoed and Indians in feathers danced among the circle we were in. When the ceremony ended Chief Yellowhorn asked me to say a few words about the plight of aboriginal people in Canada so I sprang to my feet and said, "A Native woman once told me that the Whiteman was strange. He's always running around, he tells lies and looks at his watch to tell him when he's hungry. Indians can't understand white people are always busy, why they break promises, even when there's good reason, and why they don't eat when they are hungry.

"And then there's the Whiteman who can't understand that an Indian gets quieter when he's angry and there are lawyers and judges who can't understand that when an Indian defers his eyes, he's showing respect and uncertainty.

"Most Canadians think Indians would be more likeable if they only be a little less power-seeking. And Canadians, you know, those who love to hyphenate themselves, those who automatically gravitate to their own whether it's a corporate suite or checking out potential neighborhoods to live in, wish Natives would only try to be less clannish. And, yes, 90% of Canadians say they would like Indians better if they were a little harder working. Well, so might a lot of Indians, but try working hard when you are surrounded with 80 % to 90% unemployment."

There was a burst of applause and drum thumping that made me feel good. I had been given an opportunity to say a few words about the way I felt the way Canadians treated our aboriginal people.

In 1970 I was forty years of age and had run a gamut of shifts and announcing responsibly at CJOE. Now I was the morning man and did considerable amount of news reporting too. The morning audience was considerably different and larger compared to the other shifts because people were getting into the habit of watching television during prime time and listening to the radio in the morning. If the songs of the sixties can be characterized as rampant and excessive with lyrical exhibitionism coupled with strong autobiographical instinct, beginning of the seventy's found singers and song writers seeking to restore the psyche and melodic balance.

Since I had to get up at 4:00 a. m. I gave up coaching soccer. Lorne and Lorna were thirteen years of age and Ozzi twelve. Wherever we went people would say how much Lorne and Lorna looked alike. They had the same green eyes, the same blond hair, the same facial features, yet they were different.

On the whole the children had a good time with each other and people would say they were the prettiest in the neighborhood. The kids enjoyed carousing around, climbing trees, squeezing insects and balancing objects on their nose.

Ozzie, however, was quiet, soft spoken and had a slight speech impediment in which his T's sounded like D's. He would say *dat* is that of *that*, and enjoyed playing with dolls and wearing girls clothing around the house and yard.

Lorne had a tendency to be quiet and spent hours writing and reciting poetry. He was close to Henny, much closer than Lorna was. It was Lorna who was demanding and screamed the loudest when she wanted something. Lorna was a dreamer in the family who could lay on the grass or sand on the beach for hours.

One day while the family was at the Okanagan Lake Beach, which was two blocks from our home, Henny smiled and said to me, "I was like that when I was Lorna's age."

"And what did you dream about?" I asked.

"About being an actress or a nurse. Did you ever dream about being a radio announcer?"

"I did. I had other dreams too."

"Like what?"

"I dreamed that when I grew up besides being a radio announcer I would marry some one like you."

"And what else did you dream about?"

"That some day the two of us would tour Canada in a camper truck"

Those dreams were put on hold when the following month employees of CJOE attempted to form a union and Fahlman was brainwashing them into being anitI-union.

"Our wages aren't keeping pace with inflation," Happy Buck Milton told us as a group when we met at his residence.

Happy Buck was right with that assessment but Fahlman, as manager of the radio station, refused to discuss staff discontentment with any member

As days went by we met with a representative of the Canadian Union Of Public Employees who took us under his wing and applied for certification. When we were certified Fahlman still refused to discuss wages, sick leave benefits, and number of hours worked.

The union with Happy Buck Milton at the helm of the local presented Fahlman with a seventy two hour strike notice. As soon as the notice expired a picket line was set up in front of the radio station.

The strike seemed to have little effect because Fahlman hired a staff or new announcers who were eager to begin a career in broadcasting. Fahlman also hired relatives and high school students as part-time employees. We called them *scabs*. Fahlman himself became more active with on air presentation and read the major newscasts and most of the commercials, which were taped as a rule.

The following three months were frustrating because I was unemployed and no income coming. he frustration increased a short time later when I came home from the picket line and a bank representative was waiting at the front door with Henny.

"Hi, what brings you to Naramata?" I said to the bank rep.

"Good afternoon, sir," the banker said. "I'm here to serve you with foreclosure papers. Bank records show that you have missed three consecutive mortgage payments."

After handing me the foreclosure document and the banker had left, tears came down Henny's face. "What is that supposed to mean?" she said.

"It means that because of the strike at CJOE we are unable to meet our commitment to the bank and are losing our home."

"Well, I can go back to work in order to put food on the table," Henny said.

"Let's talk about it," I said and when we did, Henny and I decided to sign a quitclaim, to store our furniture at Lehman's Moving and Storage and live with my parents at the Patricia Motel.

"And who is going to look after the kids?" Henny then asked.

"Mom and dad," I said.

Both Henny and I were under strain and Henny wanted to give me something I was losing, faith and confidence.

"At least we won't starve by me going back to work," Henny said as she lowered her voice and planted a kiss on my cheek.

"I'll do everything to restore a normal life again." I said and then pulling Henny to my side I kissed her lips.

A moment later I followed her to the bedroom but nothing happened there. It hadn't for over a month. There were too many things on our minds but at least the love for each other was still there, battered but no gone.

"Battered but not gone." is how one described the taxi which I undertook to drive for the local taxi company, until the strike at CJOE was over.

A battered wife fleeing from her estranged husband, A lawyer heading to the Courthouse, A sun bathing beauty in a bikini, A prisoner out on parole. Yes, I drove them in my brief period as a taxi driver and worked twelve hours a day to bring home the bacon without the eggs. The taxi I was assigned to drive could be driven up to sixty miles with the oil warning light flashing. Turning up the volume of the radio eliminated unusual and alarming noises. It was tough, especially working the night shift. By morning I was dead-tired and often went to bed without seeing Henny, the kids or my parents. When I did see them they would often ask questions like, "How did it go today?" "You must meet interesting people?" and "How much money did you earn yesterday?"

When you spot a cab driver seated in a cab reading a newspaper as he awaits a passenger, you may think the job is easy. I always did. Not so. I found that a cab driver makes a bare living the hard way and has to keep his cab in shape and insurance to pay. He must get out and hustle because he gets no salary and has to work on commission and tips.

Hackies must be alert and expert drivers. Besides they must be willing to be in pursuit of gangsters and hold-up criminals if a cop hails them. They are also required to pick up the sick and accident cases to be rushed to a hospital.

No matter how I felt, I had to be polite to customers, even a stuffed shirt like Judge Michael Shaw who on my first day as a driver fined me fifty-dollars for parking ten minutes instead of five in an unloading zone. One did not need a college education to become a taxi driver although one co-driver had a PHD degree because he couldn't find work in his chosen profession and another must have had more degrees than a thermometer. All that was required of me to drive a taxi was a license that was easy to get but not before I gave an account of my past life. The taxi company wanted to know when and where I as born and my social security number. I had to fill out a form if I drank or smoked, in the habit of spitting or chewing tobacco, and if I ever was bonded, not with glue but by an employer.

And then they took my fingerprints and checked the criminal files to see if I ever had been arrested for larceny, rape, and murder or child abuse. They also took a snapshot of my face to place a number on it to make sure the public knew who I was.

I soon discovered that a cabby never knows what sort of a person is going to hail a taxi. Still I admit I would rather drive one than be on Unemployment Insurance, welfare, shining shoes or digging ditches.

It's rather difficult to describe the feeling, which came over me when for the first time I heard the cry of, "Taxi! Taxi!. Oh, taxi driver! Please take me to the airport!"

This took place on a Saturday night during the peak of the summer tourist season and a time when Penticton comes alive and people are in a partying mood.

It's true that in Penticton a taxi may be difficult to find on a Saturday night because that is the night people, especially tourists, go drinking, attend sporting events, stay on the beaches past midnight and teenagers cruise Lakeshore Drive in their hot-rods with the radio turned up to full volume.

There's a mystique about Saturday night in Penticton and it's a busy time fro taxi drivers. It's a business, like radio broadcasting, and if not careful, send one to a psychiatric ward in a hospital. This nearly happened to me on the third day of driving when my first fare that day was a woman who reminded me of a female assassin. She must have been about forty years of age. When I increased the volume on the radio and a rock n roll tune was playing with risqué lyrics, she said to me, "Mr. Taxi driver. You are going to hell for listening to that type of music."

"If I'm going to Hell you must be in the wrong cab." I said but shouldn't, because at the next red light she got out and hailed another taxi.

My second fare that day, was an obese woman who must have weighed at least three hundred pounds. In her futile attempt to climb inside she looked at me hopelessly and said, "If you were half a man you would help me."
I didn't say it but thought, "Madam, if you were half a lady, you wouldn't need a taxi."
It took five minutes before I finally managed to get her inside the cab and another five to get her out once she reached her destination.

My third fare that day was a skinny woman who weighed less than one hundred pounds and said she had 12 children. As I was making my way through traffic, passing other cars, she said to me, "Hey, taxi driver, you are driving with reckless abandon. Would you please be careful?"

Can you imagine me to be careful? She's the one who had twelve children.

After a week of driving a taxi and Lorne, Lorna and Ozzie were in school, Henny and I decided to have late breakfasts together and each morning, talk, laugh and catch up on the news.

It was during our first get-together that Henny said, "Is it true that a cab driver is faced with situations that get him into trouble?"

I said that it was and told Henny about an embarrassing experience I had the night before when a young lady flagged me down and said, "Catch up to that police car. My brother is the cop driving it."

I obliged and stepped on the gas pedal heading north on Highway 97 towards Summerland. As I caught up to the police cruiser and about to pass it, so that my fare could speak to her brother, the cop flashed his lights, rolled down his window and barked at me, "Where do you think you're going at such high speed? Wise guy, you are a menace to those driving on the highway!"

"But my fare insists she's your sister," I said.

"Pull over and be quick about it," the cop said which surprised me.

I pulled over and got out of the cab to explain the matter when my passenger said calmly, "Cabby, that's not my brother after all. I made a mistake. I'm sorry."

Was my face red? Reder than a cherry. I was lucky to be given a ticket for speeding only and not charged with dangerous driving.

Then I told Henny that one of my customers was in the habit of hiring my cab each afternoon just to relax, chew the fat and tell me his troubles. The guy is known in Penticton as a big-time gangster, charged with a dozen killings and on parole from prison after serving 25 years.

"I won't mention his name," I said.

"Why?"

"Because I don't want to take the risk of being the thirteenth."

"He sounds like a dangerous customer so please be careful" Henny warned.

I said that I would and told Henny that we didn't talk about the crimes he committed but mostly about his rose garden that refused to bloom.

The following day, Henny and I had breakfast again and as she was enjoying her cup of coffee said, "Well, how did it go yesterday?"

"A bit snaky," I said and went on to say that the fare almost gave me a heart attack after I had an encounter with a three-foot cobra that the fare had left behind and hid in the back seat of the cab. I called the SPCA. They called the cops. The cops called the Game Farm where the reptile was allegedly taken from. The Game farm people blamed the snake's disappearance on the moon being in Venus with Scorpio rising. At any rate my taxi was decimated and I had to tow it to an auto dealer to put the parts together again.

There's an advantage, however, of being a taxi driver in Penticton say to New York or even Vancouver. Aside from less drivers getting murdered they get to know and see things that are not taught at school. One may call it a liberal education about off-color facts of life.

Next I told Henny about another experience I had as a taxi driver which included a fare seated next to me smoking a cigarette which was different form ordinary tobacco.

The smell was something awful. I couldn't help asking what he was smoking. The passenger politely answered while taking a puff, "I hope you don't mind old chap but I smoke marijuana."

The cigarette is commonly known as a reefer. Well, you could have knocked me over with a Canada goose feather that one often finds on Okanagan Lake Beach, sidewalks and the golf course each summer. I was driving near the cop shop and got scared because smoking marijuana in British Columbia is illegal. When the fare offered me a refer I turned him down flat. He even went further and bragged that he sniffed cocaine. Imagine reefers and cocaine. That's when I stopped the cab and said to the fare, "At the risk of offending you I don't wish to drive you any further. Take a walk and goodbye."

He did, without having to pay a fare.

The following day when Henny and I met for breakfast and discussing an eggnog recipe I told her about a former taxi driver I picked up at the airport. He looked prosperous wearing a blue hand-tailored suit with a bowler had to match.

"Cabby, please take me to the office of Best Realty." he said.

"As you wish, sir."

"Let's cut out the sir," he said, "I use to be a hackie myself until I established a business in Toronto.

The fare was a friendly type so I encouraged him to tell me something about his business and maybe I could learn a thing or two how to cope with losing a home and being on strike. His knowledge could be a turning point in my life.

"Okay. I don't mind telling you about my business." he began. 'How about stropping at a cafeteria. It's a relief to meet a cabby like you who talks the same language."

I agreed and parked the taxi next to a café and once inside the ex-cabby said to a waitress, "I'll have a bowl of your regular soup."

As soon as the soup was delivered to our table the ex-cabby put a spoon into a bowl and noticed an object floating on top so he hollered, "Hey! Waitress! There's a fly in my soup!" He then mad several rude remarks and expletives which one can not find in a dictionary.

As the waitress was rushing to serve another customer she hollered back, "Watch your language, sir, or else you'll find the soup you are complaining about on your fly."

The ex-cabby never did tell me his secret to success and didn't buy any property through Best Realty because instead of climbing back into my taxi, he paid his fare, and then climbed into a bus, which was out of sight before I could say *Caveat Emptor,* words I had learned while being a temporary real estate salesman.

Then there was a Japanese man who came to the Okanagan Valley for sightseeing. On the last day, he hailed my taxi and asked me to take him to the airport. During the journey, a Honda drove past me. The man leaned out of the window excitedly and yelled, "Honda, very fast! Made in Japan!"

After a while, a Toyota past me. Again the Japanese man leaned out the window and yelled, "Toyota, very fast! Made in Japan!"

A short time later a Nissan past me. Again the Japanese man leaned out the window and yelled, "Nissan, very fast! Made in Japan!"

When we finished the trip the Japanese man said, "How much?"

When I said, "Twenty dollars," he looked at me in a strange way and said, "How come so much?"

I pointed to the meter odometer and said, "Very fast, made in Japan."

As we were shooting the breeze I said to Henny that there are taxi drivers who will cheat and take whatever they can lay their hands on but they are a small minority. Then I said that I know of an alderman at City Hall who wants to cut the number of cab drivers allowed to operate in Penticton because he says the market is too small to pay a decent dollar to them all. I feel cabbies don't need politicians to help to see the number shrink.

The various levels of governments are already making a taxi driver's life miserable. The problem starts with the lack of definition. Nobody can decide what a cabby really is.

The Feds are most muddled. In one breath they say cabbies are employees who must pay unemployment insurance. In the next they say cabbies are an independent business and must collect the goods and services tax.

The provincial government throws its weight around too. It encouraged taxi owners to convert their vehicles to propane. Manny did with compassion. The government then turned up the propane tax.

For a brief moment I thought Henny was sarcastic when she suggested there should be a ban on smoking in all cabs.

"Henny, you are staring up a slippery slop," I said. "What about female passengers who climb into a cab in a toxic cloud of perfume or men awash in musk aftershave. And how about those who don't believe in soap and deodorant?" Henny's response was that I had a valid point.

The following morning while having breakfast, I said to Henny that I had a bad day.

What happened?"

I said that it was late at night while I was parked at the Cherry Lane Mall that the murder parolee I had talked about earlier, appeared from nowhere, climbed into my cab and while pointing a gun at my head said, "It's your wallet or your life!" I handed him my wallet and the cash, which I had inside it.

"And then what happened?" Henny said.

"A cop who was patrolling the mall, arrested the parolee and took him to jail while an ambulance drove me to the hospital to make certain I didn't have a mental breakdown."

Henny wasn't amused.

The following morning, while having breakfast, with no warning and clear out of the blue, I said to Henny that I had turned in my taxi driver's license.

"So what are you going to do now?" Henny asked.

"Next to radio announcing I also enjoy selling real estate," I replied.

But a realtor I did not become because after discussing the parolee robbery with my father he said to me, "Joe, your mother and I would like to take a holiday in Poland and research family roots,"

After thirty years of marriage my father desired to find his roots and do genealogical search by visiting the graves of his ancestors, search parish archives in Galicia, part of Poland at one time under the jurisdiction of the Austro Hungarian and Russian empires.

"Since you are out of work and the strike at CJOE continues, would you mind managing Patricia Motel during our absence?" my father asked.

I discussed the possibility with Henny, and when she agreed that night I jumped at the opportunity, accepted the offer, at the same time recalling that my father always wanted me to be an accountant instead of a radio announcer.

CHAPTER 11

I began managing Patricia Motel during the 1973 Labor Day weekend, the same day Henny returned to work at the Penticton Regional Hospital. Our children were old enough to know what was taking place in our lives. They thought it was exciting to attend a different school and help around the motel

As a child I was anxious to hear how far a radio signal could be picked up from Selkirk, Manitoba. Lorne, Lorna and Ozzie were just as interested to see which customer traveled the longest distance by checking their license plates. And Penticton being a tourist town, they came from far distances.

Our living quarters at the motel had three bed rooms and a cheaply paneled living room, a fireplace that had not worked properly for years and a dining room that had a panoramic view of Okanagan Lake and the mountains which surrounded it.

After the first week at the hospital Henny said, "Well, Joe how is it going at the motel?"

"Compared to being a radio announcer it's awful but much better than driving a taxi," I said.

"And like in radio and driving a taxi one gets to meet interesting people?"

I said, "True." and then told Henny about a customer who while registering at the front desk said, "Sir, would you be kind enough to tell me where the town of Jeopardy is?"

"I haven't heard of such a place," I said and asked why he wanted to know.

The customer's reply was, "Because I just heard on the radio the Premier of British Columbia speaking and he said that if we didn't vote for his party all the jobs in the province would be in jeopardy."

As Henny and I were exchanging our experiences at the motel and hospital, the front desk phone rang. When I picked up the receiver a customer with a French accent said, "Monsieur. "I'm in room twenty one, and would like some pepper sil vous plait."

"You are in a kitchenette unit?"

"Oui."

"Would you like black pepper or red pepper?"

"No, monsieur. What I need is a roll of toilet pepper," the customer said.

While managing the motel, the strike at CJOE continued. When it was my turn to walk the picket line I walked back and forth carrying a placard in front of the radio station.

Many of my supporters wished me luck, cars passing blew their horns but others, whom I had known for a long time, walked by and crossed the picket line as if I was a stranger.

Others said they were boycotting the merchants who advertised on CJOE. When I checked with the retailers if that was true, I discovered it wasn't.

Several, even said their sales increased since the strike began. One retailer even had the gumption to say, "As for myself, I have no use for unions."

In many ways Henny enjoyed life as a nurse and part-time mamma. Her first month on Women's Medical went well following a three-day orientation and the director of nursing, Rita Saggs, grooming her to become a head nurse of the floor.

"Do you want me to tell that to administration?" Ms Skaggs said.

Henny was surprised, "Are you nuts?"

As far as Henny was concerned her employment was meant to be only temporary until we got out of a financial bind.

"You have no idea what this would mean," Ms Skaggs continued.

"What?"

"Security, until your retirement."

"I have learned something about finance since I married Joe but more importantly is that we have three children to raise and they will be graduating from High School soon. They need all the attention Joe and I can give them."

Ms Skaggs was hard as a rock. She wanted to reach across the table and strangle Henny. "You are making a mistake," she said. "If you screw up this opportunity it may never present itself again. You have a Bachelor of Science degree in nursing and because of your previous experience you are my choice to replace Mrs. Tremblay."

"What happened to her?" Henny asked.

"She's retiring next month."

Henny was running out of reasons why she didn't want to be a head nurse when she finally said, "Let me discuss it with my husband."

And when Henny and I discussed the opportunity, I said, "No, dear. Work part-time only. What spare time you may have, spend it with the Penticton Little Theatre."

"An excellent idea," Henny said. "I'll audition for a part in *Guess Who Comes to Dinner?*

We were clinging to our careers. Henny, to be a nurse and an amateur actress and me, as a radio announcer, and part-time motel operator.

A day after Henny told Ms. Skaggs that she would work as a part-time nurse only, I received a phone call from Happy Buck Milton that the strike at CJOE, "May be over soon."

"Great," I said and was prepared to begin announcing, writing and reporting that day.

"Not before we vote on the recommendation of the strike committee," Milton said.

I was curious. "What are the recommendations?"

"That's what I phoned about. I'll spell them out tomorrow morning at ten at my home. Off the record, however, Fahlman is prepared to improve wages, seniority and health benefits with the blessing of the absentee owner who lives in Vancouver."

As soon as I was through speaking to Happy Buck Milton, a news bulletin caught my attention on the radio that was playing in the background. My interest was aroused not because Fahlman was reading the bulletin but because it dealt with a plane crash over the Baltic Sea near Danzig. When I turned up the volume my worst fear was realized, a Boeing 737 jet was filled with Canadians and my parents were among the passengers.

The fear was substantiated when I called the LOT airline and am official confirmed that Peter and Stella Rubeck were among the dead victims.

Having the plane crash confirmed, I became hysterical. Henny grabbed me by the arm, led me to the bedroom where she gave me a tranquilizer. It was a day later, when I got my senses back, that I realized the full impact of my parents' death. I was the only son and the last will stated, "Upon death of both parents our son, Joseph Rubeck, is to inherit all possessions including the Patricia Motel."

I was in a dilemma. On the heels of my parents tragic death the strike at CJOE was over. Should I continue a career as a radio announcer or manage the motel and become a businessman, and even become a member of he Chamber of Commerce. After discussing the situation with Henny, Lorne, Lorna and Ozzie, I chose the latter.

We had a memorial service for my parents at St. Anne's Catholic Church where Father Brophy's voice during mass, droned on and on mentioning their names. "Peter and Stella Rubeck killed in a tragic airline accident. Their bodies have not been recovered."

Afterward, we stood outside the church, shaking hands with people who came to pay their last respects. It was difficult to believe my parents were gone for eternity and many thoughts wondered through my mind. Can I continue my announcing career later? Should I trade the motel on a radio station? If Henny is such a good actress, why is she nursing? What careers will Lorne, Lorna and Ozzie choose after they graduate from High School?

During June 1974, with Joni Mitchell singing *The Same Situation* on the radio, Henny and I were figuring out our children.

"It seems incredible, doesn't it?" Henny said. "Lorne and Lorna are going to be 18 soon and graduating tonight from High School. It seems like yesterday when they were learning to walk."

"And Ozzie will graduate next year," I said when Lorna walked into the living room wearing makeup, which made me cringe.

"Why don't you take some of that stuff off?" Henny suggested.

"Jeez, Mom, why?" Lorna answered.

"Because it makes you look like a raccoon, that's why."

Lorna seemed to have her own ideas about everything, and only God knew where they came from. Henny wanted to scream but remained calm as Lorna dug in her heels.

"It took a lot of time to put this makeup on and I'm not taking it off now," Lorna said.

"Be reasonable, sweetheart, it looks a little overdone." Henny went on.

"Who says?"

"Come on squirt, go and take that shit off," Lorne said as he walked into the room wearing his graduation suit.

Lorna shot back, "And your suit looks like you slept in it all night."

The comment ticked off Lorne. "Well, I can tell you this sis, I wouldn't go out with a girl that looks like a floozy with all that guck on her face."

Lorne looked his twin sister over and it was obvious he didn't approve the makeup she was wearing. "And your dress is so tight. It makes your boobs stick out."

Lorna became furious too when Ozzie joined in the argument and said, "Lorna, you should be arrested for wearing an outfit like that."

"Shut up you faggot," Lorna shot back and took a swing at Ozzie but missing him. "You think I don't know you hide Mom's dresses in your closet. Just wait when the rest of Penticton finds out."

I stood up from the table and said to the three of them. "All of you shut up! This is graduation day so let's be civilized."

As soon ad Henny and I calmed our children down Henny said, "I'll go and get the car."

When Henny did, we drove to the Penticton High School auditorium. As the graduation exercise began and we were

watching Lorne and Lorna on stage we had tears in our eyes. "It's like marrying a new life and one day soon, they will be leaving to be on their own," Henny said.
"Lucky creeps, going to Okanagan College next September," Ozzie said.

While on stage Lorna was watching Jeremy Beasley, a muscular boy in the third row, who Lorna brought home on several occasions and thought he, was the best looking guy she had ever seen. Lorna had boyfriends before but according to her, "All they wanted is to feel my boobs."
Henny was worried about those things too but her mind at the moment, like mine, was set on Lorne and Lorna singing the school song.

Life was just beginning for Lorne and Lorna and we wished many things for them as tears began pouring down Henny's cheeks and I handed her a tissue. As Henny was wiping her tears she said, "And as they enter the adult world they share uncertainty about the future. They look so sweet."

Following the ceremony, holding on to a diploma, Lorne raced to Henny and Lorna to me, and they each gave us an embrace, a hug and a peck on the cheek. While other graduates were standing around congratulating each other Lorne said, "And I'm going to make it my own way."
And while Lorne and Lorna were congratulating themselves I said to both of them, "Congratulations to both of you. Now let's head back to the motel and celebrate your graduation and your entry into adulthood."

Like many parents I thought that adolescence was a hormone-soaked rebellious time in life and teenagers not only need adults in their lives, they also want adults to help them evaluate risk.

"True," Henny said, "We as parents need to steer our kids from negative risks—experimenting with drugs, gangs, sex—towards positive one's such as sports, performing arts and volunteer work."

Henny acknowledged that doing so takes time, compromise, and sometimes the help of an adult who isn't the parent. For that part we often called on Dr. and Nancy Hoffman who although childless, advised us to shift the parenting role of being benevolent directors to that of available consultants.

"Your children are entering into adulthood," Dr. Hoffman would often say, "You better watch them for rebellious reactions. They'll be making decisions what's best for them."

That night at the motel, there were at least 100 people; most of them kids, invited and some that weren't, marking Lorne and Lorna's graduation with a barbecue and a swim. It was the biggest party Henny and I had given since our house warming in Naramata. And when the patrons in the motel found out that there was a party going many joined in the celebration.

By midnight some of the graduates smuggled in cases of beer. There was screaming, hollering and pushing one another into the pool. Henny wanted to have the celebrants, all of them, thrown out but I prevailed and said to her, "Let them have their fun."

But police made that decision after Lorne asked Jeremy Beasley, "I know you drink beer but do you also take drugs?"

"I do." Jeremy replied and offered Lorne some.

Lorne and Jeremy first exchanged harsh words and then violent blows. Jeremy was considerably larger in stature and a year older than Lorne so when he lifted Lorne and pile-drove his head into a concrete slab, Lorne's body made a *plop* sound and he keeled over losing consciousness.

Lorna was watching the encounter and rushed to the living room where Henny, the Hoffman's and I were sitting, and said, "Mom and Dad. Help! Lorne is seriously hurt!"

As I jumped to my feet Dr. Hoffman said, "I'll come too." And when he did, and applied first aid continued, "I'm afraid Lorne has no feeling from waste down."

"Is it paralysis?" Henny asked.

"Could be. Better call an ambulance."

As soon an ambulance arrived and took Lorne to the hospital, Henny and Dr. Hoffman went along. The prognosis for Lorne wasn't good and it even got worse when Dr. Hoffman with the doctor in Emergency, took an x-ray of Lorne's neck confirming Lorne had a spinal cord problem.

From Penticton, Lorne was taken by emergency helicopter to the Shaughnessy Spinal Cord Unit in Vancouver. There, doctors who attended Lorne, confirmed that he would become a paraplegic and have to use a wheelchair for the rest of his life.

Next day, I asked police why they had not charged Jeremy Beasley with intent to injure or even attempted murder. The Chief of Police replied, "No chance. It was a consented fight."

"Which means?"

"It means that your son consented to have the fight and even struck the first blow."

"Can we sue?"

"I suggest you see a lawyer but offhand I'd say you haven't got a leg to stand on."

After discussing the situation with several lawyers, I had to admit that the police assumption was the correct one. I also learned that Lorne would have to spend at least six months in the spinal cord unit and then, need rehabilitation in order to adjust to a handicapped person's lifestyle.

Life can be complicated at times. Four months after Lorne was admitted to the spinal cord unit in Vancouver, Lorna won $1000 in an instant scratch lottery and quit going to Okanagan College.

On the same day that Lorna won her lottery, she packed her duffle bag and left a note on our bed which in part read:" Dear Mom and Dad. I'm gone to Vancouver. I'm eighteen now. Mature, I can make it on my own. I hope you understand. See you soon. Love. Lorna."

The night Henny found the notice she called police and when two constables arrived I was sitting in our motel suite, note still in hand.

"Lorna couldn't have gone to Vancouver. She's probably at a friends place," the first policeman said.

But Ozzie took care of that theory. "Lorna doesn't have friends," he said.

It was a statement about Lorna but we all knew it was true. Her only friend recently was Jeremy Beasley and I had banished him from setting foot inside Patricia Motel property.

When the second policeman reminded us that Lorna had reached the age of majority, and was an adult now, Henny, Ozzie and I hoped that nothing out of the ordinary would happen to Lorna, but it did.

After hitchhiking several miles the first driver, who picked Lorna up, left her where the Trans Canada and Southern Provincial highways meet, near Hope, It took several hours to catch another ride but this one brought her to downtown on Hastings street in Vancouver.

Those seeing Lorna thought she was another college kid, a flower child. She kept walking and saw people everywhere and all ages. People who were drunk and on drugs, wearing bright home-made clothes and Hare Krishna's in brightly colored robes and shaven heads.

"Hey there, what's your name?" a statuesque woman asked and Lorna in a soft voice replied, "Lorna Rubeck."

"Where are you from?"

"Penticton."

"Have you got a place to stay tonight?"

Lorna shook her head, "Not yet."

"You can stay with me if you wish. My apartment is just up the street."

After Lorna said, "I'd appreciate that." the woman identified herself as Jezebel Beaumaris, took Lorna by the hand and together they went to an apartment in a neighborhood where derelicts and kids had died from an overdose of drugs and booze, and hookers came out in the evening do their tricks.

When Lorna said she wanted to visit Lorne at the Shaughnessy Hospital spinal cord unit Jezebel drew a map on a piece of paper and told her which bus to take in order to get there. And when Lorna did visit Lorne. she was amazed that he could speak but he was in traction and his head was in a halo. They spent an hour together chatting when Lorna said, "I better go now."

"To your hotel room?" Lorne said.

"No," Lorna said, "For the time being I'm staying with a nice lady with the name Jezebel Beaumaris but at the moment I don't know the address or her phone number." And Lorna wanted it that way as she didn't want her parents to call police.

That evening when Lorna returned to Jezebel's apartment, she was exhausted and complained that her neck and shoulders were tied in knots.

"I'll help you with that," Jezebel said and peeled the blouse of Lorna's back, covered her upper body with oils, messaging her tender flesh. There were sharp arrows of pain at times, followed by waves of ecstasy. This had gone on for an hour when Jezebel said, "Do you want to learn the trade?"

"Doing what?"

"Giving a message and having sex with wealthy geezers."

Having sex no longer carried a taboo tag with Lorna. The sexual revolution was alive and well in North America. The world was changing so quickly and dramatically, teenagers had to keep moving just so they weren't left behind.

"As a matter of fact the pay is good and I have a customer at ten tonight which you can have. His name is Howard Moon. He owns a chain of radio stations," Jezebel said.

"Okay. I'll try." Lorna said and when Howard Moon did show up at the appointed time, he brought along some mushrooms and acid and both Lorna and Moon became in an enlightened state of mind. When they were finished doing their thing, Lorna's first fear was that she was going to get pregnant, and the second, Henny and I would eventually find out.

Back in Penticton, Henny was on the phone and said to a Vancouver policeman, "We know that Lorna visited her brother at the Shaughnessy Hospital but if you don't find her soon then you better give up searching for her. One can search for just so long. For all we know Lorna may have left Vancouver and is in San Francisco." But the Vancouver cop knew Henny was wrong. He dealt with hundreds of runaway kids; some as young as eleven, who thought Vancouver was city of milk and honey.

There were colonies of druggies and runaway kids. The smell of incense wafted right out into the street and so did many teenage girls who had left school, home and then became teenage prostitutes.

Each time Henny and I went to visit Lorne at the Shaughnessy Hospital.we also went to see the cops, and even spent an hour or two searching for Lorna with them. A month later when we came to visit Lorne he asked, "Have you heard from Lorna yet?"

"We haven't," Henny said. "And to tell you the truth we are giving up on her as a missing child."

"Don't," Lorne said. "The last time Lorna came to see me she said she was staying with a Jezebel Beaumaris but wouldn't give him the address or phone number."

I was thinking of asking the Vancouver police to set a trap for Lorna. The next time she came to visit Lorne, they would nab her. Suddenly it struck me. We knew that Lorna was living in Vancouver and with Jezebel Beaumaris. All we needed was her address and I found it when I realized Jezebel had filled out an accident report the time we were involved with one in Naramata. I looked up the file and there before me was her address but no phone number. Knowing the type of a floozy that she was, chances were that Jezebel had a silent number and moved elsewhere. I hoped the sinful chippie still had the same address, however, and took that chance by taking the first available flight to Vancouver.

I spent the first three hours with Lorne at the hospital. His health was improving, so much so, that he read out loud several poems he had written. Naked *on Roller Skates*, didn't have a dirty word in it.

By the time I finished visiting Lorne it was nine at night. I returned to my hotel in a red light district, where I enjoyed a dinner and then went to a bar downstairs and ordered a double scotch. As I sat at a bar enjoying my drink who should come and sit next to me but Jezebel Beaumaris.

Recognizing me she first asked if I had a tape recorder with me, she was joking of course, and then if I had a light so she could smoke a cigarette and finally. "Are you looking for company?"

I said I would consider it if the price was right.

"For $100 I'll be lovey-dovey and since you are such a goody, goody, we'll go to my apartment and have a dingy-dingy, if you what I mean," Jezebel said.

It was a risk I had to take and Henny would understand. Lorna meant so much to both of us.

When I finished my drink Jezebel and I hailed a taxi that took us to Jezebel's apartment. The address matched the one she had written on the accident report in Naramata.

We began to disrobe when an unusual thing happened. Lorna jumped out of the closet and took a flash photo. Jezebel then said I would have to pay $100 to buy the negative. "If you don't your wife will get a hold of the film and you'll have a lot of explaining to do."

Eventually I convinced Jezebel to take a post-dated cheque, left her apartment and phoned Henny in Penticton explaining what happened and that, "I found Lorna."

As Henny was deciphering what I as telling her she asked, "Is Lorna on drugs?"

"I think so."

"Heroin?"

"Probably not, more like marijuana, mushrooms or LSD."

"I'll catch the next flight to Vancouver" Henny said. And when she did I met her at the airport. We hailed a taxi and then drove to the apartment where Lorna and Jezebel lived.

Only Lorna was at home at the time and when she let us inside Henny said, "Can we take you home, darling?"

"I think she should see a doctor first," I said.

"Go away, both of you. I want to see Howard Moon," Lorna sobbed.

"Who is he?" I asked.

Henny didn't ask who Moon was but," Are you pregnant?"

'I guess I am."

Being of the Catholic faith an abortion was out of the question so Henny said while embracing Lorna, "How pregnant are you?"

"I don't know how pregnant I am," Lorna said as she closed her eyes. When she opened them continued, "About three months."

"Have you been to see a doctor?" I said as I sat next to Lorna.

"Not since I left home."

Lorna wasn't ready to be pushed and Henny knew that she could escape. I was afraid of her escaping too so I left the chesterfield and sat on stool at the apartment entrance door. From then on it was woman-to-woman talk between Henny and Lorna.

Eventually a compromise was reached. Lorna would go home on condition that she could keep her baby and in touch with Mr. Moon.

We took a cab to the airport. Lorna sobbed all the way while Henny encouraged her to cheer up as everything would turn out okay. When we boarded the plane for Penticton it was a difficult flight for all of us. When we arrived home Henny and Lorna spent the evening together as Lorna glanced at her mother occasionally.

"You 're embarrassed because you got knocked up, aren't you?" Henny said.

Lorna nodded her head as to signify, "Yes."

Seconds later Lorna asked, "What are you going to do with me for the next six months? Hide me in one of those motel rooms? Well, you can do anything you want but don't take my baby away from me."

Henny talked compassionately and while taking Lorna by the hand said, "You can keep the baby, dear. Your father and I would have it no other way."

I gave Henny support by saying that I wouldn't harp about the pregnancy and that I liked the idea of Lorna staying with us. "And if you wish, you can be the receptionist at the Patricia Motel or go back to college," I said.

"I've had it with school. I want to pilot my own jet," Lorna said and then left for her room.

A month later, Henny and I were delighted when Lorne was released from Shaughnessy Hospital and back in Penticton although in a wheelchair.

People with disabilities want to lead ordinary lives but I found sometimes it's difficult. It's difficult especially if you can't walk.

I found out when I sat in Lorne's wheelchair and tried to make a sharp curb. I found it harder still when I tried to negotiate my way to one of the rooms in the motel and couldn't. That's when I hired a carpenter and built a wooden ramp and widen the door to Lorne's bathroom.

When Ozzie graduated from High School we attended his graduation, but didn't throw on a party. Some other parents did but from what I gather it was more subdued than the one we had thrown for Lorne and Lorna.

As a graduation gift we bought Ozzie a used half-tonne pickup truck that he called "Super Dodge" and the day before graduation night he roared up and down Penticton streets. I was certain Ozzie would either crash or be arrested when he picked up several friends, cranked up the radio to full volume and they were whooping, hollering, screeching while burning rubber.

Henny and I hoped that Ozzie would drive sensibly as our intent was for him the use the pickup as a means of transportation while he attended Okanagan College in September and study management of hotels and motels. He could hardly wait before the first semester began. In the meantime Ozzie was to go north to Prince George to plant tree seedlings for the Department Of Forestry of British Columbia.

When Ozzie woke up in the morning after the graduation bash he had the worst hangover of his life. His head throbbed, his stomach was upset. Ozzie wakened up three times during the night and thrown up once, on the bedroom floor. Ozzie thought he would die as he tried to stand up at eleven next morning. I saw Ozzie staggering so I handed him a cup of black coffee and a glass of tomato juice with a raw egg in it. Just looking at it all made Ozzie feel sick again but I insisted that he force both down.

"Make an effort, son. It will do you good," I said.

Ozzie trusted me, so did his best and was amazed when he felt a little better afterwards.

I then handed Ozzie two aspirins for his headache and he gulped them down, and felt almost human by noon, as he stretched out in the sun by the swimming pool.

As he was lying in the sun Ozzie glanced towards Lorna, who was wearing a bikini which was barely more than a piece of string thus exposing her stomach which led Ozzie to ask, "When are you due?"

"Any moment," Lorna said and that precious moment came the following week when Lorna locked herself in her room sobbing hysterically, on the bed, convulsing with pain, and there was water all over the floor. Lorna's water had broken and the pain had grown severe.

When Henny knocked on he door and Lorna opened it, she cried out, "Oh, Mom, I'm scared! I'm so scared! No one told me it would hurt so much!"

Henny called an ambulance and on the way to the hospital Lorna kept on moaning and groaning. When it arrived at the hospital the ambulance was met by Dr. Hoffman who said to the frightened Lorna, "Don't be afraid. Everything will turn out okay."

Two nurses wheeled Lorna into the labor room where Henny said, "Can you giver her a sedative?"

"I'm afraid not," Dr Hoffman said. "It may slow down her labor. She'll get over it soon."

Henny wasn't that certain so Dr. Hoffman said Henny could stay and sit with Lorna. It was six o'clock and I was amazed that Lorna had not had her baby yet. I couldn't imagine it taking so long. She had gone into labor at eleven in the morning.

When Henny phoned from the hospital she said to me excitedly, "Joe, they just can't take the baby out and Dr. Hoffman doesn't want to do a Caesarean on her unless he absolutely has to."

"I hope it's a health baby," I said.

"Me too."

The nightmare went on for another two hours when a little head emerged, and the rest of him followed, causing Lorna grief until the end.

Dr. Hoffman understood why Lorna was in such agony. The baby was huge, just over nine pounds and in perfect health. When Lorna saw the child she cried out, "You're my baby. In many ways you look like Howard!"

Lorna was to be kept in the hospital for a week in an attempt to let her wounds heal, both physically and mentally. Dr. Hoffman told her both would heal with time and kept her on Valium and Demerol for the pain.

A psychologist came to talk to Lorna every day but Lorna would say nothing to him. She just lay in bed and stared at the ceiling or the wall, wishing Howard were with her.

Lorna was even more depressed when she and baby Grant left the hospital but didn't have the strength to argue. She sat in her room holding Grant in her arms for the next two weeks, refusing to eat most of the times and telling Lorne to, "Get the hell out of my room." when he stopped to say, "Hello."

Lorna steadfastly refused to be wooed by gifts for baby Grant and kept making long distance phone calls to Vancouver, sometime five times a day. While this was happening Lorne approached me about publishing his poems in book form. Knowing the problems many new authors, especially poets, have in having their work published I was less enthusiastic about the chance of finding a publisher.

I had read that large publishing companies usually had their stock of known writers and only a handful were interested in poetry because poetry books didn't sell. There were publishers who would publish a new author provided you paid towards the cost of printing and you usually ended up a roomful of unsold books.

Undaunted by my pessimism Lorne decided to forge ahead forming his own publishing company, Happy Face Books Inc., using a loan I gave him. A local printer was hired and plans set to print 10,000 copies of *Poems By Lorne Rubeck* began after Consumer and Corporate authorities gave him the green light to proceed with the project, which included a sweepstakes.

Lorne made arrangements with a major car dealer to purchase a New Yorker car, fully loaded, from the receipts of poetry books he sold. Any one purchasing Lorne's poetry book for $10 also received a coupon enabling him or her to win the luxury car.

Lorne employed other handicapped people and they went on the road from town to town marketing the poetry book in shopping malls, rodeos and conventions. The New Yorker had hand controls on it and whenever Lorne drove he tossed his wheelchair into the back seat. One week Lorne, with the help of other British Columbia Chrysler dealers who used the cars as demos, had eight malls, two rodeos and a convention going at the same time. Lorne was so happy the way sales were going, that I heard him recite several limericks he wrote. This is what I heard him say as he wheeled his wheelchair into our living room one afternoon.

> Anyone can go to the Annual Ball
> Including City Council and all
> To observe the mess
> CJOE NEWS sent its best
> What he saw, made him crawl up the wall
>
> Poet Ed was tired and sore
> His legs could walk no more
> They ached and they pained
> Each day that it rained
> He would fall asleep and snore

Henny and I wanted to spend several days alone so on a weekend we drove to Dr. Hoffman's cottage on the shore of Okanagan Lake near Peachland. We hadn't had a few minutes to ourselves since I took over the Patricia Motel and Henny began working at the hospital.

Dr. and Nancy Hoffman's cottage was an enormous place. The décor was rustic and cozy, with quilts, antlers and pewter plates everywhere. There were Indian baskets and bearskins on the floor. The cottage and the beach in front of it was exactly what we wanted to relax in and take stock of our lives.

It was early afternoon and we hadn't unpacked yet, that the telephone rang. When I picked up the receiver after the third ring and said, "Hello," Ozzie was on the line and said,

"Mom and Dad, a Mr. Moon has registered at the motel. He and Lorna have left to get a marriage license."

I was amazed and Henny nearly fell over. "Lorna and Moon, what?" I said.

"They have gone to get married."

When I told Henny what had happened she said, "Are you certain that's what Ozzie said," and took the receiver from me.

"Would you repeat what you just said to Dad?" Henny said and when Ozzie did, Henny said. "This must be some kind of a joke."

"I'm telling you Mom. They took baby Grant along and said they would be seeing a Justice of the Peace and be back at the motel by five."

"Are you certain they left to get married?"
"By the large stone Mr. Moon gave Lorna I'm inclined to say, yes," Ozzie said.

It took Henny and me another hour before we got back to Penticton. When we arrived at the Patricia Motel, a Cadillac with a personal license plate MR. MOON, was parked in my stall.
I felt like having a tow-truck haul Mr. Moon's car away but instead used good judgment because when Henny and I walked inside, and into the living room, Lorna stood up and happily greeted us with, "Mom and Dad, I want you to meet my husband, Howard Moon."

We shook hands but what surprised me was that Howard Moon was my age, forty-five. I had read about older men marrying women less than half their age. It wasn't the worst thing our daughter could do. If Lorna was crazy enough to marry Moon it was her prerogative. She was an adult now. I figured that when Lorna would be twenty Moon would be fifty. When Lorna would be fifty he would likely be dead.

Henny didn't spend much time following the introduction to ask Moon, "What do you do for a living?"
"I own a chain of radio stations throughout British Columbia. I'm also the absentee owner of CJOE, in Penticton," Moon said.
Henny and I were both in shock and when we recovered Henny asked, "Since when?"
"Since 1952."

"That was the year I joined the CJOE announcing staff," I said.

"And do you want to know something else?"

"What?"

"Harry Fahlman always had high regard for you and your versatile talent. Mind if I ask another question?

"Go ahead."

"What will it take to get you back on the radio?"

I shrugged my shoulders. "Who knows? Right now let's celebrate your and Lorna's marriage."

I hurried to the motel basement and came back with several best bottles of champagne ever vinted in the Okanagan Valley. All of us, Mr. And Mrs. Moon, Lorne, Ozzie Henny and me, drank and ate until the early hours of morning when Ozzie decided to break his silence on his sexuality and said, "Mom and dad. Do you want to hear something?"

Henny and I aid simultaneously. "What, son?"

"It's time to share my whole story."

"What story?" I said.

"That I'm gay."

Ozzie then recalled his feelings or hurt and shame after someone wrote the word *fag* on his folder in junior High School. Ozzie said there were other signs such lack of girlfriends, playing with dolls in the bathtub and getting caught wearing Henny's and Lorna's clothes.

Naturally Henny and I were devastated with Ozzie's announcement. I wept for the first time since we lost our home in Naramata but in the end I said, "Ozzie, I still love you."

Henny said something similar, including, "Being gay doesn't make you different from the rest of us. I still love you too."

And then Ozzie, Henny and I hugged each other, chatted and played checkers until the morning sun began to rise. Mr. and Mrs. Moon meanwhile with Hennny's and my approval went to sleep as husband and wife.

THROUGHOUT CANADA
(1976)

CHAPTER 12

As a young boy I dreamed not only becoming the best radio announcer there is but also to travel throughout Canada, this great, spacious, rugged land mass. A year after Lorna and Howard Moon were married and living in Vancouver, mine and Henny's life seemed to settle down. Lorne was doing well marketing his poetry books although he was beginning to get pressure bedsores from sitting on his wheelchair. Ozzie graduated from Okanagan College in Hospitality Management and was my assistant in day-to-day operation of Patricia Motel. It was an ideal time for Henny and me not to instruct others but to inform ourselves.

When I suggested that we should take a trip across Canada Henny agreed, took a leave of absence and then said, "I'm ready to go whenever you are, Joe."

Our trip, an exploration, was different from most journeys in that it was to be made in our camper truck Ogopogo 2, and I had agreed with Fahlman to phone CJOE daily reports about our travel experiences, doing interviews and even asking searching questions.

With that in mind I had Ogopogo 2 overhauled, capable of going almost anywhere under rigorous conditions, added a chemical toilet and windows screened against insects or other flying objects which may interfere with our travel enjoyment.

Since Henny and I enjoyed fishing, canoeing and golfing, we took along our clubs, a canoe, fishing rods, a camera, film and a checkerboard. We also took a .22 rifle in the event of an attack, robbery or an assault. There were canned goods in the event we got caught in a storm, an emergency or a breakdown.

There was warm clothing in the event it got cold and Henny decided to bring along pocket books, most of them by Canadian authors Grey Owl, Pauline Johnson and Stephen Leacock. I brought along a radio, typewriter, Canadian atlas, and several bottles of whisky and knowing that we would be in Toronto I brought along several air checks of my best interviews while employed by radio station CJOE. Along the way we would buy newspapers and find out what other Canadians were thinking.

As our departure date approached we studied a map of Canada and a route that would take us through hundreds of lights, detours and delays, which would mean a journey requiring slight adjustments along the way. To begin we picked a route that would take us to Banff and Jasper national parks in Alberta and then the northern back roads through Alberta, Saskatchewan and Manitoba where we would add some leisure time to relax and enjoy the scenery, stopping in Selkirk for a week realizing that through decades some things stay the same others are very different.

Our final destination would be Newfoundland and then turn around and return to Penticton. We took the old adage "Shoot for the moon, and if you miss, you'll land in the stars," to heart. One thing was certain; we would enjoy ourselves during the extended holiday.

As our parting date came we saw a rainstorm approaching Penticton. As the storm crept forward we prepared to stand the siege. The wind struck first as the weatherman on the radio said it would. The rain began that night as the disc jockey on CJOE was playing B. J. Thomas singing *Raindrops Keep Falling* and ended in the morning causing minor flooding. To see if any damage was done I drove Ogopogo 2 to the nearest commercial campsite in Penticton where a camper said to me, "I'm glad I'm not in a tent today," as he surveyed his mobile home sitting in a large puddle of water. On the other side of the puddle a Lac La Ronge, Saskatchewan resident, on her way to Vancouver, wasn't so lucky.

Maria Bitternose said, "It doesn't rain like this in Saskatchewan," as she was folding her waterlogged tent.

When I said to Ms. Bitternose that we had included Lac La Ronge in our journey she smiled and said, "You'll find it a dull place, especially on a Sunday. And the mosquitoes there, are as large as ravens."

We left Penticton that May morning after saying "Goodbye" to Lorne and Ozzie. They said "Goodbye" too and wished us a safe journey.

As we began traveling Henny said, "No wonder springtime in the Okanagan Valley attracts so many people."

The aroma of blooming fruit trees filled the air as we drove along Highway 97 parallel to Okanagan Lake and then a chain of smaller lakes until we reached the Trans-Canada Highway at Sicamous. There, we turned eastward and followed the two-lane highway wedged between mountain chains and an incredible scenic series of lakes, rivers, forests, mountain peaks and thinly populated valleys.

Along the way we met high rolling semis, slow moving motor homes and were even cut off by logging trucks, until we reached the town of Banff, the centre of the Rockies, and pulled into Tunnel Mountain Village where we set up camp for the night and I filed my first report to CJOE describing our trip thus far. Next, we had a campfire meal and as we went to bed in the back of Ogopogo 2, listened to coyotes howling in the distance and wondering what wild animals were on the prowl that could harm us. None did.

While in Banff, we did what most tourists do: ride the Sulpher Mountain gondola, relax in the hot-springs mineral pool, canoe and walk the hiking trails, take pictures and talk to international tourists.

Henny and I were surprised by some of the questions asked by the visitors. I noted a list and sent it to CJOE on my next broadcast. Some of the questions were:

1. Sir, at what elevation does an elk become a moose?
2. Are the bears with collars, tame?
3. Where can I buy Alpine flamingos?
4. Where does Alberta end and Canada begin?
5. Do you have a map of the state of Jasper?
6. Is this the part of Canada that speaks French, or is it Saskatchewan?
7. If I go to British Columbia, do I have to go through Ontario?
8. Which is the way to the Columbia Ricefields?
9. How far is Banff from Canada?
10. Do they search you at the B. C. border?
11. Are there phones in Banff
12. So its eight kilometers away, how far is that?
13. Is that two kilometers by foot or by car?
14. How large is a hectre?
15. Don't you Canadians know anything?

It was during our second day in Banff that we watched a painter who incorporated elk dung in his work. We heard about clocks being made out of cow pies but this piece of art was out of the ordinary so Henny said as she watched the artist put dung onto his brush and then onto the canvass.

"Isn't there enough perversity around without paying homage to this sort of art?" Henny asked.

The painter said that he had recently won a prestigious prize for his previous painting and went on, "I like to link my art with ordinary life."

His art involved a naked painting of a woman name Minewanka and after putting another glob on the canvass said, "What do you think I should call this painting?"

"A pile of shit," Henny said.

The naked truth about dirty art is that Henny and I didn't like it and decided to continue our journey to Lake Louis and Jasper.

Lake Louis is an inspiring sight and known, as the Jewel of the Rockies where the view is spectacular but more so, I think, fifteen kilometers up the hill and lesser known, Moraine Lake, is more impressive of the two. Surrounded by mountain peaks and deep teal in color, Moraine Lake is defyingly gorgeous. There are two lakes every visitor touring the Canadian Rookies must see: Lake Louise and Moraine Lake. Not visiting them is like going to the Grand Canyon and looking over the edge.

While at Moraine Lake, Henny and I sat and stared, canoed the lake, walked the forested shoreline and watch climbers scale the Wenkchemna Peaks above when a terrible thing happened.

Before our eyes a group of mountain climbers was scaling one of the ten peaks when a climber plunged to his death. There was nothing Henny and I could do but debate this kind of sport and mountaineering generally.

After camping three days near the Chateau Lake Louise Hotel we refueled Ogopogo 2 at a gas station where I asked the attendant about road conditions to Jasper.

"There's a lot of repair work going on and you me be in for a a two hundred kilometer dust drive, with long waits," the attendant said.

The attendant was right but despite the long delays we found ourselves on the most spectacular stretch of ahsphalt in Canada. The highway follows a lake-lined valley between two of the eastern mountain ranges that make up the Continental Divide.

The Watershed Rivers from the Continental Divide flow east towards the Atlantic Ocean and those westward to the Pacific Ocean. The mountains here are the highest and most rugged of all the Rockies.

Although there was construction it was good for traveling but slow, as bear, deer, goat, sheep and elk were beside the highway and often on it. Along the way we stopped and took pictures of Peyto Lake, Columbia Icefields, and Sunwapta and Athabasca Falls and then the town of Jasper, teeming with wildlife and less pandering to tourists than Banff.

We camped in Jasper three days and before we left the town and park, had a photograph taken to show Lorne and Lorna back home. There was an RCMP officer on horseback in front of, no, not Niagara Falls, but Malign Lake. Henny and I pretended we were thieves signifying that Mounties always get their man. In this case it was man and woman. In the background there was a beaver gnawing away on a pine tree.

The following morning, we were on the Yellowhead Highway heading for Edmonton and along the way passed small gas, oil, and farming and forestry communities. As we traveled we listened to the radio. The records played that day were the same all over the country. I think we heard *The Long and Winding Road* by the Beatles at least twenty times that day so that I was beginning to hum the tune everywhere I went.

At Edmonton, because of a convention, we had no choice but to stay at a bottom end hotel on 97th Street that had several apartment buildings next to it. From our window we could hear music, talking and laughter, which at 3:00 a. m. turned to the sound of fire engines, ambulances and police cars. We got dressed and rushed down a flight of stairs to the fire site. By now firemen had pulled two people from the ruins of a four-story apartment walkup. At daybreak distraught relatives came rushing to the scene and found that the building had all but disappeared.

A day later, we were heading north to Fort McMurray where we pulled into Rotary Park several miles south of the community and the Clearwater and Athabasca rivers meet.

If you've never been to Fort Mac you're in for a surprise. What use to be a forest village now becoming a vibrant town and the reason it calls itself *Alberta's Northern Light*. Nearby, Syncrude Canada Ltd. was building an 80,000 barrel-a-day oilsands plant.

The town was beginning to look like as if it was one huge construction project. Whole subdivisions were going up which led local residents to joke that Fort McMurray was a town of 8000 people and 10,000 construction workers, one-half from Newfoundland.

Fort McMurray was a wild frontier boomtown when we camped there. As soon as I filed my report to CJOE, Henny and I had a game of checkers and then I crawled into the camper truck bed while Henny propped up a pillow under her head and read a pocket book.

After spending a day in Fort McMurray, we were back on Highway 63 heading southward until we came to a junction where Highway 55, mostly gravel, turned eastward and would take us to Saskatchewan. Along the way we stopped in Lac La Biche, a small community filled with Alberta history. We parked Ogopogo 2 where explorer and mapmaker David Thompson set foot in 1798 and Bishop Grandin built a Catholic mission, which overlooked the lake. Lac La Biche is one of the first French settlements in Western Canada.

From Lac La Biche we drove to Cold Lake where we read the local newspaper and then toured the Military base and met CF-104 pilot Garth Polly. The flying officer said that he had five children and his wife was expecting for the sixth time.

The following day, we proceeded driving to Prince Albert, Saskatchewan where near Meadow Lake, we were listening to the radio and there was a bulletin on the air.

As I turned up the volume the announcer reading the bulletin said that a CF-104 jet had crashed and the pilot failed to bail out. Before we reached Prince Albert the pilot was identified as Flying Officer Garth Polly.

Prince Albert is the most northerly town of any size in Saskatchewan and the location of a major maximum-security prison. We were told that the locals could have opted out for a university but chose a penitentiary instead.

Henny and I wished they hadn't. It is here that a bizarre thing happened in our journey. Two prisoners had escaped the same day as our arrival and when they saw Ogopogo 2 parked at a campsite with the engine running they kidnapped Henny, bound and gagged her into the sleeping quarters and drove away.

As the prisoners were dragging Henny into the rear of the camper truck one warned me, "Don't call the police or else we will kill her."

And they could, because my rifle was stored underneath the bed along with a package of bullets.

Despite the threat I phoned the RCMP who armed with rifles and bullet proof vests immediately set up roadblocks and a hunt for Ogopogo 2. A short time later police found the camper truck abandoned near the Weyerhaeuser Pulp and Paper Mill, and two hours later, using a tracking dog, the prisoners holding Henny as a hostage were found hiding underneath a bridge camouflaged with pine tree branches. Henny was released unharmed and the two prisoners were taken into police custody.

Following the traumatic experience, I asked Henny if she wished a checkup at the hospital or even return to Penticton but she replied, "No way. I'm okay. Let's continue with our journey and see what the rest of Canada is like."

"Fine," I said as we climbed into the cab and headed north to the Prince Albert National Park, a huge wilderness tract of rolling terrain where the prairie of the south turns to woodland of the north. Among the geographic features of this part of Canada are huge cool lakes, bogs, forested uplands and plenty of mosquitoes that are large but no garage sale signs or McDonald restaurants.

This is the park where Lavalley Lake is situated and we camped there for two nights but during the second, we needed a shower but found that the shower drain was clogged. We hadn't seen lye in years but it sure did the trick when an attendant came and poured a can down the drain, which caused an eruption of gunk. With a couple of pumps with a plunger and quick wash later, the attendant was on his way with the shower draining just fine. Lavalley Lake is where the second largest white pelican colony in Canada lives, and when Henny landed a fish next morning she had a fight with one of the pesky birds.

Next stop—Lac La Ronge

Lac La Ronge is north of Prince Albert and Saskatchewan's largest provincial park. Aside from the main lake it contains about one hundred more, On the west side of the park we camped in the village of La Ronge, a small resort centre for the park and from where we had a tour of the La Ronge Wild Rice Corporation, which processes the rice gathered by local producers. Long used by Native peoples the rice is black-hulled and has a mild nutty flavor.

Those who were in the same campground as we were, said Lac La Ronge was a fishermen's delight. Set in the middle of wilderness forest, rocks and streams the community is no means a family vacation like Ms Bitternose confided when we met in Penticton before our journey began and she said, "You'll find Lac La Ronge a dull place, especially on Sunday and the mosquitoes are as large as ravens."

With that assessment Ms, Bitternose was correct because the mosquitoes were so large that a camper parked next to us said he was beginning a campaign to replace the maple leaf on the Canadian flag with a mosquito.

It wasn't a crusade Henny and I were particularly interested in, but the one by a group of trackers from Black Lake, Saskatchewan, a tiny community not far from the Northwest Territories border, which was in the same campground that we were in. What was unusual about the trek was that it was a spiritual voice to Lac Ste. Anne Lake, near Edmonton and one thousand mile in length, and all on foot by Dene Indians.

The following day, we had a wonderful outing in the park. It was a gorgeous day on a Sunday, not too hot, and a lovely picnic lunch under the pine trees when Henny and I walked up to a large orange-colored tent and peeked inside. What we saw were heads that were bowed as the Indians were listening to their two elders and fingering rosaries. A six-foot high wooden cross stood near the tent.

"There are twenty six of them, counting the two dogs, they appear to be short of food," Henny said following a cursory inspection.

As soon as the pep talk was over Henny and I spoke with the two elders. The first confirmed what Henny thought—they had run out of food and had only bannoc, a traditional bread, to eat.

"A human should never be short of food," I said to the elders who spoke English fluently, and immediately, with Henny's approval, took all the canned goods we had inside the camper truck and gave it to them.

While we were sitting around a fire with the tent in front of us, I offered to go to the camper truck and get a bottle of whiskey. The second elder stuck out his hand and said, "Please, Mr. Rubeck, don't. That's what this trek is all about."

The first elder then said that the group had been walking through knee-deep slush, brush, muskeg and a dusty gravel road since leaving Black Lake in April and hoped to reach their destination by the second week in July.

"The pilgrimage is a statement against drugs and alcohol," the first elder said and went on, "Hopefully someone will sponsor a resident from Black Lake to become a priest." Noteing that the community was without one.

The two elders said they hoped the walk would inspire the right person to take the job of a parish priest, while funds raised along the way would help to pay for his education.

The first elder continued, "As well, donations gathered on the reserves and towns along the way will be used to renovate the Black Lake church."

The elders said that the walkers had chose to use the walk as part of their treatment for alcohol and drug abuse but everyone had their personal reasons. For eighteen year-old Gilbert the trek was a spiritual statement against alcohol and drugs in Black Lake.

For twenty eight year-old Charlie, the father of six, he joined the walk, "So I can have a better life in the future for myself, my kids and my wife".

Like many of the walkers Charlie said while Henny and I spoke to him, that he had problems with alcohol in the past but the alcohol-free walk was a special experience both physically and mentally. "When you are walking it makes you feel good spiritually," he said.

Next Henny and I spoke to Archie Desjarlais, who was twenty-nine. Archie said the walk was a way for his parents to reunite after being separated for three years due to alcohol and drug abuse.

Archie said he expected he and other walkers to Lac Ste. Anne, Alberta would serve as role models for many of the residents back home in Black Lake. "I think the walk has already started to affect the hunting and trapping community of 1100 which suffers nearly 100% unemployment. What we have heard so far is that we have changed a lot of people," he said.

Dubbed the *Black Lake Spiritual Walk for Future Generations* the trek had been the two elders' dreams. The first said, "Lac St. Anne draws more than 10,000 Indians to the lake each year.

It's a celebration organized by the Oblate missionaries over 100 years ago who at the time called the lake, *Lake Great Spirit.* It's revered for what is believed to have special healing powers."

The elder said that it all began in 1898 when aboriginal people began coming to Lac Ste. Anne to pray for rain during a draught season. Since that time thousands of people have made the pilgrimage to the lake with healing powers.

The second elder then took over and said that their trek began in the spring when the sun began melting the ice on Black Lake and the walkers, all men ranging in age between sixteen and forty nine, hauled backpacks through three feet of slush on the lake. "From the other side of the lake we headed south along a power line corridor which cuts a swath to the terminus of east Saskatchewan's northern most road at Points North. The elder went on to say that supporters from Black Lake drove food-laden snowmobiles as far as the road, also making one airdrop of food at Unknown Lake. Along the way the pilgrims kept in daily contact with the community by radiotelephone.

First part of the journey, unlike Henny's and mine, was tough with some walkers choosing to add to their discomfort by going barefooted along part of the route. To help lighten the walkers' load one walker used a rope and blankets to fashion makeshift dog packs for the two dogs, Rex and Eaglehead. The packs were loaded with a portion of hundreds of pounds of food the group was initially carrying but most of it was given away when they ran into four prospectors searching for uranium and had run out of food. "That's God's way," the elder said.

The problem compounded when some of the walkers couldn't comply with the added demand of not drinking alcohol en route and the elders' sent them home. What started as a group of forty two, dwindled to a hard core of twenty six. The rest were left behind that night at Lac La Ronge because they didn't seem to be able to stop drinking. They wouldn't listen what the elder's had said.

The second elder took over and recalled tales of days of old. "Every time we camped I would tell the boys about our culture and how we use to travel, fish and hunt, and about survival skills we used. The old generation could survive with a knife, an axe and some matches. There was no alcohol and drugs at Black Lake. Nature was in better shape too."

The elder went on to say that there were fewer birds and caribou now and contamination from uranium has harmed animal life, especially fish. The elder then said that the present generation is losing its spirituality and changing the walkers or those in Black Lake is something the elders' couldn't do alone. "Only God knows what has to be changed. Hopefully people will get their spirituality back soon."

So did Henny and I. We wished the elders' luck with their journey to Lac Ste. Anne and next morning, after filing another report to CJOE, we continued with ours backtracking on Highway 2 until it met 105 which ran into 106 until we reached Flin Flon, Manitoba.

This was a lonely stretch of road and as boring as reading the ingredients on a jar of reduced-fat mayonnaise, that is until we saw bear, moose, caribou and deer crossing the highway. The traffic was sparse but we did meet a pickup with a dead deer strapped across the front bumper.

"Somebody shot a deer," Henny said.

"I doubt it. Hunter's don't shoot deer until its hunting season," I replied.

"Then why was the deer strapped to the pickup bumper?"

"The driver may have hit it on the road. Deer come near roads and even on them, most often during sunset."

"It could wreck Ogopogo 2 if we hit one?"

"It could," I said and nearly did further down the road as a buck jumped in front of us and then disappeared into a forest of trees.

And then about fifty miles further, we met up with a moose kicking up gravel. The moose was long legged and heavy bodied with a drooping nose, a dewlap under the chin, and a small tail. Its color was golden brown and the trophy-size antlers indicated the animal was six or seven years old. Suddenly a stone, the size of a golf ball, struck the windshield cracking it from top to bottom and the moose disappeared near a slough surrounded by birch, willow and aspen.

We didn't get a new windshield until we were greeted by a goofy twenty four-foot statue of Josiah Flintabatty Flontin at the edge of Flin Flon that made Henny laugh hysterically. All I could do was sigh. Flin Flon is situated on the Saskatchewan–Manitoba border and set on the edge of the Precambrian Shield. The area is noted for its distinctive greenish, fine-grained stone—greenstone.

After having our windshield replaced and going up and down the Flin Flon hills and touring the Hudson Bay Mining and Smelting Company zinc surface operations we had another headache when we drove to a restaurant for lunch, parked and had a flat tire. Henny and I changed the tire at a tire shop that shared a building with a ceramic tile store.

After picking up what brochures we could at the Tourist Office, we drove through Northern Manitoba known as the Interlake region, where we discovered diverse cultures and a variety of landscapes as one hill seemed to lead to another until we reached Komarno and a sign that read *Komarno: The mosquito Capital of Canada.* As we were driving we watched tornado-shaped clouds of mosquitoes twisting above the highway. As we stopped and were cleaning our windshield, a farmer walked up to us and said, "At dusk they form gray columns. There are hordes of them this year."

At the same time we listened to the radio where a talk-show host was receiving phone calls about the biting insects. To overcome mosquitoes biting one caller suggested using bear grease, another *Off* or *Bounce* and still another said, "We boil different types of wild flowers and coat ourselves. Avoid wearing dark clothing. Take Vitamin B daily. Your body will exude a yeast odor which repels insects."

And another caller said, "Tie your pant and shirt cuffs with duct tape and eat one raw clove of garlic a day."

About the latter suggestion Henny said, "If garlic doesn't work on mosquitoes, it will, of course, work on your friends and family."

When we reached Winnipeg, we were hopelessly lost, the city grew so much in the last two decades that Henny and I had been there, so I pulled to a side street and got out a road map. But to find where you are going, you must know where you are, and we didn't.

As Henny and I were studying the map and the radio was playing softly in the background, there was a knock on the camper truck window. The man standing next to us appeared to be under the influence of alcohol and said while struggling for words, "I see by your license plate that you are from British Columbia."

When I acknowledged that we were, the crusty elderly man pointed to the radio and said, "Turn that thing off."

Henny did, and then the stranger continued, "You look like someone in trouble. Now where is it that you are going?"

"To Selkirk," I said. "It should be tweny minutes north of here."

"Okay," he replied. "Turn around and then make a right turn. When you see a gang of street kids, go through three traffic lights, carry on past the panhandlers. Turn left when you see a psychiatric screamer, cross the Red River bridge until you see a group of thugs near City Hall. Keep on driving north, where you will see several hitchhikers and that will bring you to the Winnipeg/ Selkirk Highway."

I was never good at following directions so I thanked the gentleman and blundered my way towards Selkirk, getting caught in traffic jams several times before we reached our destination.

From Selkirk, we drove to Henny's parents' farm and camped there for a week exploring the previous past, enjoying ourselves in a leisurely way, chatting, eating, playing games, exchanging stories of pain, joy, triumph and defeat, during the past and present. It was sort of a reunion only there weren't hundreds of people that belonged to either the Field or Rubeck ancestry.

While Henny spent most of the time visiting with her parents I one early morning took the opportunity for a drive to the farm where my parents lived before moving to Penticton, and unleash my memories, dreams and reflections. The sun rose swiftly over the horizon and the one-section of land that had changed twice and the present owner, Harjit Singh, who emigrated from India purchased the property two years ago and instead of wheat was growing canola.

Walking into the new dawn I watched as the deep blue sky seemed to catch on fire. Stars that had been so bright just moments before quickly dimmed and faded like the last of fireworks celebrating Canada Day. Within seconds the clear full moon with its mountains and valleys turned from brilliance to sunshine. All around me, the sleeping earth suddenly became active with roosters crowing in the distance, field mice dashing through the grasses, various species of birds chirping on trees and catfish jumping in the Red River

There's a long, hilly drive between the town of Selkirk and the farm where I once lived. A mixture of pine and popular trees decorate the way. Unsuspecting travelers are likely taken by surprise when they climb the last rise to a feast of valley farmland glittering in the sun in peace and seclusion.

As a child, aside from spending endless hours at the library, I tromped over our farm on a mustang mare named Jenny. I recognized every inch of the neighborhood and the parts that have changed I knew them too. My secret hiding place was no longer there.

Neither was the garden patch where friends and I would raid in the middle of the night and then hold our sides in painful stitches from running and laughing at the same time.

My dog Lady is buried on the southwest side near the farm home, which was torn down recently. The day she died was traumatic and as sad as I was. The barn is gone now too.

Pigs, lambs, horses, chickens, all became part of my life with accompanying lessons that never would have come in the bustle of a city like Winnipeg.

There were other changes too. The slough where I use paddle makeshift rafts and shoot mud hens with a slingshot had dried up. The gophers were still there but there wasn't a prairie chicken or a partridge in sight.

And then I drove to where my elocution teacher, Mrs. Bunchy, lived and again I shook my head in amazement, not at the condition of the house she lived in, because it was no longer there, but that gas station operator at the site that said, "Mrs. Bunchy died fifteen years ago."

While visiting with Henny's parents, I also visited Catherine Livingstone, the librarian at Selkirk Public Library on Main Street. She was the one who told me about Marconi, Edison and radio waves and encouraged me to read books, all types of books, and to become a radio announcer. As I approached the main library entrance on Main Street I could see people, many of them students, stretched out with their faces in books, deep in thought engrossed in their world of learning. I could see shelves of books, magazines and newspapers.

The ceiling and the elegant hanging lights spoke of grandeur I had not forgotten. Art on the walls woke my senses and I had to stand there for a moment just to take a deep breath and say to myself, "This is where it all began."

Somehow I felt the sensation that I was absorbing knowledge by osmosis just by standing inside such a place.

When we met, Mrs. Livingstone and I embraced and then after being reacquainted she said, "Now most books aren't about inventors but heroes and heroines are grandpas and grandmas like me. Authors associate people with gray hair and wrinkles but seldom negatives like dying form a disorder or disease."

Mrs. Livingstone then showed me a poetry book that had recently arrived at the library and asked if the author of *Poems by Lorne Rubeck* was related to me.

"That's my son," I said gladly and then we embraced again.

"I wish Lorne all the luck in the world," Mrs. Livingstone said.

I hadn't prepared to spend an entire afternoon at the Selkirk library but easily could have.

It's true that I am older now than I was when I lived in Selkirk and haunted the halls of the library learning about radio and the world. Now I'm spending more time by going to other libraries, museums, family research centres, cemeteries and learning about myself, my parents, and my ancestors and scare up ghosts of the past who whisper to me stories they have to tell.

CHAPTER 13

We left Selkirk and Winnipeg at sunrise and found ourselves on the Trans Canada Highway for the second time since our journey began. The scenery here was monotonous without a tree in sight. The wide, bald, green turning to gold wheat, rippling the horizon in all directions, however, was a beautiful sight, and so was, Henny thought, a crop circle we stopped to see adjacent to the highway on a farm near the town of Richter. Bizarre crop circles have confounded me for years.

Seeing the circle, Henny who was driving at the time, parked Ogopogo 2 along the highway and as she was getting out of the cab said, "The circle seems incredible. I wonder who and how was it done?"

This was the first circle, about 30 meters in diameter with a hexagram inside that we had ever seen so jokingly I said, "Maybe it was the Martians who did it."

As we were looking at the circle an army of wannabe Winnipeg scientists descended to the field to try solving the mystery of how the ring was formed. There were many theories among the experts claiming the phenomenon was caused by different things: static electricity, a spinning plasma vortex, a fungus attack, electrochemical processes in the earth and the oil lay hidden beneath the mysterious ring. One even said it was a work of an angel warning an upcoming disaster on Planet Earth.

What caused the ring was beyond our comprehension too so I took a dozen photographs, filed a report to CJOE and shortly after we were inside Ogopogo 2 again heading eastward towards Ontario.

Our next stretch of highway brought us to Kenora and Lake of the Woods area in northwestern Ontario. At Kenora, one-half hour's drive from the Manitoba border, we came to a directional sign, which read: Cornwall—1280 miles. According to our travel plans we would stop in Cornwall but only after we reached Newfoundland and turned back. We did however, set our watches ahead an hour because we were in the Eastern Time zone.

Near Kenora on the shore of Lake of the Woods, we found an ideal camping site where after supper we took the canoe off the camper truck and launched it into the water. After paddling for several minutes we couldn't determine how much of a moose we were looking at. All we could see in the magnificent sunset was his head, ears and antlers. The rest of the animal was submerged in Lake of the Woods.

We first noticed the moose when we rounded a point and came upon him munching lily pad stems from a shallow bay of the lake. As far as I was concerned all moose are big.

They seem larger when you encounter one at his level in the water. This moose seemed larger from fifty yards away when we first noticed him. And he even got larger before the encounter was over.

Henny and I sat still for several minutes watching the big fellow chewing his last bite. He was regal-looking even with a couple of strands of lilly pads dangling from his antlers. His rack was still in velvet, the soft furry growth on antlers when they are still growing. They would continue to grow through the summer, and finally the soft covering would shed. That would leave the hard palmated shoves and blunt tines the moose would use to discourage other bulls and intise cows during mating time.

The moose seemed only vaguely interested in our canoe that had floated into his world. He eyed us momentarily, then swung his wrack around and dipped his entire head under the water to grab another lily pad.

While he was after another pad we paddled furiously towards the moose. When his head came up, dripping and chewing, we stopped. We repeated the sequence several times until were close enough to hear the moose chewing the succulent lily pad stems. By that time the bull had enough of his uninvited guests. He swung his large head and rack toward shore and began half-swimming, half-wading through the neck–deep water.

It was an impressive display by the largest mammal that roams northwestern Ontario and we paddled alongside in awe. The moose was all head and eyes and muzzle he left in a wake that looked like diluted chocolate malt.

While in downtown Kenora, originally known as Rat Portage, we resupplied our camper truck with groceries and did not leave before citizens that we met, reminded us that the Kenora Thistles, an amateur team formed by a group of Lake of the Woods lumbermen, gold prospectors or individuals in the mining industry won the Stanley Cup in 1907 defeating the Montreal Wanderers. The town is the smallest in population to have ever won the Cup,

The following day we drove on the Trans Canada Highway passing forests, lakes and rivers and Cambrian rocks until we reached Thunder Bay, formed by the amalgamation of Fort William and Port Arthur, making in the twelfth biggest city in Canada.

Thunder Bay is on the western tip of Lake Superior where huge grain elevators greeted us. It's the geographical centre of Canada. When we met an employee of one of the elevators he proudly said, "A billion bushels of prairie wheat are stored here, then shipped east through the St. Lawrence Seaway."

When Henny asked what other industries support the city he went on, "Thunder Bay has four paper and pulp mills."

Across the grain and freight hustle of Thunder Bay's waterfront loomed Manibijou, the Sleeping Giant, carved out of rock.

Manibijou we were told by elevator employees was the Obijiwayon Prometheus, who stole fire from heaven and gave it to men. The son of the West Wind and an ally of the thunderbird, he was a handsome Indian brave.

The Indians considered this mighty promontory resembling a prostrate human form and believed to be the Great Spirit watching over a treasure of silver held within the ancient rock. The Indians also believed that thunder came from this great headland, hence the name Thunder Bay.

When we arrived in Thunder Bay, there were barbecues, dances, parties, fireworks and a kazoo concert. It wasn't a concert per se but an attempt to break a record for the world largest band.

The 5000 red and white kazoos were courtesy of the Chamber of Commerce and as soon as the kazoo-jam played *O Canada* the MC hollered, "We did it! We did it! Thunder Bay has broken the world record for the number of people playing kazoos at one time!"

The previous record we were told was set in Warsaw, Poland when my parents were teenagers and lived there. At that time 4,179 musicians used kazoos along with wine bottles, coffee cans, lard pails and bongo drums to play the Polish national anthem.

The stretch of the Trans Canada Highway between Thunder Bay and Nipigon was slow driving because of the amount of smoke. We found why the smoke, as soon as we came to the junction where the northern section of the highway takes one to Kapuskasing, Timmins and Kirkland Lake, and the southern part, follows the north shore of Lake Superior to Sault Ste Marie and Sudbury.

At the junction there was a barrier with a provincial forest branch officer standing next to it, warning travelers. When we pulled up next to him the officer walked up to Ogopogo 2 and said, "Hot temperatures and dry winds are fanning a fire which has crossed the highway north of Nipigon. As you are traveling east its best you take the southern route to Sault Ste Marie and Sudbury."

The officer was a friendly type and said the firefighters were battling a forest fire which had gone out of control and started by a lightning flash and went on, "Water bombers and 100 firefighters had to be pulled back from the blaze because of the unpredictable winds."

We took the foresters advice and as we followed the highway we could see plooms of smoke rising towards the sky. When we reached the Soo a sign greeted us which read: Home of Phil and Tony Esposito. The Esposito brothers were stars in the National Hockey League.

What struck me about Sault Ste Marie was that it sat strategically where Lake Huron and Lake Superior meet. Once a fur-trading outpost, the Soo is an industrial town important as a shipping centre, for here on the St. Mary's River is a series of locks which enables ships to navigate the seaway system further west into Lake Superior.

Aside from the busy canal, the steel, pulp and paper, and lumber mills are major employers. The huge Algoma Steel mill is one of the city's mainstays.

Our next stop was going to be Sudbury where English and French is spoken and a four-hour drive, but it took us seven. As the weatherman had predicted it was cool and cloudy.

We were enjoying a picnic lunch when a cross-Canada runner came to our camper truck and gave herself an insulin injection.

The runner introduced herself as Kathy Forbes, a diabetic.

Ms. Forbes moved with the lightness and power of a natural athlete. She stood slightly less than five foot seven inches but seemed taller because of the way she held her head. It was set high and confident, her square jaws forward ever so slightly. She looked like a Spanish princess surveying her realm. Her brown eyes were clear and steady, her nose straight, and her thin-lipped mouth set. Her long brown hair hung over her neck. Wearing blue jeans, a black blouse covered by a blue jacket with a Toronto Maple Leafs crest on it, she was impressive.

"I'm not running across Canada to show that I'm a diabetic," Ms. Forbes said as we shared our lunch with her. "I just said to myself, 'Get off your ass, Kathy, and do something.' So here I am."

Ms. Forbes said she averaged about eighty miles a day and that she was a nurse, a poet and a computer technician and set out on her run following n argument with her boyfriend. "Two weeks later I left St. John's, Newfoundland and hope to reach Vancouver before September," she said.

When Henny asked her age, Ms. Forbes replied, "Well, I'm starting to get the occasional hot flashes and boy are they nice in this kind of weather."

Ms. Forbes went on to say that she was loosing a feeling in her toes and that her run across Canada was a personal adventure, not a crusade for diabetes cure. I wanted to know more about diabetes so I asked her about the symptoms.

"It's a leading cause of death by disease," Ms Forbes said and went on, "If left undetected or improperly managed, high levels of blood sugar can cause damage to blood vessels in the body, resulting in complications such as heart disease, blindness, kidney disease, circulatory problems leading to amputation and even impotence."

Ms Forbes paused and then asked if I ever had a diabetes test.

"That's a good question," I said. I hadn't, but would have one, as soon as we returned to Penticton. because I constantly had itchy toes and urinated often.

An hour later, Ms. Forbes continued her run west and Henny and I drove east towards Sudbury where we discovered the city sits in the rocky Precambrian Shield and for over 100 years has been supplying the world with nickel. Inco Ltd., the world's largest nickel producer, is the town's biggest employer.

Sudbury is noted for polluted air, the orange glow of molten metal on its slag heaps and its nickel production. Sudbury is also the hometown of Drew Canwin. Drew and I attended the Academy of Radio and Television Arts in Toronto at the same time so we decided to look up his mother and say, "Hello."

Mrs. Canwin was delighted that we came to visit her and over a cup of tea said, "Drew still mentions your name occasionally wondering what you're doing."

I confirmed that we both attended the Academy at the same time and I also often wondered what Drew was doing as he had such a promising future ahead of him.

"Drew is with the CBC in Toronto as an executive television producer," Mrs. Canwin said.

"We are heading to Toronto and while there, make a point to see him," I said.

"Do that. I'm certain he would like to see you and chit chat about your broadcast experiences."

We stayed in Sudbury for two days and then traveled to North Bay which, sits at the eastern end of Lake Nipissing where we found a campground and parked Ogopogo 2. It was while we were canoeing on the lake and the sun was about to set that we heard the haunting sound of a loon. I remember as a child listening to loons on Lake Winnipeg and the sound at that time made my hair stand. It was different now. I had not seen or heard a loon for a long, time so I asked the camp attendant why.

According to the attendant the shy, resilient bird that yodeled for fifteen million years and came back year after year, was disappearing because of the acid rain found in lakes.

"What is precisely killing the loons?" Henny asked.

"It's due to the fish filled with pollutants which the loons eat."

Then the attendant said that a similar loon crisis was taking place in upstate New York where the birds are also on decline. Turning towards Henny the attendant said, "Are you afraid for the loon?"

"I am, for the loon and for us."

"Why so?"

"Because besides acid rain, mercury in fish, many loons, I have read, get run over by motorboats on lake resorts."

"True," the attendant said, "Even on Lake Nipissing I have seen where loons get run over by motorboats, but also trapped in fishing nets."

The attendant also said that loons were dying by the thousands in their winter grounds in Florida. When I asked why, he replied, "The mercury loons ingest in Canadian lakes destroys their nervous system. From what I gather the destruction begins right here in Ontario."

To me a beaver builds dams, a loon dignity. I felt the loon was becoming extinct.

"You are right about that," the attendant said, "Mark my word. Soon the only way you'll be able to see a loon is on a Canadian coin."

During our stay in North Bay we visited a museum containing articles to the Dionne quintuplets who, born in 1934, became the most famous Canadian multiple-birth story.

It was at North Bay that we restocked Ogopogo 2 with groceries, enjoyed an ice cream cone and continued driving towards Toronto, a distance of 350 kilometers. Along the way we stopped at Huntsville, Orillia and Barrie.

It was while we stopped overnight at Huntsville, a shopping area for those with summer homes around the large lake of Bays.

As we were setting up camp, we discovered that many of the citizens of this town were up in arms against a realtor who sold beach property to an entrepreneur from Toronto. Henny and I couldn't figure out why the residents were so upset until we walked up to Deer Street and the sign was defaced to read *Queer Street.*

We were told that a realtor had advertised the property with a posted sign that read, *Beach Property for a Gay Community.* The property in question was a row of cottages surrounded by tall pine and birch trees. A petition was being taken and the subject of the sale of properties was discussed at Town Hall that night. When I asked one of the residents why a Town Hall meeting, he replied, "So our children won't be molested on the streets. In the tourist industry perception is an important reality. Homosexuals could affect our business."

What could I say—nothing. Henny shook her head in amazement and said, "What is this world coming too?"

For most of our journey, Henny and I woke up at the same time the sun was rising. Ogopogo 2 had to be checked for oil, windshield washer and tires. And then as a rule we would have a sumptuous breakfast of ham and egg, toast and coffee. This done we continued driving. Our next stop was Orillia, a pretty town lying on the west shore of Lake Couchiching, an extension of Lake Simcoe. Orillia is built on terraces overlooking the lake and where humorist Stephen Leacock, immortalized Orillia's golden years in *Sunshine Sketches of A Little Town* which Henny must have read at least ten times since we began our journey. The Orillia area is known for summer homes belonging to "Toronto Big Shots."

Next we drove to Barrie where along the way, since it was a Friday; we met heavy traffic that included cars, trucks, motorcycles and motor homes pulling trailers and boats. Some were topped with sailboats.

The drivers seemed to be in a hurry to make certain they would find parking space because, perhaps, they had not made a reservation. As we approached Barrie we ran into severe weather unlike we had experienced before. The temperature was at least 90F, humidity was exceptionally high and thunderclouds exploded almost every minute. The storm was so severe that we pulled off the highway and waited out the storm. While waiting Henny turned on the radio and we were both surprised when an announcer interrupted regular programming to read a news bulletin and said, "A tornado has just swept through the southern part of Barrie turning debris into flying spears and pummeling those registered at the Greenwood Mobile Home Park and Campground."

The announcer went on to say that the twister that sprung from nowhere and lasted only minutes had tossed vehicles and trailer units like Tonka toys burying the dead in makeshift graves. A heavy rainstorm with hail the size of golf balls hit areas of Barrie not struck by the tornado. The announcer still did not know of the estimate of damage but said about casualties, "There are known at least seventeen dead."

As soon as the storm blew over we were on the road again heading for Toronto where the following day my surprise call delighted Drew Canwin and after a preliminary conversation he said, "Joe, what are you doing these days?"

I gave Drew a verbal resume and then he said, "Are you interested in getting into television?"

There was that possibility I said and handed him several of my best interviews which, I did while with CJOE and told him that I was filing daily reports back to the station in Penticton during our journey across Canada.

"So you interview people?" Drew asked.

"That's my specialty."

"So what do you consider as a successful interview?"

I was surprised by the line of questioning and answered the best way I could by saying, "A successful interview is one conducted with skill and understanding. You need to put yourself in the other person's place and be fair as I would expect an interviewer to be with me."

"Interesting," Drew said and after further questions pertaining to interviewing people he asked if I wanted to audition if something came up "In the near future at the CBC."

I was caught off guard but took an audition that I found interesting. Before leaving Drew took my address and phone number and then wished Henny and me a successful trip across Canada.

We stayed at the Carlton Inn Hotel, next to Maple Leaf Gardens, and only several blocks from the CBC studios on Jarvis street. The following day, Henny and I toured Toronto and I noticed that since my Academy days were the new City Hall and CN Tower. There was talk of building the Skydome. I now thought of Toronto as a mini-New York City, not as once lampooned as a dull and ugly city whose inhabitants fled to Buffalo for a good time and where the main department store, Eaton's, had blinds drawn on Sunday, to stop anyone from sinfully window shopping.

Henny made certain that we saw Henry Fonda in a performance of *Mr. Roberts* at the Royal Alexandra Theatre and Paul Anka at the Casino. We saw other productions too—at the O'Keefe Centre and the St. Lawrence Centre, where Canadian actors performed.

Since the Academy days I also noticed a substantial infusion of other cultures. Once a quiet, conservative community dominated by Anglo's, there now was an influx of Italians, Chinese, Portuguese, Hungarians, Greeks, Poles, Filipinos, West Indians and Jews.

Our final day in Toronto, before leaving for Ottawa, we dined atop of the CN Tower, the world's tallest freestanding structure.

From the tower's 1100 foot-high restaurant and observation area we could see for a distance of about seventy miles miles but not as far as Ottawa, our next important stop.

Trucks as long as freightersm delivering goods across the nation, with a wind-like blow of a fist.

Highway 401 between Toronto and Kingston is wonderful for moving goods but not inspection of the countryside. As soon as we left Toronto I was bound to the steering wheel and my eyes to the rear-view mirror for traffic behind me, and the side mirror for cars and trucks about to pass.

At the same time I had to read all the signs for fearing of getting lost or missing some of the instructions or orders. There were times I couldn't differentiate between ground vehicles and low flying aircraft.

"Brace yourself," Henny said, "This is the heaviest traffic we have encountered on our journey."

I always had sympathy for truck drivers who replenish the country with food, merchandise and fuel. They are a breed set apart from any other occupation and in hauling loads a long distance are separated from their families and I was when I drove a taxi. I noticed that truck drivers are clannish, stick together and speak a language of their own. Many times I was amazed and wondered how a *Safeway* truck, for instance, could maneuver a vehicle so long, through traffic and into a congested loading zone.

Traffic on 401 was heavy as Ogopogo 2 was following a semi-tractor with a load of steel pipe when suddenly, near Trenton, the highway turned into a disaster zone. The semi trailer was passing a bus when unexpectedly it spilled its load of steel onto a bus and both burst into flames.

Henny and I were horrified and stunned by the most terrifying highway accident we've ever seen. I slammed on the brakes and Ogopogo stopped just short of the inferno. Then, without hesitating, Henny and I raced to the truck and bus as an explosion violently shook the site. Without thought for our safety we were smothering the flames with our coats and trying to get the bodies inside the bus, which we found later, was filled with people on a pilgrimage to Ste. Anne de Beaupre just east of Quebec City.

Soon other motorists stopped behind us and they too offered assistance and first aid.

"I have never seen anything like it. This is the worst motor vehicle accident I have ever seen. It's like in a Hitchcock movie," Henny said. "Pray to God, oh please, don't anyone die. Help!"

Miracously several doctors and nurses came upon the accident and heard the cry for help from Henny and those trapped inside the bus. Still others traveling in campers similar to ours, stopped. Several people who couldn't stand the horrible scene stayed back to control traffic. Soon there were many people helping in different ways, running around, grabbing first aid kits and blankets. During the accident Henny and I lost track of time in a desperate effort to treat the injured before police and ambulances arrived.

As police, doctors, nurses and paramedics took over we continued out journey until we reached Kingston, solid and enduring like the gray limestone on which it is built. We registered at Wolfe Island. A bridge connects the island with New York State.

Handy if an overnight camper wants supplies. As we had plenty of supplies there was no need for us to cross into New York State so we had a campfire dinner and then I filed my radio report to Penticton.

As we were crawling into bed Henny switched on the radio where a Kingston radio station, in a regular hourly newscast, said that there were nineteen people killed as a result of the semi-trailer-bus accident on Highway 401 near Trenton.

The day we arrived in Ottawa there were striking workers protesting in front of the Parliament Buildings. The public servants carried placards signifying that they wanted an increase in pay. The demonstration, however, did not interfere with our member of parliament giving us a tour of the buildings, overlooking the Ottawa River.

The Eternal Flame in the centre symbolizing Canadian unity, the blooming gardens and parks, and the thirty-minute changing of the guard ceremony performed at 10:00 a. m., complete with pipes, drums, bearskin hats, and flashing red coats of the General Governor's Foot Guards and the Canadian Grenadier Guards from Montreal.

Statues abound on Parliament Hill grounds. Among the more notable figures immortalized here are two fathers of Confederation who were assassinated. Behind the Centre Block's northeast corner is George Brown, the Toronto journalist. Brown was a reformer who helped shape the Liberal party. He also championed runaway slaves who wished to settle in Canada. He died in 1880 after an employee he fired from the newspaper he owned, presently the *Globe and Mail*, shot him.

Diagonally across from Brown is the Irish-born D'Arcy McGee, another reformer who drew the wrath of the Irish Fenian group criticizing tactics. One Fenian, acting on his own, shot McGee in 1868.

The statue of Sir Wilfred Laurier, Canada's first Francophone prime minister, can be found in the extreme east corner of the grounds. At the southwest corner of the block Henny and I spent some time looking at the statue of the hard-drinking visionary, Sir John A. MacDonald, Canada's first prime minister.

After a week in Ottawa Henny and I were looking forward to next leg of our journey. When morning came we left Ontario by crossing the Ottawa River into Hull and following the north shore of the St. Lawrence River until we reached Montreal. In Montreal we were told, couples kiss on the street and strangers talk to each other. We didn't camp but treated ourselves by staying at a luxury hotel.

CHAPTER 14

What makes Quebec so different from all the other provinces in Canada is its French heritage. Not only is French spoken everywhere but many of their roots in Roman Catholic France rather than in Anglo-Protestant Great Britain. From the moment Henny and I crossed the border at Hull we fell in love with the province—for its French character, for its peacefulness, for its beauty, for its storied past.

Kebek, an Algonquin Indian word meaning where the river narrows, is the heart of French Canada. This is the country's largest province with nearly 7-million people and for those who love history it's unlike any other in North America with its old-world feeling, its ramparts, and its winding cobblestone streets. For those who want fun and excitement Montreal is as cosmopolitan as New York, and as chic as French in Paris. For those who yearn serenity of nature, that too is in Quebec in its unaccountable lakes, streams and rivers, in its mountains and forests, in its rugged coastline and its farmland and villages.

I had heard from those who visited Montreal during
EXPO 67 that it was actually a grumpy self-absorbed city
where people avoided speaking to strangers, especially if
they spoke English. After staying in Montreal for several
days I learned the reason why some felt that way.

While Henny and I were sitting in the lobby of our hotel a
journalist who introduced himself as Pierre Lapointe, said
to me, "You look as if you are lost in Montreal. Where
are you from?"
"Penticton, British Columbia," I said.
"I have been there once," Lapointe said and when I asked
him what was the purpose of his visit he want on, "A
radio station there was offering $5000 if someone came
up with an authentic photo of Ogopogo, who it is said
lives in Okanagan Lake."
"And now I'm sending reports from Montreal to the
same station which, prompted the Ogopogo contest," I
replied.
"So you are a journalist too?"
"Sort of," I said. "I prefer to be known as a radio announcer
who does the work of a journalist."
"If that is the case you are one of us. Can I buy you and
your wife a drink?"
"Certainly," I said and the three of us went into the hotel's
bar and as we were chatting and enjoying ourselves when
Lapointe said, "I'm a Quebecer first and a Canadian,
second."
"What is that supposed to mean?" Henny asked
Lapointe's reply was, "Just as I thought. You do not
understand Quebec. We are a coalition of people who

want to control our destiny. We are Quebecois dead or alive."

"Oh, you are members of the FLQ?" Henny said. "We have heard about your group many times in newscasts. You are a terrorist group?"

Lapointe rejected the suggestion that he was perhaps, a member of a terrorist organization.

"But you guys blew up a monument of General Wolfe in 1963 and in the year that followed took to bombing anything that represented English, including the Royal Canadian Mounted Police headquarters," I said and reminded Lapointe that in 1967, during Canada's 100th birthday, Charles DeGaulle of France visited the province of Quebec and while in Montreal the World War 11 hero at the time said, *Vivre le Quebec libre*, which in English means Long Live an Independent Quebec.

I remember DeGaull saying that too," Lapointe said. "And a year later Rene Levesque left the Liberal Party and found the Parti Quebecois."

"And reminded Canada that Quebec was discovered in 1534 by French explorers and Levesque wanted Quebec to go alone as an independent state, "Henny said.

Later we talked about the October 1970 crises which culminated in a FLQ cell kidnapping British trade commissioner, James Cross, who eventually was released unharmed, and a member of the Quebec cabinet, Pierre Laporte, who wasn't as fortunate—he was assassinated.

At that time the Federal government in Ottawa, under Prime Minister Trudeau, himself a French-speaking Quebecer, imposed the *War Measures Act* on October

16. This permitted police to breakup civil disorders, arrest 500 people and suspects, and led to the arrest of the murderers of Laporte. The political crises ended but left vibrations that could be felt throughout Canada. The Federal government redoubled its efforts to correct the Quebec grievances but many, like our journalist interviewer, Pierre Lapointe, weren't satisfied.

That night when I filed my report to CJOE I told my audience that in my opinion Montreal was a hotbed of French nationalism and I wouldn't be surprised if there wouldn't be future acts of arson and bombing. I concluded my commentary by saying, "Mark my word, there will be a sovereignty referendum held in Quebec soon."

Henny and I left Montreal the following Saturday and while traveling along the north side of the St. Lawrence River we stopped at a campsite on the outskirts of Quebec City. We had a commanding view of ships plying the St. Lawrence. When we woke up next morning we noticed a large crowd in the picnic area and a photographer determined to take its photograph.

When I enquired of the campground custodian what was happening he said, "It's the Dubois family reunion."

In a conversation that followed with the Dubois descendants one said the original Dubois lived in Quebec City from 1685 to 1721, and had approximately 900 descendants throughout North America. When I said that the original Dubois family must have been a large one, a second descendant said, "It was, and now there's a challenge to survive because we are different from rest of Canada as far as language and culture is concerned."

"Why so?" Henny asked.

"Because we want to be Quebecois and not Canadians. Those who let go their language. Let go their roots."

It was a typical comment as we traveled throughout the province of Quebec. Quebecois wasn't a romantic belonging but to take control of major institutions that are run by the English. I smiled when one of the descendants said, "I can spot a Dubois anywhere."

Henny said, "How?"

"A big nose, blue eyes, they're proud of their heritage."

"That's for sure," Henny said and then went on to relate how a group of Quebec fruit pickers, some with the sur name *Dubois,* arrive in the Okanagan valley each summer and get into trouble with the locals on Ste. Jean Baptise day.

"Is it true that those living in the Okanagan Valley of British Columbia resent the Quebec fruit pickers because they speak their own language?" the Dubois descendent said.

I replied, "Not really. There are over 15,000 French-speaking in the valley who settled there, so that's not the problem."

"Why is it then when the fruit pickers come home to Quebec they say they were treated like migrants and even sprayed with insecticide?"

"It's certainly not because the fruit pickers come from Quebec," Henny said.

"Why is it then that they are mistreated?"

"Because some are criminals and others well, what can I say about them?"

"Please go on."

"Because most of them are young men and women who are promiscuous, they sleep in pup tents. The women walk around beaches topless and both, men and women, have no respect for the locals when it comes to their sex habits," I said.

Out next stop—Quebec City

Like in the Okanagan valley, there is much to do and see in Quebec City and vicinity. Canada's destiny was shaped on the famous battlefield, the Plains of Abraham, now a national historic park.

The image of General Wolfe and his army of 4000 men crossing the St. Lawrence River and scaling the cliffs under the Plains on the moonless night on September 13, 1759 live in the memory of every early Canadian school child. Both the general and the Marquis de Montcalm died heroes in a battle here. The Citatdel, Martello Towers, and other fortifications built to protect the city from American invasions are part of the remarkable fortification systems in the park.

Just outside the walled city are modern Quebec, the highrise hotels and government buildings with architecture of the past. Quebec's location on a steep hill gives it a split-level character. Probably the most photographed building in Canada, the Chateau Frontanac, is a massive green-turreted castle that dominates the city.

Following Quebec City, Gibraltar of North America, we arrived at Sainte Anne de Beaupre, a gaudy little tourist town, renowned for its immaculate and mammoth church and an annual religious pilgrimage. The beautiful basilica has excellent tile-work on the floor, stained glass, and ceiling mosaics.

From the mid 1600's the village has been an important religious site and it all began, according to legend, when French mariners were sailing the St. Lawrence River and ran into a terrifying storm. They prayed for their patroness, Ste. Anne, to intercede for their deliverance.

Surviving the storm the mariners dedicated a wooden votive to Ste. Anne near the site of their perils. Not long afterwards, a pilgrim to the spot was cured of an affliction while praying there, and since that time, pilgrims have come to pray and pay their respects to Ste. Anne, the mother of the Virgin Mary, from throughout the world. We were told that more pilgrims come here than in Lourdes, France. Two million make the pilgrimage annually and the great heaps of crutches, trusses and surgical boots, testify to the comfort received by the faithful.

Henny and I combined our visit to Ste. Anne de Beaupre by attending mass in the Basilica and then picking up a bottle of holy water. Since we had no proper container I poured the water into an empty whisky bottle and placed it in the camper truck refrigerator.

As we were about to leave Ste. Anne de Beaupre and head east towards Newfoundland an unusual thing happened. Maybe it was a miracle? As we were listening to the radio we heard an English announcer say, "Here's an urgent message for Mr. And Mrs. Joe Rubeck of Penticton, British Columbia, believed to be holidaying in Quebec. Would Mr. or Mrs. Rubeck please call the nearest detachment of the RCMP concerning an urgent family matter? I repeat . . ."

I made a U-turn and pulled into a service station and rushed to the nearest public telephone booth. After looking up an RCMP number, I dialed it. When a voice answered, I identified myself.

The constable who took my call said, "We do have an important message for you Mr. Rubeck. The message reads, Please call home as soon as possible."

Many thoughts ran through my mind while placing the call. Did someone in the family die? Did Patricia Motel burn down? Was Ozzie in a traffic accident? And how about Lorne and Lorna?

When the call went through Ozzie was at the other end and said, "Dad, Drew Canwin called from Toronto and wants you to call him as soon as possible."

I did.

The message was that I had won an audition for a television network program *Entertainment Now* and to meet Drew Canwin in Toronto to discuss a contract.

"Drew, I'll be in Toronto within two days," I said and minutes later heading west where that night we checked into Wolfe Island Campground at Kingston. Since it was still daylight I wheeled Ogopogo 2 across the bridge connecting New York state and a custom barrier and the Stars and Stripes stood shoulder with the Maple Leaf.

When we stopped we found the American officer polite as he asked where we were going and how long we planned to stay.

"Just across the border to purchase groceries for tonight and then we're coming right back," I said.

The customs officer gave Ogopogo 2 a thorough inspection and came up with a bottle with the *Seagram's* label on it. "What is this?" he said.

"Holy water from Ste. Anne de Beaupre," Henny replied.

"Holy what?"

"Holy water, it's the gospel truth," Henny repeated.

"Looks like a bottle of Canadian whiskey," the officer said.

"If it is it's a miracle," I said. "Really, it's holy water."

Giving Ogopogo 2 a more thorough inspection the officer next came up with a box of bullets and a .22 caliber rifle he had found underneath the bed. "Is this gun registered?" the officer asked.

"We do not register guns in Canada but some day we may," I said.

Upon hearing our conversation another officer came outside and said, "Look, we advise you not to cross the border."

He eyed me as if Henny and I were criminals.

"But we want to cross the border so we can get some groceries for our camp-out tonight. We have never smuggled anything in our lives," I insisted as a sense of guilt crept over me until the first officer said, "We understand. You have a choice, however. We indict you with illegally trying to export a firearm or you return to Canada. Which will it be?"

"Let's go back, "Henny said.

These were two friendly and helpful men. We didn't want to hassle so Henny and I climbed back into the cab. I then made a U-turn and headed back to the Canadian side of the border where a Custom's and Immigration officer greeted us with, "Where have you been and have you anything to declare?"

"We have been nowhere and declare we are a bit peed off," I said.

"What do you mean, sir?" the officer continued.

"I mean that the Americans refused us to cross the border."

"Better step into the building?" the Canadian officer then said.

The request had the effect that Henny and I were smugglers. It raised my panic, anger and guilt. My voice took on a strident tone of outrage when I said, "I'm telling you the gospel truth, we haven't been outside Canada so an inspection of our vehicle is unnecessary. We turned around at the U. S. Customs."

Pointing towards me, the officer continued, "Step this way please, sir." The officer then placed a phone call to his counterpart 500 feet away. I heard him say, "B. C. license plates with a sketch of Ogopogo 2 on the left door of the camper truck."

As soon as the officer got off the phone he looked at me and said, "They say you didn't cross the border into America. Technically you are still in Canada. You may proceed."

We did and stayed overnight on Wolfe Island but instead of Henny cooking up a sumptuous steak on a picnic fire spit we had to contend with wieners in a bun and play checkers until we crawled into bed.

In the morning, we rose early and drove to Toronto to discuss a contract with Drew Canwin. As I walked into the CBC studios, Drew congratulated me. Then while we were in his office he said, "CBC is pleased to confirm your temporary assignment as host of *Entertainment Now* on the full television network."

"Temporary?" I said. "Why temporary?"

"Because the CBC does not believe in jumping in and committing itself to something that it might regret later."

"Well, I'll have to discuss this offer with my wife," I said.

"And where is she?"

"Waiting in the lobby."

"Go ahead and when you speak with her, tell her there's a condition attached."

"Condition? What kind of a condition?"

"That you start on Monday."

"But this is Friday!"

"I know it is. If you aren't interested in being the host of *Entertainment Now* there are other announcers, some right here with the CBC, who are."

"I understand, but before I discuss it with Henny, would you be kind enough to tell me what happed to the previous host, George Lamont?"

"Television killed him."

"Television what?"

"I said television killed George. The whole country is stunned by George's death yesterday morning. I don't think I have felt a greater loss."

George Lamont's death had a sobering effect on me and I suppose on the entire broadcast industry. Drew said that

George would come of the show soaking wet, perspiration dropping and clothing soaked right through after each program. "I know that the cost of his nervous system, he being overweight, plus tension of doing too much simply snapped his strength and his heart couldn't take it."

When I discussed the television offer with Henny she encouraged me to accept, and I did. Temporary or permanent, it did not matter. What did was that I would be back in broadcasting.

I kept Ogopogo 2 in Toronto next to an apartment we had found that day. By evening Henny was on a flight to Penticton to resign as part-time nurse at the Penticton Hospital and to join me as soon as possible.

While Henny was flying home Drew and I were lining up guests for *Entertainment Now*. As we were lining up guests Drew pontificated, "Joe, the television audience will never accept an announcer who wears glasses, has a mustache and a receding hairline. And, hey, how about losing some weight?"

So intimidating was the new media to me that at the first opportunity I discarded my horn-rimmed glasses for contact lenses, shaved off my pencil-thin mustache I had grown, had hairline fill-ins to compensate for my V-shaped forehead and joined a fitness club in order to lose weight.

TORONTO
(1976-1978)

CHAPTER 15

My transition from radio to television with cameras, lights and all sorts of wires was an intimidating one. Those who were associated with *Entertainment Now* felt that anyone who needed a cue card or a teleprompter was an idiot. In fact that's how the name originated—idiot cards. It was damaging to my ego, with years of experience in radio, to be termed mentally deficient because I suddenly was expected to memorize everything said on camera, aside from the interview itself.

Radio was the last experience in the world that taught me to expand my memory. An actor learns a new role in a short period of time is said to be a quick study. Due to the protective arm of radio, and never being an actor on stage, I had not acquired the skill of a retentive memory.

In radio, if I didn't ad lib, I read everything. I spent years to *lift it of paper* and suddenly there was no paper to lift from. And even with cue cards or a teleprompter, there is a definite technique to using them. You need practice, it's not easy to use these and still make the TV audience unaware of their use.

I pleaded with Drew to leave me alone for a few minutes while I ran through the card copy or prompter roll, even marking them with a felt pencil when necessary, just to get the feel of the lines and put them directly into the lens. But no, it was impossible. "No time." Drew would often say. "No cue card holder or teleprompter operator. Besides they are on their break and aren't due until show time."

I remember an *Entertainment Now* program when a teleprompter operator was available but he had difficulty in rolling the machine to my pace of reading. He had trouble with a switch so that it would stop and start erratically. Then the final disaster, the copy roles simply left its container above the lens and rolled down across the floor like a roll of toilet paper.

There were other times when *Entertainment Now* tried to humiliate me. I missed cues, lost my place in the script and guests didn't show up for an interview. There were several times when we had power failures.

Radio was gentler to me than television. Most of the radio shows were put on the air by two people: the announcer and the operator or technician. The announcer paid attention to the operator's hand signals and that was the end of it. In television there seemed to be at least ten people each assuming he has the right to guide and instruct the person on which the camera is focused.

Everyone with a radio voice sought a sound, a distinctive style that would set him apart from anybody else. It was a phase in radio that most announcers wanted to sound like Lorne Greene, and then when rock n roll came the trend was to scream. My style was neither. I spoke and read naturally. In other words although Lorne Greene was my idol, I was myself, Joe Rubeck.

Since I became host of *Entertainment Now* Henny moved to Toronto while Ozzie kept managing Patricia Motel in Penticton. We exchanged phone calls frequently. Henny was fortunate because she won a part in a play which was filling the St. Lawrence Centre. To her, nursing was now a second profession. Every critic gave her an excellent review. As for *Entertainment Now* the same critics seldom gave the program good reviews. Ever since that time I thought of a critic as someone who would tell Don Juan how to make love, but I think, the Irish writer, Brenend Behan, had the best description of one. He said critics were like eunuchs in a harem, they saw the trick done every night but couldn't do it themselves.

Although I had difficulty adjusting to television, eventually things were going smoothly. Henny was getting great reviews at the St. Lawrence Centre and me interviewing guests on *Entertainment Now.*

Whenever Lorne Greene appeared as my guest on *Entertainment Now* it was like a father/son relationship. Mr. Greene and I had known each other since my Academy days and I was one of his last graduates. His voice was deeply resonant and during World War 11, I remember him reading the CBC News where he was dubbed *The Voice of Doom*.

Canadians, including my parents, literally came to a halt each night when the news was on. In addition to his marvelous voice, Greene had an unquenchable dramatic flair and later put his talent into great use as a dramatic actor on stage and screen, culminating in one of the best-loved television characters of all time—Pa Cartwright on *Bonanza*.

I should explain that there are celebrities who hate interviews. They resent their privacy has to be interrupted at ungodly hours in order to hype the publicity of whatever vehicle they're appearing in. Sometimes it's their contract; sometimes its necessary if frantic theatre management sees that the advance isn't to good at the box office. In any case my sympathy is usually with these people so I tried to be especially polite and courteous in order to make them feel welcome.

There were times when my interviews were difficult because the guest would answer with a *Yes* or *No* to the question I asked. I always thought the audience wanted to hear the guest and not me giving answers to my own questions.

As a television interviewer I had an experience I shall never forget. This happened when I was interviewing a retired Hollywood actress and said something to the effect that she was still beautiful.

"I'm not beautiful. I'm a rolly polly," she insisted.

I countered with, "You aren't a rolly polly. You are beautiful, beautiful."

The actress who was in her seventies, then said, "Joe Rubeck. You are nuts, nuts."

Another time I asked a Hollywood actor who just completed an epic movie, "What's the hardest part about being a star?"

"Sitting next to you," the Oscar-winning actor said.

In another sequence I said to a lovely actress, "I'd like to ask a question I'm sure you have been asked many times."

Even before I asked the question she said, "No. I will not marry you."

Another time, I interviewed a rock n roll star that was performing in Toronto for the first time. I asked him what he thought of Toronto as a whole.

"As a hole I think it's a big hole," he replied.

I then worded the question differently and said, "What do you think of Toronto?"

I was shocked when the rocker, who had three, hits on the *Billboard* top-ten list, when he said, "I think Toronto is the largest cemetery with lights."

Entertainment Now was on the air from 9:00 a. m. until 10:00 a. m. The guests on the program were people who entertained the public or enriched the public in one way or another. There were record artists, stage and screen actors, politicians, sports celebrities and those in the literary field, which included my son Lorne about his unique way of publishing and marketing books. Following the interview

Lorne took me aside and said, "Dad, I have something to tell you that I couldn't say on television."

"Well, what is it?" I said.

"It's about our family."

"What about our family?"

"It's about Ozzie."

"What about Ozzie?'

"He says he's supposed to be a girl."

"He says what?"

"Ozzie says he's supposed to be a girl, a female."

"Why should he say such a thing?"

"I don't know. But one night he was wearing Mom's dress while registering guests into the motel. I even overheard him say that he was going to have an operation."

What could I say about Lorne's allegation? "Lorne," I said. "Ozzie is an adult now. Stop making up poetry about your brother. Let him sail his own ship in life."

Interviewing is an art of making a stranger tell you things he/she wouldn't tell his best friend. My mother taught me that everybody is admirable in some way, and that we all have soft, vulnerable core that must be treated with kindness and respect. Before doing my interview, however, I had to do my homework and know my guest as much as possible before I met him or her. Not because it saves interviewing time by letting me concentrate on issues in question, but also because the trouble I take to prepare the interview inspires confidence in my thoroughness and encourages the subject to talk more freely to me that he/she would to someone less informed.

I began by hunting information in newspapers, libraries and newspaper morgues, even encyclopedias, if necessary, then talk to mutual friends or just we informed people about the subject's specialty: age, lifestyle, habits, quirks, hobbies, and various accomplishments.

All in all, a successful interview conducted with skill and understanding is not hard. All you need to do is put yourself in the subject's shoes and be as fair as you would expect an interviewee to be with you. That way you will find, as I have, that as a result of the interview, you have gained a friend. By now I had interviewed bankers wearing jeans and plumber in tuxedos but the interview I enjoyed doing the most was when my guest was Hollywood movie director, Alfred Hitchcock.

Scenes from several of Hitchcock movies are forever memorable so I asked him, "Is the politics of your movie *Topaz* just window dressing?"

In reply Hitchcock said, "When you get, for example, a spy story and you say to yourself what are the spies after? It really doesn't matter what they are after. It matters to the character in the movie not the audience. The public doesn't care about *paper* or the *plans* or the *forts*. It's the suspense regarding them. that matters."

Hitchcock told me about making the movie *Notorious* in which the plot revolved around the discovery of uranium. "A year before Hiroshima we made the picture," he said, "And wanted to show what these Nazi's were up to in South America. Ben Hecht, the writer and I visited a scientist and we asked him what size of an atom bomb would be and how it worked. The scientist spent an hour telling us the whole thing was impossible. Well, we made the movie anyway and I was later told the FBI had shadowed me for three months. They figured I was trying to sell atomic secrets."

I then asked Hitchcock about the famous Cary Grant scene in *North by Northwest* in which Grant is pursued across the open prairie by a crop-dusting airplane.

"That scene was done in a way to avoid falling into the usual cliché," he said. "Here was a situation in which a man is to be put on the spot. The typical scene would call for a darkened shot, on eerie street light, cobbles washed with recent rain, a face would appear from a window and a black cat would slither by. That's the cliché. I tried to imagine a scene as far removed from the cliché as possible. Bright sunshine, no trees, anywhere to hide. Being chased by a plane over flat fields created it own terror."

I asked about fear and Hitchcock's use of this emotion in movies. He illustrated an example with a remark about the movie *Psycho*. "It was made with a sense of amusement on my part. It was like taking the audience through the haunted house in the neighborhood. It amuses me to watch people being shocked as much as it amuses them to be shocked."

Another question I asked Hitchcock why fear was such an important thing in life. He said, "We all have fears. We had them since we were babies. Our mothers threatened us with the *bogyman* if we didn't behave. Later we paid money to enjoy fear—we went on a swing and went higher and higher to scare ourselves. Later we paid money to go to the haunted house or a roller coaster at the fairgrounds."

Before the interview ended I asked about his next movie and Hitchcock replied, "It will deal with fear, of course, but at the moment I'm having difficulty in finding a leading lady."

My interest in the movie rose. "What is the movie about?"

"It deals with a horrific traffic accident just as a tornado rips apart a community."

"I may have the actress you are searching for," I said.

Hitchcock said, that's interesting interesting, who?"

"My wife, Henny Rubeck. She went through at least two horrific incidents during our recent journey."

"Was there fear involved?"

"There certainly was."

"Tell me more."

I told Hitchcock about the tragic accident on Highway 401 near Trenton, the kidnapping in Prince Albert, and going through a tornado at Barrie.

"Give me her telephone number and I'll phone her," Hitchcock said.

As soon as the program ended I gave Hitchcock our phone number but didn't mention it to Henny.

"You want me to do what?" Henny said when Hitchcock phoned her. She was at home at the time doing her fingernails while listening to a Beatles record on the radio.

"I want you to read for a part in a movie I'm directing," Hitchcock repeated.

Henny began to laugh. "You obviously got the wrong number."

"This is Henny Rubeck. Isn't it?"

"Yes."

"I'm serious, Henny. This is Alfred Hitchcock."

"A good impersonator. This is a joke."

"It's no joke. I was interviewed by your husband and he says you are an actress who has experienced fear during a recent journey."

"That's true."

"I want you to read a script at 9:00 tomorrow morning."

"What am I supposed to read?" Henny said trying to convince herself that she indeed was speaking with the famous movie director.

"It's a leading part in a new movie."

It was the strangest thing Henny ever heard as she finally agreed to show up at the Hilton Hotel where Hitchcock was staying, the next day but she couldn't resist by telling me first.

Henny hardly slept that night, and was up at six in the morning, washing and drying her hair, doing her face, checking her nails again. She decided to wear a plain black dress, just in case Hitchcock was serious. I thought it was a little dressy for nine o'clock and it was low cut, showing a cleavage.

When Henny arrived at the Hilton Hotel, she went straight to Hitchcock's suite where she knocked on the door and was greeted by Hitchcock with a, "Good morning, Mrs. Rubeck, please come inside and be seated."

As Henny was sitting she noticed two other men in another part of the suite conferring quietly, with a table in front of them, and photographs of other actresses spread on it. When Hitchcock returned he said, "Mrs. Rubeck, I understand that you are presently acting at the St. Lawrence Theatre?"

"I am."

Hitchcock spoke in a soft, gentle manner as a professional. It was as if he was trying to tell Henny something and giving her all the encouragement he could. By now Henny had lost her nervousness and began to feel comfortable and calm. She forced herself not to think of herself as a movie actress but that of stage, and only the script. Suddenly the script meant everything to her. She knew she could act.

"We'd like you to read the part of the nurse during a tragic highway accident." Hitchock said handing her the script.

"What kind of a part is it?"

"About a nurse your age who while traveling comes upon a tragic highway accident and rescues the passengers from a fire."

"Can I have a few minutes to study the script?" Henny asked.

Henny's eyes were intense. She knew she had the experience after taking part in a similar accident and rescued passengers from a fire that followed. It was the strangest development of her entire life. Suddenly she wanted the part more than anything else. At the same time she wanted to show the public that an acting career in the movies can begin when one reaches their forties.

"Take fifteen minutes in the other room and come back and read to me," Hitchcock said.

When Henny returned she read the part clearly and with emotion. There she was as if on that day on Highway 401 near Trenton, Ontario. She was saving children and adults trapped in a tour bus after tonnes of steel pipe jettisoned into the bus's window and then caught on fire. Henny's heart went all out as she ranged and stormed and then there were tears streaming down her cheeks.

There was pride too. And she expressed fear, cried and then laughed as Hitchcock watched her. At the end of several scenes she said to Hitchcock, "Well, do I get the part?"

"You certainly do," Hitchcock said, embraced Henny and then said, "I have never seen anyone reading a part like that. You were great."

"Thank you, Mr. Hitchcock."

"My pleasure. I'm proud of you."

"When do we start making the movie?"

"Next week."

"Where?"

"Hollywood."

HOLLYWOOD-
TORONTO-PENTICTON
(1979-1980)

CHAPTER 16

"**A**ction!" Hitchcock said as Henny began working on the movie she convinced the director to title *A Bad Day on Highway 401*. It was the month of October and Henny never worked so hard in her entire life, even as a nurse. Hitchcock demanded the most from his cast, working for long grueling hours. The film was completed in fifteen weeks and two weeks after that, the first sneak preview was held in a Toronto theatre.

I got there late and and the studio publicity man let me in. "There are only a few seats left," he apologized.

I looked down and saw a section roped off in the centre for the studio guests. I went up into the balcony as the lights went down and the picture came on. I then found my way in the dark to a seat in the middle of a bunch of movie buffs and looked up at a screen. It felt strange to see the name *Henny Rubeck.* But that strange feeling left when the credits were over and the movie began. After ten minutes had passed, I sensed restlessness by those around me. "Aw, shit," I heard someone say. "I thought this was going to be something different. It's just another friggin mystery."

Then Henny came on the screen and five minutes later, when I turned around, those near me were staring at the screen, their mouths partly opened. There wasn't a sound except their breathing. I could see one of the buffs squirm as he whispered to another sitting next to him, "Oh, my God. This is a terrible way to die."
Nobody had to tell me that *A Bad Day on Highway 401* was going to be a box office hit. The plot was filled with fears, turns and twists, only Hitchcock could dream up.

After the movie was over and I came down to the lobby where Henny was standing with Hitchcock signing autographs. Reporters surrounded Hitchcock and Henny minutes later.
"Congratulations, Henny." said one critic. "I'm certain your performance deserves an Academy nomination?"
"Thank you," Hitchcock said.
"Henny, are you going to make another movie?" another critic asked.
Henny responded with, "I'm not certain."
"Why so?"
"Because living in Toronto and commuting to Hollywood poses a problem."

On the morning I was scheduled to interview Henny on *Entertainment Now* and the possibility of her winning an Oscar, I showered, shaved, got dressed and then became aware of something strange happening to me. I felt irritable, tired, had blurred vision, felt extremely hungry and made frequent trips to bathroom. Then as more time passed, it became perfectly obvious I wasn't feeling well so I discussed the problem with Henny and we agreed it was probably some momentary phenomenon that would disappear as quickly and mysteriously as it had come.

At 8:00 a.m. we drove to the CBC studios and as soon as I parked Ogopogo 2 and climbed out of the cab, my dizziness continued so I sought Drew Canwin, my producer, and said to him, "I can't do *Entertainment Now.* I feel unsteady on my feet and I'm afraid to walk for fear I'll fall down."

"Fear?" Drew said in jest. "Maybe Hitchcock should make a movie about you." Then in a softer voice continued, "Take it easy, Joe. You'll be okay. Sit down and rest. By the time you and Henny are on camera your sense of imbalance probably will be gone."

Drew was hopeful. At the stroke of 9:00 a. m. the camera's red light came on. Henny sat to my left side. Every time I shifted my chair I felt that I was about to collapse. Even seated perfectly still, I felt like toppling forward. But the spirit of the *show must go on* still existed and I managed to interview Henny for ten minutes, and then, I keeled over. As soon as I recoveredm I apologized to my audience but by that time there was no red light on the camera. The remaining portion of *Entertainment Now* was replaced with a filmstrip that dealt about Canadian national parks.

Seeing the condition I was in, Henny rushed me to see Dr. Henry Charles where in his office he gave me a physical examination, sent me to a laboratory for urine and blood samples. When I returned, was told to come back the following day for the results. And when I did return, the doctor diagnosed my disorder as Diabetes 2 and, although Henny warmed that I was a good candidate, I wanted second opinion so he referred me to a *specialist* Dr, Swartz where I was subjected to a battery of tests.

The specialist confirmed what the doctor had said earlier and that diabetes 2 occurs mainly in adults and could go undetected for years. "Decades can pass before it shows signs and damage to the body have already been started. It can also lead to heart and kidney failure," the specialist said.

Then when I asked, "What is diabetes?" the specialist replied, "Diabetes is a genetic disease and a metabolic disorder that affects the way food is converted into energy. This means your body makes some insulin. In type 1 debates, which frequently begin in childhood, the pancreas makes no insulin as it has to be injected into the body. Type 2 diabetes usually occurs in midlife. The pancreas still produces insulin, but the body cells cannot make use of the insulin as it should and one most likely overweight."

The diagnosis was depressing. I was devastated and even more so the following week when Drew said to me on the telephone that because of my absence I was no longer host of *Entertainment Now.*

"Who is?" I asked, disappointed.

"Another announcer, who is prominent around the CBC."

Upon hearing Drew's news, Henny and I gave notice to our landlord, packed Ogogpo 2 and returned to Penticton where we waited for the Academy Award presentations.

The night at the Academy Awards, Henny turned to me with a worried look and asked, "Joe, do I look fat?"

"Not fat, you look beautiful," I said as we were in a hotel near Sunset and Vine where Henny was wearing a pale blue dress with jewelry on her hands, ears and throat. It was a great night of glamour in Hollywood.

"I have never seen you so beautiful," I said. Henny didn't look as skinny as she had been when we first met but she wasn't fat either. I felt she looked content, peaceful and everything about her glowed.

"You look better than most movie stars," I said helping her put on a white mink coat, and then called a taxi which took us to the Grumman's Chinese Theatre where the Academy Awards were held and Bob Hope was the emcee.

"How exciting," Henny said as she saw Hollywood luminaries sitting around us and a camera zooming in on her face. We sat through the boring Academy part when awards were presented to special effects, sound effects, the screenplay, the song. The award for the best director went to Alfred Hitchcock although the movie *A Bad Day on Highway 401* was named one of the best pictures categories, it did not win.

As soon as Bob Hope announced, "Time now for the Best Actress Award," Jane Fonda and Clint Eastwood came onto the stage and Fonda, after opening a sealed envelope, announced, "The award for the best actress goes too . . ." There was a dramatic pause as those in the audience were kept in suspense, and seconds later, Fonda continued, "The winner is Henny Rubeck for her portrayal as nurse, Candy Britain, in, *A Bad Day on Highway 401.*"

The screams in the Patricia Motel could be heard from one end to the other as Ozzie and his girlfriend, Helen, danced around the kitchen table, overwhelmed by the news. Lorne, meanwhile, pounded his wheelchair, and together they tossed all the popcorn in a bowel onto the floor.

In Vancouver, Lorna and Howard Moon shouted and screamed until they woke up Grant who was asleep at the time, and in Hollywood, Henny and I were exited too. Henny ran headlong towards the stage with a lost look over her shoulder towards me. Hundreds of cameras' were taking her photograph as she blew a kiss and then joined Fonda and Eastwood on the stage.

The Oscar was handed to Henny and tears streamed down her face as she attempted to thank everyone. "I want to thank Alfred Hitchcock for giving me the opportunity and my husband, Joe, for his encouragement."
Henny then held the Oscar aloft and continued, "I want to thank also my children Lorne, Lorna and Ozzie. I love you."

Following the presentation of the Oscar and a celebration that followed, Henny and I returned to our hotel room and phoned Lorne and Ozzie in Penticton, but there was so much excitement that what conversation we had, didn't make sense. Next we phoned the Moon's in Vancouver, but our conversation didn't make any sense either.

After we returned to Penticton, I asked Henny if I should go back to announcing for CJOE but she shook her head and said, "No, dear. You are my Oscar and I'd like you to retire."

"How about yourself, do you want to go back to nursing?"

"No," Henny said. "I want to be just an ordinary housewife, close to our family."

I shared Henny's philosophy and after we purchased a home on Ridgedale Avenue in Penticton, we dealt with, not our retirement or that I had diabetes 2, but an unusual family matter. Whenever the feeling welled up in him, Ozzie immersed himself in doing chores around Patricia Motel wearing female clothing. On the plus side Ozzie affiliated Patricia Motel with an American base chain of motels. He did research and lay out an extensive advertising campaign. He even prepared a speech he was to give to the National Motel Operator's Association which had its annual meeting scheduled for Penticton. Ozzie worked. He worked long hours. It was one of the reasons for Ozzie's success. He was in his own words, "A driven man."

So that spring in 1980 when the impulses threatened again to disrupt his life, Ozzie spent the afternoon talking bookings for the tourist season which was about to begin. He pushed himself to the point of exhaustion, only this time it wasn't working. The emotions passed his exhaustion, overwhelming him, until he no longer could suppress them or keep them from Helen, his friend.

"I have to find out who I am," he said to Helen, who was in the motel with him at the time. "I have to."

"What the hell do you mean by find out, I have to?" Helen retorted.

In his heart Ozzie already knew who he was. He had always known but Henny and I failed to acknowledge the symptoms, just like I failed to acknowledge I had symptoms that could cause diabetes.

At age six, Ozzie was playing with a flower bed outside our home in Naramata and awareness hit him with such force that years later he would remember the color of the flowers, the look of the dirt, the way he walked inside the house and asked Henny and me to buy him a doll for Christmas.

Ozzie also remembered the time when he was in elementary school and someone printed on his lunch box the word *faggot,* Ozzie realized that he was supposed to be a female.

By age ten he had Lorna's clothing hidden in his closet. On one occasion, Halloween, he got dressed in her clothes and went from house to house saying, "Trick or treat?"

Ozzie sometimes prayed that he would awaken and find his body transformed into that of a little girl. When Henny and I heard the prayer we dismissed it as a child's far-flung imagination, a form of creativity, a trivial thing.

At High School, Ozzie immersed himself in schoolwork and neither was unhappy nor an outcast. He was just one of the boys who always had a book to read, an essay to finish or a sketch to paint.

When Ozzie finished High School, he took a course offered by Okanagan College in hotel/motel management. When I became host of the network television program *Entertainment Now*, Ozzie took over the operation of Patricia Motel and held the title of manager. Ozzie by all accounts, was at the top of his profession, and at an early age. But as Henny and I found out he was leading a double life. The feeling suppressed since childhood resurfaced again. In the evening he tried to on Henny's clothes. When that failed to satisfy he tried to explain the situation to Helen.

"I find it odd that you want to dress like a woman." Helen said and went on, "My love for you will not change no matter how you dress, like a man or a woman."

The next time they met Helen even brought along some of her own clothing and gave Ozzie a woman's name. "From now on you'll be Angela," she said.

But soon wearing Helen's clothing around the motel wasn't enough. He continued wearing women's clothing, and with Helen, visited Penticton nightclubs. They knew the gay community accepted transvestites, the transsexuals, the drag queens. It was a perfect place to investigate his feelings and it was at this time that Ozzie decided to leave Helen.

Ozzie befriended the transvestite community, men who enjoy dressing up in women's clothes, and, for the time hoped he was one of them, since it might permit his marriage to Helen. But the other men differed from him in one respect: On Monday mornings, they returned to the world of men. Ozzie felt only frustration and began hating the life of man-by-day/woman-by-night. He wanted to be a female all the time.

Helen continued to visit Ozzie on weekends and he returned to his former life for social engagements requiring couples. Then in the spring of 1981 Ozzie and Helen traveled to Las Vegas on a holiday that rekindled their love for each other. Despite the upheavals of the previous months, they loved each other more than ever.

But near the end of the Las Vegas holiday Ozzie finally said, "Helen, I love you no longer. I no longer can be your boyfriend."

"What do you mean by that?" Helen protested. They knew it was over and took separate flights back to Penticton. A month later Helen said, "The hell with you guy. You are a weirdo, a wacko, a sicko."

This time, Helen promised not to see Ozzie again and from then on, Ozzie existed at the Patricia Motel only during office hours, the rest of his life belonged to Angela. A month later, still Ozzie entered the Penticton Hospital clinic where doctors' assess people confused about their gender.

Dr. Don Watson said to Ozzie during the assessment, "The exact cause of transsexvitism remains unknown, although some researchers believe it stems from biology rather than social experience."

The second doctor, Wayne Alverez, continued, "One theory exists that severe stress in the early months of your mom's pregnancy may have interfered with the normal production of hormones."

"Whatever the cause I want an operation," Ozzie said.

"Well, you are an excellent candidate for one, we'll be in touch with you soon," Dr. Journal continued.

Ozzie had no problem with having a surgical sex-change operation. Most of his friends already knew what he wanted to be. And unlike many transsexuals who endure rejction from their parents, Henny and I accepted Angela without question. It was, however, a significant and a radical change, and an agonizing one for all of us. The main problem was that Ozzie as Angela wanted to manage the Patricia Motel and had no idea how Henny and I might react.

Before we had time to say how we felt, Angela met a traveling salesman from Kelowna who registered at the motel. He was, as it turned out, an employee for the American motel company with which Patricia Motel had affiliated itself. The two went out to a nightclub and danced and talked most of the evening. Several nights later, the salesman phoned again They chatted for several minutes before Angela decided to set the record straight.

"Do you know what I am?" she asked the salesman, and paused.

"Well, you are a lovely person and a good dancer too."

"Besides that I'm a transsexual. Do you know what that means?"

"I think so."

Angela continued, "I use to be a man. You are quite welcome to hang up right now and I'll understand."

But the salesman didn't hang up. He told Angela that he still wanted to see her and during the following several weeks, they dated and everything went smoothly until when Ozzie's and Angela's separate lives suddenly crashed headlong into one another.

Ozzie was required to attend a meeting of the national Motel Operator's Association which one of the member motels also employed Angela's salesman friend, and had no idea how to tell him that sometimes he was still a man. The salesman took one look at Angela and felt that she had deceived him. Ozzie for his part saw the look of betrayal and knew what had to be done—an operation.

Following the National Motel Operator's Association meeting, the Penticton Regional Hospital Operating Room nurse phoned to say that a booking date had been set for Ozzie's operation, but before he was admitted, he came to our home on Ridgedale, to have a meeting with Henny and me.

"You may be thinking that I have come to tell you that I'm quitting as manager of the motel," Ozzie said as soon as we were seated in the living room Henny and I remained silent so Ozzie continued, "If you are thinking that way, it's not true. But after I tell you what I'm about to do, you may wish it were."

"What's the problem?" Henny said.

"I'm a transsexual and have reached a point where I can't live as a man."

"Too bad," I said.

"And sad," Henny continued.

After Ozzie summarized his life, I asked him with candor, "Are you going to continue managing Patricia Motel?"

"I'd like that very much."

After I said that he would have Henny's and my support, Ozzie said, "Thank you Mom and Dad."

Ozzie then went back to the motel.

The following day, Ozzie talked with friends, counselors, psychiatrists to determine his next step, and that step was taken when Dr. Watson said to him, "Ozzie Rubeck, it's time to take care of Angela. Your operation is booked for tomorrow morning."

As soon as Ozzie spoke with Dr. Watson, Ozzie phoned me and wanted a conference with all the employees at Patricia Motel. That afternoon the entire staff, including maids, crawled into a small meeting room where I said. "This meeting has nothing to do with the excellent service our customers get, but about Ozzie. And what he's about to tell you has the support of the Rubeck family."

When it was Ozzie's turn to speak, I could see his legs shaking. He began with, "Very few people ever have reason to question their gender, but I'm one of those people. I have felt all my life that I was a female instead of a male."

Ozzie went onto describe his diagnosis and his plan to proceed with surgery in the morning. "You are going to have to know me as a female, not as a male. I ask for your support and your patience. I'm going to make mistakes, so please bear with me."

When Ozzie finished speaking, to him the applause seemed as if it lasted for hours.

In a sense it was his last moment of glory as a man and already he had his business card printed to read: O. A. (Angela) Rubeck. "It will save the staff a few awkward moments when someone telephones for Ozzie," he said while displaying the calling card to everyone.

In the morning, Ozzie had his surgery and became transgendered. It was a surgical sex change procedure that lasted four hours.

When Angela woke up from her surgery she looked at Henny and me in the recovery room and said, "Mom and dad, say hello to your new daughter."

Angela returned to work a short time after operation and became one of the most respected women in the service industry. Every once in a while she got teased, however, even Lorne said to her, "Women certainly go to great lengths to climb the corporate ladder these days."

As for Henny and me, we are retired and genealogy is our passion. I like my elocution teacher in Selkirk, Mrs. Bunchy, find genealogy fascinating because as I search my roots and develop a family tree I find mysteries: the origin of the

Rubeck surname, the roots of the clan and discovering unknown relatives in Poland and throughout the world.

There is a curiosity about the blood, body and spirit and collecting facts, which are found in church and civil archives throughout the world as I pry, probe and question relatives about my family history until I'm blue in the face—alas to no avail.

Then one day, something happens, I mention something simple and all of a sudden a key turns and the floodgate opens.

Genealogy is not only a kind of science that engages reason, but also the activity, which like in radio announcing, brings many positive emotions. My emotion hit a low when I discovered that during World War 11 in 1942 two Rubeck families were executed by the Nazi Death Squad in the tiny village of Koszoly, Biala Podlaska in the wojewodztwo (province) Lubelskie, in southeastern Poland where my parents came from.

First there was a tragic event in the Rubeck Family tree when on July 28, 1942 my uncle Jan Rubeck, 66 years of age, his son Jakub,43, Jakub's wife, Paulina, 40, and their two sons Stanislaw, 13 and Jozef 17, were victims of Nazi terror and executed by the German Death Squad. Initially they were buried on the spot of the tragedy but later their bodies were exhumed and buried in the nearby Huszcza cemetery.

The barbaric Nazi executions in Koszoly during the German invasion were rampant and similar to other Polish communities. The so-called "foresters" (partisans) visited the village, but the Germans controlled it. In the beginning of 1942 there was a battle in Koszoly forest between the Germans and the partisans from Major Iwan Sadykow's Russian division. Two members of the division were killed. In July 1942, the German Police, *Shultzpolizei*, from the nearby town of Lomazy kept capturing Russian prisoners. During one of these captures the Nazi's surrounded the Jan Rubeck family household, ordered everyone to go outside and then, burnt their farm buildings.

The Nazi's did that, according to information I have gathered, because there were machine gun shots coming at the Nazi's from behind the Rubeck home. The partisans were doing the shooting. Death was the punishment for aiding Jews or the Russians not only for the helper but also for his/her family. The Nazi's literally clubbed and then shot the Rubeck family.

In the second tragedy, another uncle of mine, Antoni Rubeck, died due typhoid fever on January 19, 1942 and then on August 20, 1942 his 45 year-old wife Antonina, was executed by the Nazi Death Squad. The most dangerous and yet most frequent form of help given Jews or Russians in the area was the offering of refuge in private buildings. Nazis applied the death penalty for anyone aiding Jews or Russians. Apparently the Germans felt Antonina, a widow, had collaborated with the Russians and sheltered a Jewish couple. Because of her assistance she was executed in front of her five young children who suddenly became orphans.

And then, I did a genealogical search of my father's family tree and discovered that Piotr Rubeck was one of three sons and a daughter born to Konrad Rubeck and Dominika Czubla in Koszoly (Galecia) Poland. My father married Stella Maslowska.

The decision to leave Poland was not an easy one, and once made, was beset with a variety of obstacles. Mom and Dad had to apply for identity papers, visas and medical documents and then choose a route to travel. Since they lived inland they had to arrange transportation. To finance the journey they sold all their property, all that is that my parents couldn't carry and pack up the remainder in makeshift boxes and bundles.

The overland journey to Canada began with at the port of Danzig and was disheartening because on arrival they, like all immigrants at the time in Europe, were harassed by hordes of pirates, swindlers selling counterfeit tickets and unscrupulous agents selling passage on ships that some were barely seaworthy. It was normal for high-pressure jobbers to buttonhole immigrants and take them to disreputable inns or other places where they could be fleeced by lively assortment of thugs, thieves, and prostitutes.

My father and mother received their passports June 5, 1928 and a month later, set sail for Canada as they took a feeder ship from Danzig to Copenhagen, Denmark. On July 4 they boarded a larger ship, *S. S. United States 2,* spending ten days crossing the Atlantic. The ship docked at Pier 21 in Halifax July 14, 1928.

As immigrants passed through the portals of Pier 21, some came to seek shelter from ravages of war and oppression. All came in search of a better life, an opportunity for a new beginning, a Mother Country for future generations, the nearly free land and an opportunity of homesteading. They came in groups large and small, some bringing a sizeable collection of possessions, others only clothing on their backs, which was the case with my parents.

Pier 21 opened in March 1928 and was a two-story complex of buildings connected to an overhead ramp to the Halifax railway station. It housed the Immigration Services, Customs, Health and Welfare, Agriculture, the Red Cross, a waiting room, dining room, canteen, nursery, hospital, detention centre, kitchen, dormitories and a promenade overlooking the harbor. Tickets were purchased at the Canadian National Railway ticket office and their destination according to the Canadian Immigration Service manifest was directed by the CNR Department of Colonization to Winnipeg, Manitoba. A CNR Redcap helped my parents to get onboard a train destined for Winnipeg.

The immigrant train or *colonist* trains as they were called were primitive. Coal burning stoves at each end of the cars provided the only heat. Dining facilities let much to be desired and most immigrants brought their own food. The seats were made of wood and a platform was located above the seats where a brave soul could climb up and attempt to sleep. Babies cried as the odor of dirty diapers and unwashed bodies permeated the cars.

Anticipation was great and excitement intense, however, even as the train chugged along the lonely and desolate section of the Canadian Shield through Northern Ontario.

What lay ahead? Had Piotr and Stella Rubeck made a wrong decision? No time to think about it now.

A new life was about to begin. And it began when my father paid $10.00 and was successful in obtaining a 160-acre homestead near Selkirk, Manitoba on which he built a home, farmed, and eventually prospered enough to own more land, become a Canadian Citizen and later, purchase a motel in Penticton, British Columbia.

As a part-time genealogist I wrote a letter to Santa recently. It read:

Dear Santa,
Don't bring me new dishes,
I don't need a new kind of game.
Genealogists have particular wishes
For Christmas I just want a surname.

A new tape recorder would be great,
But it's not the desire of my life.
I just found an ancestor's birth date,
What I need now is the name of his wife.

My heart doesn't yearn for a ring
That would put a real diamond to shame.
What I want is a much cheaper thing,

Please give me Mary's last name.

To see my heart singing with joy,
Don't bring me a leather suitcase
Bring me a genealogist's toy,
A surname with dates and a place.

I find that Genealogy is time consuming, complicated and demanding work. At the same time, its result is often uncertain because, besides practical experience, special skills and knowledge, as well as persistence, it requires luck.

Aside from working on my Family Tree, Henny and I enjoy listening to music and playing checkers. As I walk through the twilight of my life, and knowing that I have diabetes, I watch my diet of course, and exercise each day by looking for my glasses. And once I find them, and because I'm impotent, I keep jumping Henny in a game of checkers, with a king, that's all.